THE GLORY OF THE HUMMINGBIRD

Books by Peter De Vries

THE GLORY OF THE HUMMINGBIRD

A NOVEL BY PETER DE VRIES

LONDON
VICTOR GOLLANCZ LTD
1975

Printed in Great Britain by
Lowe & Brydone (Printers) Ltd, Thetford, Norfolk

THE GLORY OF THE HUMMINGBIRD

1

WE MUST LOVE ONE ANOTHER, yes, yes, that's all true
enough, but nothing says we have to like each other. It
may be the very recognition of all men as our brothers
that accounts for the sibling rivalry, and even enmity, we
have toward so many of them. Gotcha! The same construction to be put on the perpetual wars waged and
squabbles conducted among what are, all too truly, a
family of nations.

I never much liked any of my family, though I loved
them, at least do now in retrospect, and always allowing
for this emotion to be experienced with gritted teeth, etc.
I cottoned most to my father, with whom I could empa-
thize as a basically fine-grained and superior sort, one in
whom had once burned the same romantic flame sensed
to be consuming myself, to be safeguarded at all costs
from the early marriage and imprudent multiplication
that had snuffed out his own untimely. We were just too
goddamn much family, even for each other, let alone

Popsicle, and the specter of ever getting the equivalent on my own back as its breadwinner was enough to make my flesh creep. I had simply had too traumatic a bellyful of the mucilaginous togetherness of Home, and at too early an age, being the youngest of eight. I would march to a different drummer, at least one different enough to get me out of 315 Jefferson Street three blocks from the Second Presbyterian Church of Wabash, Indiana, and into a bachelor apartment on the East River, or at least the Chicago Lake Front.

I doubt that any of my brothers and sisters sensed as keenly as I how we gravelled the author of our being, as he called himself in moments of ironic belittlement, giving his Ascot a fidget or shifting in his lap a tattered copy of Bliss Carman — response to whose own call to the gypsy life was something for which it was now, in his case, too late. We surrounded him, we smothered him, we completely encircled him, like the sousaphone tuba he played in the local marching band, for his near disappearance into which, in public and private, learned metaphorical explanations are now of course available. He is getting back into the womb, or, for the even more flamboyant among us, retreating into some kind of cloacal hideaway. For the tuba is certainly the most intestinal of instruments, the very lower bowel of music. His connection with it, in any case, was snuggling and intimate; it seemed, as he oompahed away up Main Street on festive days, his face red as a beet and his legs pumping like pistons, an organic extension of himself, or he of it, pneumatically wed to it, the veins in his neck like copper pipes through which additional air pressure was pumped, rather than blood, his private tubes and veins and ducts for an hour one with the brass entrails to which he com-

4

mitted the wind mustered from the depths of his own, from his own regular entrails that is, his cheeks rhythmically inflating and deflating like a pair of bellows, transmogrifying him rather into one of those breeze deities visualized as propelling ships across the — oh, this figure of speech is much too complicated. But the point is that he was too. Suffice it to say that the regret with which he emerged again from under and within the instrument's Fallopian — or duodenal — shelter was as visible as the joy with which he entered its welcome embrace.

I never told my father his pleasures with the band were intra-uterine — why should I, what purpose would it have served? — much less explained it in those terms to my mother, who would have resented it even more. "Womb, why should he want to get back into the womb I'd like to know, haven't I given him eight fine children? What more does he want? Aren't they all healthy, growing up here in a decent town?" Such discussions would have got us nowhere. Besides, I had another angle, another fancy, more suited to the layman, which I put not to my mother, but to one or two carefully selected friends. The tuba was not a musical instrument at all but an enormous piece of plumbing out of which he was trying to blow a terrible obstruction — *us*! All eight of us. Nine, counting my mother. Nine! each arithmetically setting him back from any hope of pursuing with Bliss Carman the joys of the open road ("For him who travels without a load"). We clogged his drains, we bogged his brains, who had been meant by nature to be a free spirit, blowing where the wind listed, a wandering minstrel fingering a flute from cottage to cottage for a crust of bread and cheese (in some representations washed down with gouts of wine squeezed from a goatskin slung round the neck). Or a doer and dreamer both, now Lawrence in Arabia, now Harold in Italy, the melancholy wanderer whose oyster the world is, to be eaten whole or not at all. What was he doing here in Wabash, Indiana, for Christ's sweet sake? Where am I? Who are all these people, what do they want? Children with braces on their teeth for which bills are being waved in his face or huddled over croup kettles in the upper respiratory season; pimpled pubescents miring him ever deeper in cliché, "Pop, can I have the car tonight?"; humid female in-laws with goiters, one of them threatening to recite "To a Waterfowl" *with expression*; persons in mackinaws appearing at the door with stories that they are relatives from even farther west, and requisitioning on that flimsy ground a night's lodging.

No, it was not for him.

Obliteration on that scale, of an individuality that strong, could only be explained by an equally vital impulse running counter to the anarchic one I have made out: a recognition that in a family lay the sole immortality open to it — for Oompah wore the look of a man who does not take the Third Law of Thermodynamics at all well. He went to church only rarely and then to keep peace, believing in neither a God nor an afterlife, in contrast to my mother who had faith that after death married people would meet in infinity, like railroad tracks. But he took entropy personally, as I suppose we all do, and wore himself out in the effort to slow down his extinction, or in some relative way momentarily to qualify it. Anyone informed that the universe is expanding and contracting in pulsations of eighty billion years has a right to ask, "What's in it for me?" A piece of the continuity can reasonably be asked. Therefore, just as he now regretted the freedom he had given up for the privilege of marching us all once a year to Shoe Town to dicker for a quantity discount, as a vagabond he would have pined for the hearth and home necessarily waived in the pursuit of that condition. The actual case being what it was, the family he would have longed for under the alternate life style were now on hand, and being treated to an unending flow of sardonic comment. "You not only *can* go to the movies, you may." Or, running a palm over the thick straight black hair that stood up like a fright wig, or as though he had his finger perpetually in an electric socket, "You know you all have my swerving devotion." Etc.

So Oompah was an apt and ever-visible object lesson, a warning of what I should be like myself forty years hence if I got myself saddled with the likes of me.

"It's the old story," Oompah would say, answering himself the fictive who-am-I, who-are-all-these-people-what-do-they-want outcry, as of one suddenly stricken amnesiac at table, or at a family reunion where the fungoid sister-in-law is about to begin William Cullen Bryant, but regrettably finding that he has his wits all too clearly about him, "It's the old story. I chased her till she caught me." Oh, Oompah! This was the humor of his day, of course further forfeiting my esteem. There was no excuse for it, he might even now have risen above it, sparing me this. Might all his troubles be little ones! As though he had not only not made any headway, but had backslid into a twenty-three-skidoo type of situation, wave length, who should have taken the golden road to Samarkand ("For love of knowing what we should not know"). The vein in the marble had become the fat in the ham — was that marriage? No, thanks! I would have respected him more if he had never had me. Just as he must have sensed in me the pristine hankerings of his own youth, I saw in him a clear blueprint of what to avoid if I did not want to wind up (a rather more palatable metaphor) a lark in a cage. And it seemed to me that this slant on things vouchsafed me a clue to his trouble. If you think trouble is the word for what I'll now go on to relate, an incident illustrative of which, at any rate, starts our story off.

2

MY FATHER WAS A SOMNAMBULIST. His sleepwalking had long caused us consternation, but none so great as that occasioned by his rising from our pew and picking his way out of church, one Sunday morning, in the middle of the sermon. We had been aware of his commencing to nod, directly the minister had begun to drone his exposition of the text announced (ominously enough the verse from the Psalms running, "A day in thy courts is better than a thousand."). Oompah had often nodded, in the years of his exposure, under matrimonial duress, to Reverend Slosch's preaching, but he had always managed to come to with a start, usually with an adroitly timed left hook to the ribs from my mother, a sort of jerk which long practice had enabled him artfully to convert into a kind of bob of approval, faked but vigorous, of what the cleric was saying. This time, however, he was (as later declared) dog-tired, and unable to keep his wits at the surface level adapted to congregational tedium. He sank into a genuine slumber. Then suddenly (after, as might be said, a month or so of this day that was more than a thousand) he stood up and made his way out of the pew and up the aisle toward the door, holding his two arms straight ahead of him like a protagonist in a magazine cartoon, almost as though subconsciously striving to conform to the stereotype of the somnambulist laid down by that art form (a popular representation based on fact).

My mother, who had dealt with more years of this tendency than my father had of Brother Slosch's "messages," knew precisely what to do and what not to do. Signalling for us children to remain behind, she rose from the pew herself, as numberless times she had from the connubial bed, and fell in beside Oompah, requiring a trot of only three or four neatly executed steps to draw abreast of him. She did this in the casual, fluid manner of the trained bodyguard, which in effect she was, acknowledging a smile here, a nod there among members of the parish privy to her cross, as though nothing were amiss in the manner in which they effected egress from these particular "courts" — to offer an example of the kind of language that gave Brother Slosch his sedative powers. People effected egress (or burglars ingress), instead of went out or got in. My mother, who never tried to waken her charge untimely, deeming it unwise to do so as well as knowing it well-nigh impossible, must have been as aware as the rest of us, as they went up the aisle toward the door, of Reverend Slosch pausing in his treatise and plaintively watching their exit, his bovine brown eyes liquid with reproach. He knew of Brother Tickler's sleepwalking as well as the next, and so this little flurry was one of the more bitter pills to be swallowed in a ministry replete enough with intimations that he was not a winner. Hints that he was less than a spellbinder often bordered on the explicit, some even going so far as to threaten legal reprisals if he didn't ginger things up, get the lead out, oratorically speaking.

Joe Tickler had appeared at the doors of more than one of those present, in his night excursions, ringing their bells or rapping at their windows, like Wee Willie Winkie in his nightgown, to fetch them down on some purpose that made sense only, of course, in the context of whatever he was dreaming. For such nocturnal tangents must be in the nature of dreams acted out. Surrealist charades it might not be too fanciful to call them. Once he had made his way through a light fall of snow, clad in pajamas and robe and slippers, to the home of a neighbor who owed him some money. I don't recall how much. Maybe twenty or thirty dollars. Another time, he had risen in the middle of the night and successfully eaten a bowl of Shredded Wheat and milk; still another, got up and packed a Gladstone bag while my mother sat on the edge of the bed and watched. It was useless to remonstrate with him while in a trance, since sleepwalkers apparently do not hear, or at least do not understand, what is said to them (words uttered in their presence being roughly as incomprehensible as those of a man talking in his sleep to a conscious listener). My father's streak of the repressed wayfarer being as strong as I have made out, there is no obscurity in the symbolism of the suitcase, dexterously loaded with a good week's change of clothing before being snapped shut and set behind the bedroom door, as if in readiness for the morrow. My mother showed it to him the next morning, asking whether he remembered having packed it. He replied that he did, vaguely.

"Where did you think you were going?" she then put to him.

"French Lick."

"Was I going along?"

He shrugged and mumbled something to the effect that he wasn't sure.

He had lately seemed to be outgrowing the tendency. More than two years had passed without a single recurrence. Then, whammo, suddenly the incident at morning worship. As I said, it dashed poor Slosch, to whom some amends certainly seemed due. Yet making any great point of it could only heighten embarrassment, already keen enough all around.

Hotfooting it home as soon as the service was over, we children arrived to hear our mother earnestly discussing the crisis with Oompah — who had come to as he sailed out of the midsummer heat into the cool vestibule of the house, and was now smoking a cigar in his favorite chair, deciding also that a whiskey and water would not come amiss. What made matters worse was that Slosch was due to take midday dinner with us — unless that made them better by insuring speedy resolution of the contretemps. Get the whole thing over with. As a bachelor, and presumed celibate, Slosch broke bread with some family of the congregation nearly every Sunday, rotating more or less alphabetically among those willing to shoulder this social chore.

"We must all take it in stride," says Oompah, returning to the chair with whiskey in hand. He sank into its leathery depths with a characteristic sybaritic "Ahh!" which rather belied the excuse that he had been dog-tired; at best indicated that he was now greatly refreshed by the forty winks and in the market for more such renewal via a few of the well-established physical pleasures.

"You could at least have kept awake," Mother said.

"Could I? That end of it might be considered his responsibility," my father answered, blowing on the coal of his cigar in one of those echoes of an urbanity perhaps not all that lost to the paterfamilias, thought to have been cultivated for a brief period in London in early manhood, and very possibly to be recovered *in situ*. It was not entirely to be ruled out.

"But you ought to apologize."

"I can do that. But it'll be rough."

He did exhibit regret over the episode, at the same time displaying helpless relish of it, as a form of comment. Still, on balance, it was as the guilty party, definitely the wrongdoer, that he prepared to face the oncoming cleric, who could be seen from the curtained window at which we all rubbered to be even now approaching up Jefferson Street toward the house.

The term "take it in stride" certainly had a literal applicability here. Slosch moved with his familiar long-legged gait, in his customary dark suit with the thoroughly incompatible straw hat he always wore in summer. The brightly banded boater, or "skimmer" or "katy," was of the kind more normally associated with young blades rowing their girls across lakes, or singers belting out a chorus of "Hello m'baby, hello m'honey, hello m'ragtime gal!" An even more raffish note was struck by the way he swung the headpiece in his hand. Nevertheless, the moment bore a weight of drama. Now he had reached the house, now he was coming up the broad wooden stairs, now crossing the porch, now handing the hat to my mother to hang on an antler of the moosehead dominating the hall. He forged briskly on into the parlor — and there whatever courage he had, or had been trying to pluck up in the resolve that he was the injured party to whom some remorse was due, failed him. As we stood flanking Oompah, himself extending the hand of Christian fellowship, we must have struck him as a family that had closed ranks in our counter-determination that *he* was accountable for what had happened. Not for nothing was he known among regional wags as the Sandman. Slosch's capacity as a Sad Sack could hardly be exaggerated, and was never more in evidence than then. He entered with such a hangdog air as to make my father's protestations of apology all but meaningless. The roles were reversed. It was Slosch who shuffled forward to stand accused — as he might even before the bar of Judgment — of being soporific.

The dinner my mother served was, at any rate, all the restitution anyone could ask who was willing to take it in home cooking. I don't remember specifically what we had to eat except for the dessert, a peach that tasted as though it had been poached in cologne. It was one of my mother's canning specialties, the preparation of which involved a secret ingredient imparting that high, florid flavor which I can still in memory vividly taste (and even have conjured up by certain fleeting whiffs of female toiletry). Our Sunday table was even without guests of honor the kind giving rise in the fiction of those days to the term "groaning board" (a name also bitterly applied to itself by the ad hoc committee saddled with the thankless task of slugging contributions out of the congregation for a new car for a pastor who scarcely deserved even the modest salary the gift was meant to supplement).

Over what was, in any case, probably either pot roast or fried chicken the conversation turned to the Bible, and then to the Old Testament, of which Reverend Slosch knew more than was good for him. But his familiarity with it wasn't a patch on my mother's, who took literally the injunction to search the Scriptures. She had bits of information of the most obscure kind, with which she liked understandably to show off with chapter and verse. One of those Good Women whose backsides for some reason look as though they are made out of cardboard — insuring the stiff gait of rectitude — my mother was a mainstay of the Women's Auxiliary. Today she fed Slosch one of her customary arcane nuggets. The remarkably detailed pedigree of Christ, as given in the first chapter of Matthew, was for some reason mentioned. My mother cleared her throat.

"Jesus was not completely Jewish, you know," she said, with rather the air of a gossip disclosing the reverse of a local acquaintance trying to pass himself off as a Gentile.

Slosch looked up, half a cologne-poached peach arrested halfway to his half-open mouth. "No kidding."

"Fact." She closed her eyes as she smiled, the better to savor for a moment the suspense on which she had impaled one and all. "Why not?" she prodded pedagogically, "Where did He get his non-Hebrew blood?" Class?

Slosch returned the laden spoon to his dish and "thought," one of the dull scholars being encouraged to do so. Or as one posed a riddle. "God," my father muttered under his breath. He had done so out of feeling for Slosch's being unmasked as an ignoramus when he had just been publicly dramatized as a bore. But my mother must have thought that he too was "guessing" this as the source of non-Hebraic blood, because she said, "Noo," shaking her head with a smile. "Give up?" We all gave up, my father in the sense conveyed by rolling the eyeballs to the ceiling and throwing up the hands with a sigh.

"From Ruth. You will remember she is, or was, a Moabite." She ran off a brief but impressive string of begats from the relevant section of our Lord's bloodlines, very much to her credit you had to admit, beginning with the son of Ruth and Boaz — Obed I believe — who was then only two generations from King David, whom we all know to have been an ancestor of Jesus.

Slosch smote his brow in self-flabbergastation. "Well, I'm —" You thought for a brief second he might be going to say, "Well, I'm a son of a bitch," thus revealing himself in a new and more palatable light. But he went on, "I'm glad to be reminded of that. Which I knew, of course. We all know that Ruth was one of His ancestors, it's one of those things that just slip our mind. Ruth, who 'gleaned in the field of Boaz,' of 'whither thou goest I will go' fame?" he expatiated by way of jogging our memories, at the same time threatening fresh proof of his sedative gifts. But of course to save face he had to take the ball and run with it. "She was a Moabite. Or Moabitess," he said, pronouncing the word as though it had some kind of lubricious, even perverted, connotation. "A Semitic tribe, but not, to the best of my knowledge, Hebrew."

My father smiled and nodded, feeling no pain. Apart from the fleeting moment of exasperation, he was by now expansively genial under the influence of wine unsuccessfully pressed on our guest, whose share he was therefore free to drink. As a carnal substitute, he pressed on him a second and even a third helping of the heady peaches.

"Enjoy. It's later than you think."

"What time is it?"

Slosch screwed about to consult the banjo clock on the wall and reminded himself, and us, that he had another sermon to preach at the evening service (the one from which people stayed away in droves) and of his habit — his "wont" he actually put it — of returning to the parsonage early for that reason on Sunday afternoons, especially after such a heavy dinner. It wasn't just to brush up on the message. "I always take a nap beforehand," he said.

Oompah himself generally napped after such a meal, on the parlor couch, a section or two of the Sunday paper (in this case the Chicago *Tribune*) placed as a tent over his face to discourage flies, as well as sequester himself from the surrounding domestic jumble, almost Hogarthian in its wealth of steamy detail, of family members spread about on chairs or lying on the floor poring over other portions. I remember no such deferential respect as implied in Emily Dickinson's, "When Father napped on the couch the house was full." — or however her remark went. Our father preferred the noisy cool parlor to the muggy quiet of the bedroom upstairs. He could sleep in any din anyway, and until slumber overtook him might even participate in the conversation, at least to the extent of firing some observation into it, from under the newspapers, until he had dropped off and could no longer be reached for comment.

I've said that my mother had eight children. But she was proud, and would never be seen in public with more than two at a time, if it was at all possible. She considered herself a woman of breeding. Anyone could sense that seeing her promenade into the center of town, twirling a parasol, flanked by a pair of the progeny carefully selected and washed up for the occasion, the residue left behind in no particular shape, and usually under the charge of the oldest. Of course there were times when visibility with the entire pack could not be avoided, as when we all went to church, where everyone knew anyway how much breeding she did, as well as had.

On this particular Sunday afternoon, perhaps feeling good over her triumph of Scriptural erudition, she sprang up and began to dance to the strains of some music my brother Tom had on the radio. She always made a point of showing that piety need not preclude *joie de vivre* by any manner of means, in this instance circling the room with her skirts lifted nearly to her knees. The impression given was less that of a lady dancing than picking her way gingerly around pools in the street, or through a pasture beset with worse hazards to grace. The result was entertainment by any standards. I paused in my perusal of "Gasoline Alley" to smile approval from the corner of the floor on which I lay on my stomach. This had the unfortunate effect of making her stop to catch hold of my hand and snatch me up into the whirl of her rhythms.

There was a reason for her choice of partner from among the available brood, other than my ill-timed blandishment. I was the only boy she could get to dancing school, and the last of the neighborhood enrolled in a class where anything like classical dancing was taught. *Après nous, le déluge.* Like a tidal wave the age of the slob was to sweep waltzes and two-steps into limbo, and Miss Primrose's Dancing Academy into oblivion. Already presaged by such omens as actors mumbling their lines, the permissible chewing and even popping of gum in normal society, girls going off to school dressed in their fathers' shirts with the tails hanging out of their jeans, the era came to full bloom "terpsichorean-wise," as my mother put it, in boys and girls simply hunching and shuffling about on the floor in one another's general vicinity, physical contact more often than not consisting in the circulation of cans of beer or bottles of Coocamonga wine from which slugs were fraternally taken with little or no interruption of these unilateral gyrations as the drinks passed from hand to hand. It was a development with which I later caught up, of course, but not without having acquired some firm foundation in the traditional disciplines my mother espoused and Miss Primrose taught, the timely inculcation of which, Miss Primrose told me with tears in her eyes as I watched her blow out the candles on her last academy party and lock the door for good, would make me better at the free-form than the Neanderthals themselves. There would be style in my abandonment of it. I would be like those people who may say "ain't" because they know better, and so on.

"Your father is a frost on the ballroom floor," my mother said as we sailed in three-quarter time about the room. "Most intellectual men are."

"I've got two left feet," he concurred from under the newspaper, his path still not quite vague in distant spheres. "But you dance divinely."

"This one has manners. *And* a manner. The old-fashioned kind. True grace. We could be under chandeliers in old Vienna. His destiny will be among the refined and the cultured. He will walk with the swanky."

The praise of my style undoubtedly arose in part from

19

the distance I instinctively kept from my mother, whose sizeable bulk (itself recalling her description of someone as "a large, statutory blonde") I resisted gathering into my arms and whose perfume I found well-nigh asphyxiating. This one held his head back as far as he could get it, smiling like a stuffed lynx the while. Technically "leading the lady" — a concept also by implication now to be laughed out of court by the rabble young, as well as assumed to be abrasive to the sensibilities of feminists — I did so in a purely mechanical way, manipulating her about the room like a piece of machinery, such as a vacuum cleaner or floor waxer. It was just as well that she thought my holding her at arm's length an echo of bygone elegance, the high tradition lamented, and not for reasons I'm giving, not without a twinge of guilt at the memory. Perhaps the essence of which Mother reeked was the same as that in which the peaches were poached. To minimize its increasingly woozy effect, I began to avert my head as well as tilt it back, though rocking it as I smiled in order to mask the reluctance under which I functioned. Arching my spine as far over as possible, while squeamishly holding her wrist betwixt thumb and fingers, also contributed to an overall result easily mistaken for a revival of past decorums and vanished felicities.

These are all recollections against which objections can be legitimately filed, though at the same time no excuse need be made for the universal resistance to physical contact with his mother in a boy of twelve. That is quite normal. Nor need Freudian explanations be resorted to. Invocation of the "incest barrier" would seem pointless in view of one's flinching equally from his father's bear hugs, and from embraces with one's brothers and sisters too for that matter, as I have been at pains to say from the outset. No, it was my whole fam damily got under my skin, and on some occasions set my teeth on edge, not this or that member in particular, and collectively made me boggle, then, at the very notion of ever starting one of my own. "No way," the son of such a father would say, today, at the thought.

Oompah stirred underneath sheets of the *Trib.*

"Did I ever tell you about the time I got sick in Miss Haley's dancing class?" He shifted his cover slightly to facilitate narration, lifting it off his nose altogether now and then to call out some cardinal detail crucial to its comprehension, and raising his voice in order to be heard above the music which I longed to have stop, as he launched a story some of us had heard before.

As implied, I could appreciate its background as one of the dwindling alumni of those genteel after-school or Saturday-morning sessions to which boys were dispatched in the dark suits and white gloves my father was supinely recalling as atmosphere, to be taught the dances we were also groomed to "ask the girls for the pleasure of," after properly traversing the no man's land of the floor itself from the boys' side to the girls', and with suitably low bows, one hand on our back, the other on our stomach, through a season's suffered instruction culminating in a party at which were gobbled the iced cakes and pink punch which, my father now related as the climax of his anecdote, he for his part had quite copiously upchucked as he was piloting around the room a girl named Celeste Brady, who was inspired by his example to do the same, a slip of a flaxen-haired sprite who, had the deflating incident not occurred — and here Oompah lifted the newspaper well off his face in order to be heard quite clearly — "just damn well might have been your mother."

"Hot diggety dog," said Tom, turning off the radio as the number came to an end. I gave my mother the ritual bow of gratitude, and withdrew.

Tom is now a "flourishing car salesman," as my mother had it with her compulsion to euphemism, quite needed to put a good face on what, measured against her or any mother's loving ambitions for her young, are a rather lackluster lot of us, I fear. Jack moved to Portland and is "in cement." She means he's in the business of selling it, not lying at the bottom of the Columbia River encased in a block of concrete, a victim of gangland vengeance. Bill, rather than owning a lucrative fleet of garbage trucks, is "in sanitation," sometimes "in refuse," which evokes a Samuel Beckett character buried to his chin in abominations somewhere in the remote back stretches of the city dump, wildly transfigured in damnation. "Nick is a successful exterminator." "Clara's marrying a promising steamfitter." "Josie teaches classical piano." "George is a fine detective." Oompah is "with the McKesson Robbins people" — or alternatively "in pharmaceuticals" — a salesman with a job that by entailing some little car travel to surrounding drug stores appeases to that extent the vagabond in him, always within the cruel limits of Wabash County as his territory.

And what of Jim? What of this one? What, indeed?

3

I CANNOT WRITE, APPARENTLY. "And the style," one reader commented in a report on the partial manuscript of my novel, *Munching on Mrs. Dalrymple*, "fairly turns your stomach. Every sentence like a mother cat nursing a litter of cozily squirming subordinate clauses."

Well now. When we are parsing another we ought really not in our pursuit of woozy conceits omit that inseminating principle known as a verb, ought we now, as who should say the tom entrusted with the impregnation without which there is nothing syntactically to conceive, birth and suckle, what?

No matter. *Munching on Mrs. Dalrymple* had been about a third along when I had submitted it, not to a publisher, but to an artists' and writers' colony in the nearby Indiana countryside, in application for a grant-in-aid. The colony was a non-profit foundation set up by a greeting-card tycoon named Robert Wellington, as a sort of pet cultural project for his wife. Daisy Wellington ran it with robust regional chauvinism, proclaiming that the East, with its more prestigious colonies and literary capitals, was celebrated for displaying and publishing talent drawn in large measure from the rest of the country. "They may bottle the wine; we grow the grapes," she said, perhaps oftener than was necessary. The Wellington Colony consisted of twenty-five wooded acres where writers, artists and composers were housed rent-free in small private cottages, fed and otherwise supported for periods ranging from a few months to a year, depending on the length of time required to finish some creative endeavor for which the resident fellowship must be approved. The completion of *Munching on Mrs. Dalrymple* was not deemed a burning enough priority to warrant such a grant, but I did get something equally important to me at the time, a job at the Colony.

I rose swiftly from the rank of clerical menial to what was called administrative coordinator (allowing Mother to say, "He's in administrative coordination, you know.") which meant responsibility for handling all requests for grants in all three departments. One thing sought was a balanced variety of practitioners toiling in their hutches or trailing their coats in the woods. I had a private office, a free hand, and the chance to trail my own coat or otherwise steal a little time for work on *Munching*. Thus the authorities were in effect partially subsidizing me anyhow, though unbeknownst to themselves. I had access to the files. That was how I managed to see the report on my own application. I ran across it accidentally while looking for it in the morgue, as we called the limbo to which the records of rejected hopefuls were consigned. I stayed late one evening when there was nobody there but us chickens. It had been drafted by a man named Wesley

Bunce, a frustrated writer no longer with the Colony, given, as has been evidenced, to vertiginous locutions that can be doing him very little good out there in the literary jungle we may be sure.

I now had an A.B.-degree from Northwestern University and one foot on the bottom rung of the ladder Mother enjoined us to "set firmly on the ground of truth, prop solidly against the house of faith, and point straight up to —" I never heard what to point it toward, being on my way out of the room, in fact the house, and headed for my new digs at the Colony. They let me have one of the two or three cottages empty at the time. They were all named after famous American artists, writers and composers, mine being "Sarah Orne Jewett." "The stars of something or other," would no doubt be how Mother's triune piece of counsel ended, reasonably enough.

All applications crossed my desk, for notation and then transmission to subcommittees of the respective departments for review and decision. I had no vote, nor even a consultative or advisory voice, but I sometimes put in my two cents about literary aspirants via Tewksbury, the head cheese who ran the whole show as president of the foundation. He was a long drink of water, about forty years of age, one of those celibates — in this instance still living with his mother — about whom we say that something or other, in this case the Colony, is "their whole life." He was the sort who yawn without opening their mouths, which had the effect of tightening his nostrils into a terribly sneering expression.

One day an application with a supportive sheaf of verse arrived from a Joseph Tickler. The name in the upper left-hand corner of the large Manila envelope in which it came naturally caught my eye; my first thought being that one of my numerous cousins, I had over fifty in all, had taken to writing. Then I saw with a start that underneath it was my own home address! Oompah, no less, was writing poetry again, returning to the first love of his youth, put by in order to support a wife and author the likes of oneself. I'd had no idea. He'd never dropped a word. The poems were all written out in longhand, many of them, as later revealed, in motel rooms in his nights on the road. I read them with trembling hands and thumping heart, as can be imagined, hoping as I had never hoped for myself.

The first one was entitled "Transitional":

> Autumn dies from the ground up.
> Seedling and sumac flare in the breeze,
> Their flame runs up the wicks of creepers
> Twined around the trunks of trees,
> Catches the leaves of elms and maples which,
> Blazing and billowing on the hill,
> Burn out, leaving the bones of these.
>
> Winter blooms from the sky down.
> The first flakes, tumbling from a warm,
> Premonitory heaven, bud the top boughs;
> Wind blows such foliage as this; till trees
> Stand muffled in the shuttled wool of storm,
> And woods voluminous and pale
> Content me with the ghost of form.

"Whew!" I thought when I'd finished it, having been rooting line by line for the author, relieved when he'd made it, gone the whole distance. It wasn't great, but it was creditable. It was poetry. It was a lyric. We hadn't known he'd had it in him, old Oompah. Our impression had been that all he'd tried to bat out as a young man had been greeting card doggerel, serious poetry something he'd only read, never tried to write. The next was also about autumn, and the joys of tooling through it by car. "I ride the tattered county," it began, and continued somewhat in the vein of his old favorite, Bliss Carman. The next was one of those poems on death almost inevitably to be found in any poet's *oeuvre*. "I am the breathless gardener, say, who prunes the summer's mad excess." And so on. "Good going," I cried aloud at my desk. Then followed a poem entitled "Gardener," with the Earth itself apparently doing the talking on a somewhat similar theme. It was a long sequence of rhymed quatrains, of which the last went:

> *She's nurtured me so tenderly*
> *I regret that in my greed*
> *She must herself be gathered in*
> *The gluttonous lily to feed.*

There was an erotic effort of which the *double entendres* weren't as shocking as the author probably thought; indeed, to one of my age they were quite tame, in an unconsciously amusing way. What is so quaint as yesterday's wickedness? But it was followed by some more pretty good nature lyrics, and then a batch of light verse wound up the exhibit. Typical of the rather jumbled assortment, but suggesting a range of talent, was "Obituary for an Insurance Broker":

> *With covenants so well-devised*
> *You over me have hovered*
> *It pleases me to be advised*
> *You're adequately covered.*

A couplet detailing instructions for his own headstone inscription:

> *Here lies one who got no laughs*
> *Out of funny epitaphs.*

Well, here was a surprise indeed. I got my father on the phone as soon as I could, which was that evening, in his hotel room in North Manchester, a city on the northern rim of the territory he was working at the time. He was delighted I liked the stuff, though knowing the decision wasn't up to me. "If it was, I wouldn't embarrass you by applying," he said. "That would be nepotism."

I asked about what seemed an obvious complication that might result from his being awarded a grant-in-residence. "Won't you lose your job?"

No, it seemed he had taken the matter up with his superiors at McKesson Robbins, who had charitably agreed to give him a six-months' leave of absence, during which they would use his territory to break in some new and younger salesmen.

I took the manuscripts into Tewksbury's office, together with the letter describing the project for which the grant was being requested — "to finish a long narrative epic at which I have been working, a saga dealing poetically with elements rooted deep in our American ethnic past." I told him that, the applicant being my father, I would offer no opinion, serving merely as an office channel in a completely routine fashion. He came into my own office the next day, saying that he'd read the poems and considered them "not at all bad, not bad at all, really." He twitched and twisted about as always, giving the impression of a man perpetually writhing in a too-tight suit of long woolen underwear, to use Daisy Wellington's own description of him. One drawback was that there was no sample of the "long narrative epic" the applicant wanted to finish. I had asked Oompah about that myself, and been told that he "wasn't satisfied with any of it yet." Concentrated prolonged work free of financial worries, in an atmosphere such as the Colony had been founded to vouchsafe artists, should do the trick.

Tewksbury hefted the material in one hand, wriggling the shoulder of the other arm as though he were trying to work it into his jacket. He seemed at such times like one of those window mannequins that are screwed together joint by joint, in this case unskillfully. "If he were from somewhere else, I'd say it would count against him. But you know we're more or less on orders here to be infected with Daisy's regional bug, and to go just bonkers over any home-state talent. We don't have any Hoosiers at the moment, and few poets at all. So there's just an outside chance."

Tewksbury proved right. The application was approved by a committee no doubt also captivated by the idea of a poetry-writing travelling salesman. In the endless stream of poets with academic backgrounds, that appealed to them as a refreshingly grainy bit of Americana. Tewksbury told me as much, enacting again his nervous ballet. So Oompah arrived with his two bursting suitcases and other assorted impedimenta one Saturday afternoon and moved into Nathaniel Hawthorne, the cottage assigned him.

I had a date in town that night, but before picking the girl up I made a point of stopping around to look in on Mother. She had never shared elation over this turn of events. "Is that so," had been her inflectionless response when first I had burst in with the news that the fellow-ship had been granted. She was equally a wet blanket tonight, for reasons that, obtusely, I had failed to take into account. She had been given copies of the poems to read at her leisure, but had been noncommittal. Now I read one or two aloud to her, pausing over particular lines or effects, such as "the gluttonous lily."

"Isn't that good?"

She agreed that it was forceful, also as a gardener confirming its accuracy in fact. For the lily it turns out is a great feeder, with an enormous appetite, so that one must remember in fall planting time to put in plenty of fertilizer for the ravenous bulb. Still, she remained adamant in withholding approval. She set her knitting down and rose.

"The moderns have nothing to tell us," she said tersely, as though Oompah were already installed among the ranks of Cummings and Pound, and now she had *that*.

"But aren't you glad for him? At his time of life?"

"Are you glad for me? At mine?"

I all but smote my brow. Of course. That was it. And who could blame her, given the circumstances. Why, her own reasoning went, couldn't he just as well stay home and do his writing? Apply for a financial grant as such? It was no use telling a woman of her limitations and background that all such Arcadian retreats, be they Yaddo, MacDowell, name it, existed in order to vouchsafe temporary havens from the rude world not only for single artists, but for perfectly respectable married men, and women, enabled thus for varying periods to wrestle with their muses undistracted by other anguishes. This was Jefferson Street in Wabash, and "What will people think?" was, and remained, her wounded objection to

Oompah's up and sailing out of the house on her. "And him only here half the time anyway, all our married life. On the road all the rest. Free as a bird. Wasn't that enough getting away? No, it's a slap in the face."

"But look on it as a new lease on life, not only for him but for you," I said, glancing at the clock. "Think of it as your own chance to get away."

"I may do just that," she rather enigmatically replied.

So when my father moved out I moved back in. I couldn't bear to see my mother that unhappy, and my Sarah Orne Jewett snuggery didn't mean all that much to me. Too, the job was only a forty-five-minute commute by the car to which this shift in arrangements would now seem clearly to entitle me. That was commandeered from Oompah who was left with a bicycle, which he pedalled about the grounds and out of them, wearing a turtleneck sweater and a beige beret, tilted to one side in suitably Gallic fashion. The car came in handy in my sexual prowling, then still kept short of entanglements likely to encumber me with domesticity of the sort I was more than ever being given a cautionary dose of, but active nonetheless. One of Oompah's "light" quatrains ran,

> *Through folderol and rigmarole*
> *This shall stand eternal;*
> *I'm the captain of my soul,*
> *She's lieutenant colonel.*

This seemed particularly to stick in Mother's craw, whether because it had been written by a man making the wife out the proverbial battle-axe, or because events had proved her by no means wielding the power so imputed, was hard to determine. Speculation leant to the latter.

I took her out to dinner once a week, and to the movies about as often. She appreciated the display of loyalty and affection in "the last one left in the nest," yet I could sense something ominously smoldering beneath the outward manifestations of gratitude. You couldn't call her state of mind depression (a word far too loosely used). It was something else. *I* was depressed, Christ knew. Free evenings I spent drinking beer in a nearby bar or reading in my room. I batted out a couple of more chapters of *Munching on Mrs. Dalrymple* and then burned the manuscript. It made a satisfactory glow in the back yard incinerator, one starless night. I had never showed my mother any of it, not only for fear of its falling short of her austere critical standards, but because it was full of swear words, to say nothing of characters thrashing about in the sack like harpooned whales. Too, the moderns had nothing to tell us. There was always that. Her manner continued one of taciturn preoccupation in which some kind of secret determination could be sensed brewing — even a plot being hatched. She had, like most in the family, a strong streak of the Dutch *stijfkop*, or stiffhead. A stubborn pride that augured some kind of counterstroke when crossed. It erupted in the curious obsession that now began suddenly to fill her evenings. She sat at the kitchen table hour after hour pasting up her books of Blue Trading Stamps.

How about that? She had amassed hundreds, thousands of them over the years, tumbling them into the drawer of a kitchen cabinet on every return with a fresh batch from the supermarket. She had never redeemed any of them, or even collected them into books. She had hoarded them, like a miser his money. They became a family joke. "Why don't you cash them in, Mom?" "Oh, I will. Some day." "What you got your heart set on, a Mack truck? A locomotive? Must be something big." "We'll see."

She must have made a decision now. That was clear to me who watched as book after book was pasted up and tucked back into the drawer, this time in neat stacks, in readiness to be redeemed — for what?

"You got something in mind, Mom?" I asked at last.

"That's right," she answered, tight-lipped as again she brought a fist down on a page with a resounding thump. The book, finished, was set aside and a fresh one drawn toward her across the oilcloth.

"Must be something big. Important."

"That's right."

"What is it?"

She paused, with the timing that had always figured large in her communications. "A divorce."

I circled the table and took a seat across from her.

"Surely this is a joke?"

"Not to me."

"That part of it we can discuss later. I mean that you can get a divorce with trading stamps."

Nevertheless, such appeared to be the case — and still is. A glance at the premium catalogue she shoved in my direction proved it. A divorce isn't specified in so many words, of course, rather conveyed by suggestion, a word to the wise. "Round Trip Fare and All-expense-paid Stay in Reno" was one listing. It took a hundred and ninety books. A similar stay in Mexico City, another Mecca for claimants leaning to south of the border dissolutions, required two hundred and twelve books.

"How many have you got? Or will you have when you paste these all up?"

"I've got eighty-three filled out. There's probably enough stamps here for another sixty." That would put her in fair sight of her goal, unless some more exotic locus such as the Virgin Islands was to be opted for. That was in the catalogue too, at two hundred and twenty books. I shifted the subject of inquiry.

"What grounds will you give? I mean wherever you go."

"Desertion."

I expressed flabbergastation with one of those long whistling exhalations that sound like a tire going flat. "You mean to sit there and tell me that just because he's moved out of the house — I mean forsaken you for his muse —"

"Not that alone. There are other things between us. Over the years. It's nothing to discuss with children."

"Children!"

"So you're all grown now and don't need me any more."

"Has he had other women?" I asked, wondering whether she took seriously all the travelling-salesmen-on-the-road jokes we had as youngsters heard and bandied about our father.

"Plenty of opportunities out of town. True or not, there have been other things. Building up. I may want my freedom as much as he seems to want his."

Was Mother going into some kind of tailspin, such as women in her time of life often do, men as well for that matter, as I was to see soon enough in the case of Oompah himself? "Women my age can become an endo-crinological mess overnight, Dr. Jasper says," she had once remarked, almost proudly, or at least as though impressed with her sex's melodramatic potential in mid-stream. Was she on the verge of what is called involutional melancholia? Now she wanted her freedom — from what? Into what? Was she sick — or had she never been saner? Any union has elements in it that are finally inscrutable, even to offspring presumably witnessing it at close quarters. She frankly drove me crazy, but that didn't put me in my father's shoes, or hers, or absolve me from the obligation to show her a little affection. I felt that more keenly now in the revelation that she had been secretly brooding on such a move for years; had possibly long entertained it as the objective for which she had been accumulating the means obtained in the course of feeding the family acquired in a marriage she now wanted to dissolve.

But with trading stamps! If that don't beat the dogs afightin', as Grandpa Tickler used to say. Here is a twist on the American Dream. A divorce barefacedly offered as the ultimate prize among the glittering toasters and percolators and floor lamps and orange juice squeezers and combination clock-radios and color television sets spilling from the cornucopia for which housewives shop and shop and shop. The plum of plums in the land of opportunity, the jackpot in that God's country to which she had emigrated with her poverty-stricken parents as a little girl, led on by the lure of a better life. That had somehow eluded the old folks, now gone to their rest of course, but it would not elude Johanna Vanderhoff Tickler. Another few score books, and then a bride's dream come true.

That this was so grossly inconsistent with her religious beliefs, at least up to now espoused, made me hope she was playing some kind of emotional game with everybody including herself; indulging herself in a grandstand play for the sympathy to which we are all at times entitled, but to which we often go to illegitimate extremes to extract. That she didn't really mean to get a divorce but derived some sort of satisfaction from pretending to, the way people threaten to commit suicide who have no intention of actually doing so. Yet sometimes going so far as to scare themselves by inflicting tiny cuts on their wrists, of a self-tantalizing nature. I asked a psychiatrist about this at a party once, and he said "experimental slashes" were more widespread than thought. Pressed for some interpretation of motive, as he might have found it in the course of his practice, he said, "Oh, I think it just makes them feel alive," and moved off across the room toward an unoccupied lady.

That Mother was going through a period of self-pity cum pity-extorted-from-others was evidenced by the emotional dividends to be found in a greatly exaggerated burn sustained on one arm at the kitchen stove, for which her good friend and neighbor Lolly Drummond had driven her to the doctor. She took some satisfaction in his declaring it a first-degree burn, unaware, or forgetting for purposes of hypochondria, that that is the least severe. She confused it with the third degree. I had more sense than to straighten her out, of course. Treating it with an antibiotic salve was not enough. To avoid infection she kept it sheathed in a garbage bag, one of those polyethylene liners for refuse cans, which she decided would keep it hygienically sealed up — as well as supply some operatic color. She replaced it every twenty-four hours without fail, so that "changing my garbage bag" became a daily ritual at which I had to officiate on return home for the evening meal. The old one was peeled off and the fresh one slipped on and tied at the elbow with a string.

The sight of her shuffling about the house with one arm so swaddled as she went about chores no one was pressing her to discharge, often muttering things like "I don't want to be a burden," or "I've tried, God knows I've tried," so depressed me that I seized every chance to get out of the house without being considered a monster. Fortunately she had her Lolly Drummond. Lolly was also a martyr, to circumstances chief of which was a deplorable husband, and their visits grew more frequent as the two became increasingly compatible by reason of companionate grievance. A large, broad-shouldered woman possessing what Mother called "salient features," Lolly came almost every evening to set a spell now, and eager though I was to make the getaway this afforded me, I would sometimes lurk about in a nearby room to catch the drift of conversation of which I have never heard the beat.

"To spite me," Lolly confided in low tones one time, "he went to work and sliced bananas into the spaghetti sauce." "Went to work" was a locution she used constantly. "He went to work and drew out half our savings to buy a snow blower," "I went to work and spilled coffee all over my new dress," "She went to work and put my name up for treasurer without asking me," and so on. One morning Mr. Drummond went to work and wouldn't get up (presumably to go to work). Though dying to be off on a date or get over to Tony's bar and lift a few, I could at the same time never resist hanging back a moment to get yet another earful.

Mother was regarded as infinitely more *au courant* than Lolly, and so would often be called upon to explain the new expressions to her. Once, eavesdropping from the dining room, I heard her define "closet queen," a term Lolly had been encountering with great frequency of late.

"Means someone with a terrific wardrobe," Mother said. "A lady of fashion, you might say, who queens it over you with her dresses and furs and hats and what have you. In other words, what we used to call a clothes horse."

I suspected Mother had vouchsafed her plans for redeeming the Blue Stamps to Lolly, who became increasingly graphic in revelations about her own married life, widely held to be arduous by reason of marriage to a husband afflicted with satyriasis. Possibly slicing bananas into the spaghetti, as well as other such surrealist improvisations, were expressions of sexual frustration continually endured by Drummond — "not getting his will of me." Lolly who held this to be her cross, not his, said that Drummond's Gargantuan appetite had been an early-blooming thing. "Elsie Wallace told me once after she retired from liberrian — Yes, I'll have another cup, Jo. Thanks. She went way back, you know, and she remembers him as a little shaver coming in for his first liberry card and to take out his first book. It was one he had heard about. You know what the first book was he asked Elsie for?"

"What?"

"*Rider Haggard.* He thought it was the name of the story, you see, not the author."

"My dear Lolly."

"And him only a shaver of six or seven."

At last, however, I managed to tear myself away and

shove along to Tony's, where I went to work and knocked back a good half-dozen steins.

The situation was resolved, for the time being at least, by a means often employed by life for doing so: by blowing everything sky-high.

I had always had an uneasy feeling that I was involved in something odd, there at the Colony. Some four or five weeks before the end of Oompah's six-month term of fellowship Tewksbury called me into his office. Oompah himself was sitting there when I arrived, and I knew by both their expressions that something was amiss.

"I will be brief," Tewksbury said, pacing the floor as he gestured me to a chair, "but I will have to begin at the beginning. You will remember that we waived submission of excerpts of the" — he paused to consult something in a folder on his desk — " 'long narrative epic' the applicant declared as the work-in-progress for which a residence grant was requested. We customarily like to see some samples, but he said that none so far satisfied him, in the sense of meeting his standards as a craftsman."

"That is correct," said Oompah, who was nervously kneading his beret in his two hands.

"We respected the artist's reluctance to show portions of work not in sufficiently polished form, and accepted him on the strength of the lyrics and because we felt, at least earnestly hoped, that here was a true primitive, worthy of a little unorthodox latitude."

"I was grateful for that."

"All right. He was installed in Nathaniel Hawthorne. Weeks passed. Months. Without anyone ever hearing the sound of the typewriter supplied by the Foundation."

"I never use a typewriter. I find it too mechanical. It stifles creation."

"That was the explanation. That he composed in longhand. Well, cleaning women under interrogation testified that neither did they see any evidence of anything in longhand either. Or shorthand. Or anything whatever in manuscript form. Those reams of foolscap have remained virgin to this day."

"I've been in a kind of slump. I'm having a block."

"Which you try to break by pedalling off on your bicycle every day and tooling into town, there to seek inspiration among the crowded streets, close to where the heart of humanity beats."

"That was well put."

With an air that was becoming more witheringly sardonic every moment, Tewksbury again addressed himself to me.

"You know we have informal get-togethers in the lounge on weekend evenings, sitting around the fire and all, at which writers favor us with readings of new work. Mr. Tickler was asked several times whether he didn't have some new stuff to share with us, but always some excuse. At last — a week ago Sunday to be exact — he did read a few new things. Quite good of their kind, and well received, but there was something funny. They rang a bell with one or two of our other poets. They had heard, or more accurately read them somewhere. At last one of them remembered. It was in a past copy of *Harper's*. We dug it out of our library, and sure enough, there was the sonnet sequence so roundly applauded. Then one of the chambermaids, instructed to keep an eye peeled, yes, spy if you will, found the same magazine back on a closet shelf in Hawthorne."

With a dramatic flourish, Tewksbury prestidigitated the periodical in question from a lower drawer and set it on the desk-top, open to the sonnet sequence in question — "Mixed Blessings." Beside it he then lay the copy exhumed by the informer. They matched, except that the latter had the two-page spread scissored out of it.

"Now the question remains — indeed the certainty develops — that all the poems submitted with the original application had similar sources. They were copied out of periodicals dating far enough back so that the chances were slim that anyone on the committee would remember them even if they had seen them. Oh, yes. Somebody else in the audience at the reading had the same feeling about another poem — that he had read it in *The New Yorker*." Tewksbury paused, facing me squarely. "I think we have been the victims of a hoax."

I turned sternly to Oompah. "Is this true?"

His air of protest had progressively weakened. Now he pulled himself together, and retorted in the tone of an accuser rather than the accused.

"I had my reasons. And I had my justification. Years ago I used to submit verse to the Wellington Company. Yards and yards of it. They never paid me for it, but they used it. Lots of it. I recognized it again and again on greeting cards I'd read in the stores. Everywhere. Over and over. Not whole stanzas, maybe, but sections, lines, turns of phrase. They stole no end of my stuff. Without paying me. I figured they owed me something. I was just getting my own back."

"But greeting card doggerel is all the same!" Tewksbury returned. "Anybody would 'recognize' his stuff in any amount of it. Mother's Day, birthdays, the passing years. It's all perfectly banal twaddle —"

"Mine wasn't."

"It all sounds the same," Tewksbury continued, ignoring this. "You can't call that plagiarism, man!" His face had worn its customary pallor, more or less. Now some color seeped into his cheeks.

"Besides, that's no justification," I said, sailing into Oompah myself. "You've abused our confidence, betrayed our trust . . ." I gave off, aware of falling into platitude myself. I turned to Tewksbury again. "I can't tell you how sorry I am about all this. I regret it so keenly I'd be glad to offer restitution myself in the amount —" He waved that impatiently off. "Are you sure there's no sign of this 'long narrative epic' anywhere?"

"I'm glad you asked that." Tewksbury's lips twisted into a rather relishing grin. I sensed his *pièce de résistance* in the offing. He now conjured from the desk drawer a small book, which he held out for my inspection. "This is apparently the long saga he's been wrestling with."

I bent forward in my chair to peer at its title, and saw that it was a copy of *Hiawatha*.

"I don't understand. You mean he's been snitching from that, or something? Purloining passages from it?"

"No, no. He's *reading* it, is all. That would appear to be the jape additionally played on us. That is the sum and substance of it, my dear Jim. This is the saga he came here to 'finish.' "

"I never said I was writing it," Oompah said. He pointed to the file of correspondence on the desk. "If you'll just read my statement there again, you'll find I never used those words —"

"*Shall* we not compound a felony by invoking the semantic subterfuge by which it was accomplished." Tewksbury sighed, again revolving in my direction as he flapped his arms at his sides. "There you have the gist of it. He came here to finish *Hiawatha*, by Henry Wadsworth Longfellow."

"Have you ever tried to read it?" Oompah said.

"No more, please." Yet Tewksbury seemed to want to hear more, as one fascinated by an outrage of which he is the butt, determined to gorge himself on the last crumb of that infamy. He closed his eyes and drew a long quivering breath, like a man having a Franklin Pangborn type of conniption fit, the dramatics of which lay in the very attempt to control it. It even gave him a momentary resemblance to the actor. "What did you hope to gain by this, in addition to room and board, the free use of recreational facilities, and the modest honorarium for pocket money? Was it a purely vindictive retaliation at the Wellington Greeting Card Company, for a grievance fancied or otherwise, and not dissimilar to the crank grudges held, over long years, by mad bombers? Or might it also have been a blow aimed at cultural officialdom, the establishment, say, at whose expense it purported to be a stroke of satire?"

"And on top of all that, I felt it was a valid purpose for a fellowship."

"A grant-in-aid to get some reading done."

"Yes, sir. I sincerely felt that. For the public is important too, the consumer without whom the creative artist labors in vain. As Whitman said, 'To have great poets there must also be great audiences.' That audience must be cultivated, for it's slipping away from the artist in our time, at an alarming rate, especially the poets. How many of us are there left who don't spend all their time in front of the television set, that ectoplasm the spread of which will yet destroy this country's very —"

"Then why didn't you simply come right out and ask for a grant-in-aid to get some reading done?"

"Because I doubted you would see eye-to-eye with me in this area."

"Ah, I see. But you felt the end justified the means. That so much does the reader deserve to be subsidized, as well as the artist in these arid times, that any means may be resorted to to obtain one. A subsidy I mean."

"Something like that."

"Something like that."

Tewksbury, with a histrionically skillful gesture of defeat, typical of deportment suggesting he had at one time been on the stage, or aspired to it, gave off interrogation. He moved to the side of his desk, and gazed down at the miscreant with such an air of lugubrious despair that Oompah hung his own head. Tewksbury seemed spent of speech. Then, as though summoning from somewhere within his depleted emotional resources the strength for one last reproach, he said:

"And to do this, to do this with a poem that is part and parcel of our national heritage, dear to the hearts of school children. One that celebrates the glories of innocent human nobility. What do you think Hiawatha would think of you? Or Nokomis, or Gitche Gumee?"

"Not much, I'm afraid."

"I guess. Or your son. Whose trust you so woefully betrayed."

"He will be dealt with," I assured Tewksbury, deeming it wisest not to point out that Gitche Gumee was not so much a character in the poem as a body of water on the shores and surface of which much of the action took place. Lake Superior, actually, if memory served.

Oompah himself came to life again. He stirred about

in his chair, as though preparing some fresh counter-attack.

"It's not exactly true, or fair, to say that I never got any writing done here at all, or that all I wanted to do was wade through *Hiawatha* on the fellowship. I engaged in some experiments with it. Editing it, you might say, toying with certain variations, like, that might improve it or bring it up to date."

"Oh? And can you show us some of that?"

"I don't have it on paper. I composed them in my head. Lots of poets work that way, you know."

"So that you might be hard at work while appearing to the casual observer to be merely tooling toward town, or looking for a lady artist to walk in the woods with."

"Some of it while lying in bed at night, waiting to get to sleep. I'll be glad to recite a little if you'd like."

"Please do."

"One section in particular, about how Mudjekeewis was chosen, and then divvied up the Winds of Heaven. You probably remember he was father of the Winds of Heaven."

"Vaguely," said Tewksbury.

"Let's see. Oh, yes." Oompah cleared his throat and began:

> *"Thus was Mudjekeewis chosen*
> *Father of the Winds of Heaven.*
> *For himself he kept the West-Wind,*
> *Gave the others to his children;*
> *Unto Wabun gave the East-Wind,*
> *Gave the South to Shawondosee*
> *And the North-Wind, wild and cruel,*
> *To the fierce Kabibonokka.*

> *To the rest he gave the good winds,*
> *Both the brasses and the woodwinds,*
> *Gave to Johnny Dodds and Satchmo.*
> *Blew they clarinet and trumpet*
> *To the virgin and the strumpet,*
> *Who could either like or lump it —"*

Tewksbury sank into his chair. He was ashen. He passed a hand across his face as though brushing invisible cobwebs from it — or as though on the verge of apoplexy. "That will . . ."

> *"Did they gigs in Escanaba,*
> *Oshkosh and Balenciaga,*
> *Ish Kabibble and Pellagra —"*

"When can you take him away?" Tewksbury seemed quite ill, now very like the Franklin Pangborn of *The Bank Dick*, in the saloon-booth scene in which W. C. Fields has contrived to slip him a Mickey Finn, in hopes that, on the morrow, he may not be in shape to audit the bank's books.

"Right away," I said. "Mr. Tewksbury, are you all right? Can I get you a drink of water?"

"No, I'm all right. Or wait. Let him finish the week out. That'll bring him to within a month of his six-month semester. I don't want his departure to seem too precipitate, as though there has been a fracas." He pronounced it in the British fashion, frahkah. "We must at all costs avoid any appearance of that, for the good of the Colony. And we won't prefer charges, though one of conspiracy to defraud could be brought."

Whether Tewksbury's restraint in not bringing action

46

was prompted by motives of charity, or in order to prevent the incident's being recounted in future as one of the more humorous chapters in his career, remained a subject for speculation. In any case, I thought it best to wind this part of the episode up with all haste. Protesting again a thousand apologies, I rose to do so.

"I don't hold you to blame," Tewksbury said, rather as one not meaning to imply something left to be desired in the way I had brought my father up. "I regret the whole thing for your sake as much as ours. More, actually. Goodbye to both of you — and here is your copy of *Hiawatha*, Mr. Tickler."

"I want you to have it."

Tewksbury turned an ominous shade of purple, threatening relapse. "But I don't want it," he said quietly. "Or any memento of your stay."

"I feel I owe you something."

"*I don't want it.*"

I took it, thrust it into my coat pocket, and piloted my father out the door.

We hurried along one of the winding paths toward Nathaniel Hawthorne, the gravel crunching under our feet in rhythmic unison. He had by now put on the beret, making the customary rakish adjustment. We marched along in silence till we neared the cottage steps. I felt something admonitory must be said, on however elementary a plane.

"This is a hell of a note."

"There was nothing personal in it. I want you to know that. I mean if you were one of the judges I'd never have put you on the spot — just as my cause was."

"What magazines did you copy them out of?"

"Like he said. *Harper's, The New Yorker, The Atlantic.*

The best. I made a sort of game out of it with the judges, putting them on their mettle, if they were all that well-read. Authorities in their field. I never used any obscure magazines. Only ones they were expected to be up on."

"Gave them a sporting chance."

The problem of digesting this wonder was overshadowed by the almost worse one of breaking the news to Mother. My jangled emotions were hardly improved by the sight that confronted me when I arrived home that evening. She was sitting in semi-darkness at the kitchen table, her good elbow on it, "favoring" the burnt one by resting it in her lap. A large sack of groceries stood on the table — no doubt with a fresh string of Blue Stamps among the provisions. She had a tale of her own to tell, it was clear from her general mien when I pulled the light-string.

"As it must to all men, I nearly got run over just now as I was crossing the street on my way home from the store. Some boys zipped around the corner on two wheels — peeling I think they call it — nearly knocking me down. Scared me out of a year's growth. I'll be all right in a minute. I'll fix supper, somehow." She rose and toiled toward the cabinet where she kept her kitchen supplies. "But first, I've got to change my garbage bag."

I wanted to put my head in one, pulling it on upside down, tying the end securely around my neck, and then breathe deeply with my mouth shut, sucking the polyethylene up into my nostrils till my wind was shut off, and I knew no more. Dead and done with it. Crossed over into Camp Ground.

We had a steak as tough as life itself, my end of which I washed down with a bottle of claret worthy of it, to the back of which was affixed a label extolling its merits as an ideal compliment (sic) to any red meat, duck, or spaghetti. Sitting across from Mother, eating in silence, I knew I couldn't tell her — and suddenly thought of a way of turning this whole wretched business to account.

"Mom, I've got news for you. Good news I think. Pop's leaving the Colony! He's coming home! Yep. He feels — well, not guilty exactly, but unhappy out there. Lonesome. He's coming home to you Friday, or at some point over the weekend. He's cutting his fellowship short. He's coming home. In a nutshell, he misses you."

"Oh, if I could just believe that."

I looked him up first thing the next morning, and laid it on the line in precisely those terms. Not a word of the truth must be breathed to her. Rather his story must be the same as mine. He wished to spend the last remaining month of his leave of absence from McKesson Robbins at home. Better yet, go away on a trip with her somewhere, a second honeymoon. Then back to work at his old job. That, and that alone, was the price of my silence.

That was how the mess was resolved. Seizing on the apparent reconciliation, permanent or otherwise, I even persuaded my mother to use up fifty books on a matched set of luggage for the resultant holiday in Bermuda, thereby forestalling at least immediate threat of divorce proceedings. I quit my own job at the Colony, where it would have been a bit sticky to stay on, and made hell-for-leather for my old college scene. That seemed best. A former roommate had stayed on in a Chicago suburb near Northwestern's Evanston campus, in a small apartment for which he needed somebody to share the rent. I took the first stopgap job I could get, in the office of a turpentine factory on the nearby outskirts of the city. The only letter I wrote home about it was full of euphemistic evasions and mealymouthed misrepresentations of its importance of the sort I felt my parents were entitled to, with a definition of the smelly derivative we sold that was calculated to send Mother to the dictionary, which she felt to be one of the rewards for having saved to send me to college — a confusion as to what I was talking about that she thought of as a personal fringe benefit due her. "It's an oleoresin exuded from the terebinth, you know."

I could hear her sigh in a transitional way, as for a chapter in my life completed and a new one begun, and imagine her telling her friends, "He's got his A.B., and is now in turpentine."

Not for long. A fluke of fate gave my life a fresh twist of fortune that made my head swim.

4

ONE SATURDAY MORNING I wanted to, had to, cash a paycheck, but having overslept I found myself galloping breathlessly up to the bank door at three minutes after noon, to find it closed. I remembered the bank had a drive-in branch a short distance up the street that was kept open half an hour longer on Saturdays, so I hightailed it for that without delay.

There was a long file of cars turning off the street into the driveway ramp, making for a minor traffic snarl there being briskly presided over by a cop. I sensed absurdity in the making already as I slipped into line between a red convertible and a station wagon into which a large family was crammed. Reason told me to drop this project, but need propelled me on, though certainly at a snail's pace. Pauses necessarily alternating with spasmodic forward jerks, as customers up ahead made their deposits or cashed their checks, I filled by gazing nonchalantly around, as though being one of a queue of motor cars was an everyday occurrence in my life. Nevertheless, I was aware of gathering onlookers, uncomfortably so of the policeman's gaze fixed on me between gesticulations and whistle-blasts at the traffic he was trying to keep in order. I turned my head and smiled over at him, as who should be passing the time of day. He gave a sharp shake of his own head, with a frown of warning, the gist and purport of which became clear the instant I reached the wicket in a cloud of exhaust from the departing convertible.

"I'm sorry, this is for motorists only," a female voice said crisply through the intercom imbedded in the plate glass that divided us. The teller was a stunning girl with green eyes and a crop of auburn hair, which shook briskly in the negative when I explained that I had no car. "You'll have to cash this check at the bank," she persisted.

"But —" I reached up to adjust a gooseneck mike, the better to speak into it. "But the bank is closed."

"I'm sorry, it's a rule." She smiled and shrugged helplessly, as though to certify us as jointly locked — as though in an Existentialist drama — in a net of officialdom both lunatic and inscrutable. "It's just that we keep open half an hour longer for the convenience of customers in automobiles."

"Or the bank closes half an hour earlier as a discourtesy to the other ones." Such forensic skirmishes could but lead on to the inevitable "I only work here," though this girl continued for the moment in a vein of reasonable remonstrance, albeit with a pest pigheadedly refusing to realize when he was up against City Hall. I explained once more that I had no car, and that my business must perforce be transacted on the hoof. A blast from the horn of the station wagon at my rear — a fashionably antique "aa — oo — ga!" — indicated that I was wearing the driver thin — or his children were.

"Look, I only work here," at last came out, the girl adding, rather through clenched teeth, "and this is my last day, thank God."

"Very well. We shall see."

My problem was to become mechanized by half past twelve. I would do so by hitchhiking a ride the fifteen or twenty feet from the sidewalk to the wicket, and in so doing simultaneously subject the bank authorities to a scathing satire. They would be made to look like damn fools, and for all to see.

I took my station on the curbstone at the point where it bevelled away to the ramp up which the cars were still turning off the street. Standing there trying to thumb a ride, I became more aware than ever of onlookers gaping at the sight, again not least of them the traffic cop, who finally came over, shoving his cap back to scratch his head in a tradition seemingly derived from slapstick silent two-reelers, in which such constables are always contending with public nuisances.

"What's this all about, Mac?"

"My name isn't Mac."

I continued to sweep the old thumb through the air in the classic arc of hitchhikers the world over. The idea was to strike a car with room for another passenger, and piloted by a driver willing to meet the spectacle presented with something other than what I was drawing: namely expressions that were in turn something to behold. Some averted their faces. Some exchanged with other witnesses that smug glance peculiar to two people deploring a third in public. A finger was revolved at a temple. At last a car rolled up that was empty except for a woman at the wheel. She reached across to the far door, I thought to open it and let me in. Instead she snapped the lock shut, looking apprehensively from me to the cop. I remembered radio bulletins about some inmates who had escaped from a state correctional institution and were still presumably roaming the countryside.

"Look, Bud, this window is only for cars. Can't you buy it? It says it right there," the cop persisted, pointing to a sign. "Why cause all this trouble? Why do you have to be a wiseapple?"

"I'm the one who's having trouble caused him. I have to cash this check. All I need is a ride up to the window."

"Hitchhiking is illegal here. I can run you in for it, if you don't move along. Now I mean it."

"Very well," I said for the second time. And yet again, "We shall see."

With that I flagged a passing cab, or rather one just at that moment nosing into a nearby curbside parking stand. "See you," I called over my shoulder at the cop as once more I broke into a trot, warning that he too must now be drawn into the circuit of official folly under lampoon, while the travesty itself must be escalated. The screw must be given another turn. All then would be laid low. None would escape the fallout. At the same time that this intellectual construction was being put on the measures irreversibly embarked on, their effect on the girl personally was very much on my mind. Very much indeed. I would rush up to the wicket in this taxicab, fracturing her with a gag she must find irresistible had she a heart in her breast and blood in her veins. An encounter of a freshness and hilarity that might even mark the beginning of an acquaintance. Romances had blossomed from less . . .

"Where to?" the cab driver asked as I climbed in.

"There," I said, pointing at the drive-in a few yards away.

"There?"

"That's right. I want to go there, to that drive-in." I pointed again so there would be no mistake about my destination.

"O.K."

He pulled the flag down with a glance back at me, seeming to answer by his manner a question that has often occurred to me. Whether the stories of "this wonderful cab driver" with which the lady chews your ear off at cocktail parties have their counterpart in tales about "this fare I picked up today" brought home to wives at evening by men who hack for a living. The answer would seem to be yes: such wives are regularly regaled by accounts of eccentrics revealed as such within the course of breathtakingly short intervals.

This fare leaned back, knowing that the destination named was not all that easy of access, from here, and that the driver must have realized it, too. There was no question of backing up and darting into the drive. We were past that point, in a one-way zone of town where we would have to execute four right turns in a several-block circuit before a final left-hand turn bringing us off the street into the bank drive I had traversed in vain by shank's mare.

"Some weather we're having," I said.

"No comment."

The driver's face was invisible save for a potato-shaped nose dominating the rear-view mirror in which it was to be glimpsed, and which, together with the back of a very squat and thick neck bore out the general supposition of a laconic, even troglodytic, temperament. This was clearly a Balkan bruiser who moonlighted as a tavern bouncer. I was surprised to see the name Montmorency under the photograph beneath the glass partition, a frontal view confirming the above impression.

It had in äll conscience taken us long enough to turn the first corner; but midway the block that lay ahead we ran into a real jam. Another cop was directing a dense flow of traffic streaming from the parking lot of a church from which a wedding party were just then debouching. The cabbie rested one arm along the back of his seat, watching the scene. The meter ticked away, and with it, of course, one's wristwatch, at which one durst not glance.

"What church is dis?"

"Christ and Holy Trinity," I said, making it sound as much oath as information. One began to have second thoughts. Perhaps the authorities had been made to look like asses enough, and the lampoon ought to be called off. Just then the cab shot forward on command from the traffic cop, directing vehicles, as such functionaries often do, with the flamboyance of a symphonic conductor. "You new in town?" The words came out as I was whiplashed against the back of the seat.

"Yes. We just moved here. I like hacking here a lot better than in Chi, though of course I take fares into there all the time. I've met a lot of interesting people." As he offered this tribute to the suburb serving as our *mise en scène*, I caught him stealing another eyeful of me in the rear-view mirror. It seemed a good idea to let him in on what was afoot, if that was any longer the word for it. So I did. He thought it a great gag, at the same time one with valid social content. He was tickled to death to be a part of it — in fact a collaborator on the satire. To prove his sincerity, he whipped through the remaining streets with all the speed possible, even running the risk of a ticket in beating out a yellow light. He was anything but the phlegmatic type I had originally thought him. On the contrary, exhilaratingly mercurial.

"Shaving it close," he remarked as he jammed on the brakes for our last traffic signal but one. He consulted his wristwatch. "We got three more minutes. Two . . ." Even that finding seemed sanguine, judging from a tower clock in another church up ahead, the big hand of which was creeping ominously close to the six mark. It boomed the half hour as we skidded around the last corner on two wheels. The sight of the original cop cutting off the line of would-be depositors at the driveway, waving them by with shakes of his head while the teller accommodated those lucky enough to have got in under the wire, suggested the jig was up.

"No, wait," said my collaborator. "Look, the cop's walking away. Maybe if I poke along the curb here we can still peel in there before they actually close."

He lurked along the gutter as proposed, waiting till the last admitted car still in line had been served and left. Then he veered suddenly and shot up the ramp. Hunched over, he looked and acted like the wheelman in a heist. I had the check, already endorsed, in my hand. Now to flash it triumphantly out the back window at Jade Eyes, and watch her expression. But the operation could hardly go smoothly. Since we were pelting hell-for-leather up the drive, we had to stop on a dime squarely before the wicket. There was a screech of tires as I was dumped forward out of my seat, landing on all fours on the cab floor. By the time I had recovered myself and the fumbled check and poked my head out the window, like a bird in a cuckoo clock, a shade had been drawn behind the window and a "Sorry Closed" sign propped against the pane.

"Too bad," said the driver as I sat back, swearing a blue streak. "Anyway we tried. I'm wit you. You got a pernt. You got a beef. The fare's a buck forty, witout tip, and wurt every penny of it. Wait till I tell my missus about this caper. She'll split a gut. She likes a guy can hand her a good laugh. She'd like to meet you."

Speculations on possibly burgeoning acquaintance with the Montmorencys were perhaps best withheld till he heard the news I had for him. It was going to be a buck fifty *wit* tip, that being all I had on me and the reason I had had to cash the check.

But he took it in good part, waving amiably as he pulled on out of the drive, leaving me standing on it. I started toward the sidewalk. As I did so, I heard the door of the drive-in open. Turning, I saw the girl coming in my direction.

"Oh, it's you. Look, I hope you don't think I'm so dog-in-the-manger that I'd balk at cashing your check. But the boss was in there with me. I mean there was nothing personal about it."

"The one who made the rule?"

"No, just *my* boss. A feisty type, who wouldn't have been above making trouble about cashing my own pay-check if I'd broken the rule. Which isn't as idiotic as it sounds by the way. You can't have both cars and pedestrians at the window. Dangerous, besides making a hell of a mixup."

We stood in the middle of the now otherwise deserted

driveway as she went on with this apologia for superiors I had been at such pains to take off. She was shorter than I'd fancied — a good four inches under my own six feet — but the eyes were as incandescent as I'd remembered. They crinkled with amusement under the auburn thatch now being rumpled in a soft summer wind, and her face broke into a grin as she said, "The last I saw, you were out there trying to hitch a ride. Cracked me up. I made a mistake counting. If I hadn't caught it I might be there the rest of the afternoon balancing the books."

"And I'd be out here waiting." That was a lie, as I'd been on my way when she emerged. Close up now, though, I decided it would have been worth it. Her smile was as radiant as her gaze, and I was so sure she smelled good my loins began to tighten.

"What finally happened? Cop shoo you away?"

"I took a cab."

"A *what*?" She broke into peals of laughter.

"I thought you'd like it." I now viewed the escapade purely as a jape enacted for her amusement, all the more to be relished for the enormous risk undertaken of its falling flat. That was happily not the case. It went over with a bang. "Only missed it by a split second, too. But now where can I cash this?" I went for broke in the slang sense. "So we can have a bite of lunch."

Her expression sobered, and, looking away, she said, "Well . . ."

"I know. Bruno will trust me." I pointed toward a German restaurant up the street. "How about it. Some knockwurst and a stein of cold beer."

"You don't tempt me with those, exactly, but all right. What's your name?"

"Jim Tickler. What's yours?"

"Amy."

"What kind of Amy?"

She drew a deep breath, as though steeling herself for an ordeal. "Wintermoots," she said, with visible strain. Then the smile broke out again, and she heaved her shoulders with a charming sigh. "Well! It's always a relief to get that over with."

5

I HATE AFFECTATION OF ANY KIND, and so could only inwardly deplore the studied dash, the forged air of long-possessed negligent charm with which I sailed out of my open convertible, not swinging the door out but vaulting it still sitting, like a swashbuckler in a television film, landing lightly on the balls of my feet on the asphalt before proceeding across the road to dine with the Wintermootses. Strolling through a lull in the traffic, I suddenly found myself being borne down on by a car materializing at high speed around a curve, and, being a health nut, sprang nimbly out of its path. I told the vanishing motorist what he was like, shouting particulars from the farther curb, which I had of course thus gained with more expedition and less unction than intended. I hoped now that my arrival was *not* being observed after all.

The MG wasn't mine but belonged to the classmate necessarily generous with it because of the frequency with which I, in turn, coughed up the rent money for the apartment we shared. I'd had to park it on the street because the Wintermoots driveway was visibly choked with such possessions. I now wanted to kick myself for letting Amy think I owned it (it just hadn't been handy to pop into when I'd wanted to cash the check), but my doing so was a measure of my desperation to pass muster with a family more than a cut above me socially. This was, as said, the North Shore tenderloin, well past the city limits where the houses gave way to homes, as one's people called them, circles of the sort in which impassioned youths of low degree find themselves making a sortie on a family, not just courting a girl. He has tribal approval to win, of a kind not a factor in the case of promising steamfitters necking in the parlor with one or another of one's sisters, one's mother's pretensions to the contrary notwithstanding. Her pinky-lifting inquiries about what "stock" such a lounge lizard came from being forced in the nature of matters to stop at assurances that the mother isn't put away in the booby hatch or the father walking "funny" around the kitchen in the last stages of the pock, the result of indiscretions in Peoria. Her interrogations about the Wintermootses were on a permissibly higher level, but they made me want to put my head under a cold tap. "Are they refined? I'll bet they are." "Yes, Mother, so refined they never use the word. It would never cross their lips." Baffled look, irony wasted. Pursuit of the point hopeless. Yet hers of her investigation continuing unabated, by mail thank God. "One thing I don't understand. Why does a girl from a swanky family like that have to work in a bank?" "Mother, college girls from the upper crust" — one winced at the term necessarily resorted to — "take jobs like that for the summer to broaden their horizons. She doesn't need the money, she gives most of her salary to charities . . ."

By the time I gained the serpentine walk leading to the Wintermootses' Georgian house, I had also recovered my momentarily fumbled aplomb, in a manner once more exciting my amusement with human hypocrisy in general. I gazed upward through a flowering catalpa at the sky, as one alive to beauty in all its forms; one who, though worldling enough, let's never forget it, is not above Drinking Things In. He is capable of enthusiasms. He has fire in the belly. The response to nature was slightly overdone. The evening, though pleasant, was far from gangbusters. A nasty turn in the weather was hinted by a chill in the air, white clouds graying with a threat of rain. I took the three stone stairs at a skip.

I rarely press a finger to a doorbell without a rather charming association linking it, as unconscious folk symbol perhaps, to something my Amy had, certainly, a more opulent pair of. My mood of happy anticipation was again jarred by the memory of Mother's assurances that my progress here would be well lubricated by my having "loads of personality," as well as "plenty upstairs," as indicated by my being capable of such imaginative flights as the above mammalary metaphor. I involuntarily grimaced, as often when fleeting echoes of home in Wabash cross my mind, like shadows racing over a sunny meadow. The letter in which she had given that guarantee of acceptance was not without its quota of "Hot diggety dogs!" The exclamation was one that particularly bugged me, in those days, as representative of origins I was trying to rise above. The metaphor for this program which I found instructive was the idea of myself as a ship going through a series of locks, each higher than the preceding, and each to be hermetically sealed from the last as ascent is made to progressively greater water-levels.

The door was flung wide.

"You were nearly run over!"

"Yes. You see, my dear Mrs. Wintermoots," I replied, instantly striving to qualify for the salon I heard she ran in those parts, and thus the next "lock" to be gained in the arduous passage up life's canal, "there are indeed only the quick and the dead, and these days if you're not the one you're jolly well the other."

It's hardly possible to exaggerate the drive of a young man on the make to impress the parents of the girl he's courting, especially the mother, and not just the girl herself. The desire to be thought a good catch — to "glitter with the glory of the hummingbird," in a line of T. S. Eliot's that smartly defined this one's consuming wish — will make him strut his stuff with anyone encountered in any house he's storming as a suitor, cousins, uncles and aunts, name it, certainly younger or older sisters conceivably languishing away for not being the lucky one. The pleasure Mrs. Wintermoots took in my greeting made me positively shimmer, though again, like a mocking leitmotif, I heard my family exclaim in chorus at Sonny Boy's entrance, "Hot diggety dog!" A flicker of shame as quickly gone at sight of Amy tripping down the curved stairway into the entrance-hall.

It is written that a short girl can be pretty but not beautiful. Be that as it may, Amy managed a regal elegance on little more than five and a half feet of stature, a kind of condensed aristocracy no doubt aided by a patrician tilt to the chin and nose, and a long, slender neck. The result was almost an optical illusion. To say that she had her mother's teeth and her father's hair will be only to recall, I fear, those two-liners in down-home newspapers, involving progeny of whom callers say, "Oh, *that's* who's got them," or "I figured someone must have it," or snappers to that effect. Again no matter. That the mother must have in her own rather taller prime been a beauty could be read in her own face still, without recourse to the daughter's perfect teeth, which became suddenly visible when her full lips parted in a smile, like seeds in slashed fruit. Amy had more sense than transparently to be giving herself the extra two inches of height to which short girls often aspire by twirling their hair into a knot on top of their head. She let hers fall in a welcome cascade to her shoulders, on the bare, fair skin of which its curled ends lightly bounced as she herself did down the stairs.

"What's this I hear about you almost getting hit? Mother let out a yelp."

"Everybody drives too fast. The only safe time, you know, is rush hour, when everything slows to a snail's pace. My God, you both look ravishing. Like sisters!"

"Hello, hello, hello."

Wintermoots now appeared, adjusting a cufflink under a coatsleeve of bleeding Madras, the light sliding across his bald dome as he emerged from some back recess of the lower floor. He paused to complete the last-minute touch to his toilet, smiling apologetically at this delay in having a hand ready to extend in greeting. Then he continued across the intervening parquet in what looked like bowling shoes.

"What's this I hear about your nearly getting yours?" he said, shaking my hand.

By now one was certainly depleted of epigrams on the

subject of speed and the hazards to life and limb, as well as tired of it. So I mumbled something about the grace of God, and suggested we change it. We moved along into the drawing room.

Wintermoots was a winebibber, impatient for that reason to hit the table, so we were not long over cocktails. The single martini he rationed himself he chose to drink standing up, as though we were at a large party, so there was nothing for me to do but follow suit. As we chattered constrainedly away on a variety of themes, each topic like a block of ice at which we chipped unsuccessfully away with our conversational picks, I was uncomfortably aware of Wintermoots sizing me up, running his eye over me from head to foot, as though I were a column of figures to be added up.

"Tickler is a rather unusual name," he said.

I made what has necessarily become a set speech.

"It's an Americanization of Tichelaar," I said, spelling it out. "Tichel is the Dutch word for brick, tichelaar for tile worker or bricklayer. That sort of thing. So we must have had ancestors in Holland pursuing that craft." I spelled out for them some variations come across in phone directories scrounged around in in various towns — Tichler, Tigchelaar, Tiggelaar, till their heads swam. "Anyway, I might as well have been seachanged into Jimmy Bricklayer — or James Mason — as Jimmy Tickler, which is simply a phonetic spelling of the way the name has always been pronounced here in this country anyway."

Whether this explanation, no doubt more exhaustive than required, judging from the way my audience's attention began to wander, made them more amenable to the prospect (if any) of the name's passing into the daughter's possession I couldn't say. But anybody named Wintermoots seemed to me in a damn poor position to be squeamish. Their curiosity produced one of those expiatory waves of loyalty toward my own kind — abruptly again routed by the memory of my mother once talking about a Wabash priest named Winterfield — Wintersomething anyway — having been "disrobed for immorality." Again the customary reflex shudder, accompanied by an involuntary shake of the head.

"What's the matter? Is your drink too strong?"

"No, no, just right. If anything too . . . No, everything's fine, Mr. Wintermoots."

I threw the burden of conversation onto him.

"Amy tells me you're in something called market counseling. What, exactly, does that cover?"

"Everything," he said, sitting down. I dropped into the nearest chair myself. "Almost any service you can imagine for a client selling a product or a service. Everything an advertising agency does and more. A customer might ask us to supervise or conduct a test-marketing for a new item. Or pick our brains for a slogan for it. Or a name. For example, we have a food company right now, Wholesome Brands, who are anxious to launch a new frozen weiner. But they don't have a name for it yet, and want us to come up with something for this frankfurter. They want something nifty, different, catchy." He smiled over at me. "Any ideas?"

I laughed right back at him. "How about Hot Diggety Dogs?"

Nothing was ever to be the same again. My life had changed. Its direction was set. The awe with which I was now regarded, the downright reverence, could hardly be exaggerated. I had only been joking. I thought the name awful myself. But I didn't let that on when I saw Wintermoots's response, which was the gravity appropriate to the recognition of creative genius, suddenly so revealed. Amy probably sensed my actual thoughts, and may have shared them, judging by the laugh with which she met the suggestion, swiftly blending into the murmurs of appreciation all around.

Freud says that wit (on whatever level, but in the sense of an instantaneous retort) is the work of the unconscious. Cognitive thought is not lightning enough for the purpose. My response had certainly been an automatic association, and one having, God knew, little connection with cerebral evaluation! So as far as all that goes, psychoanalytical theory may be right.

My triumph was short-lived. It was followed by a disaster so grotesquely comparable in the interpretation to which it lent itself that I'm not sure to this day there wasn't some cunning, subterranean connection between the two. I mean it was something few parlor intellectuals would have hesitated to label one of your Freudian-slip type of accidents.

Here, at any rate, is what happened.

My first dinner in the bosom of the Wintermoots family was to be made completely that by its taking place on the cook's night out, with Mrs. Wintermoots herself doing the honors with one of her specialties, a spaghetti with clam sauce. She excused herself and went into the kitchen, from which cries of dismay presently issued. She always grated her cheese fresh, and there was no Parmesan. Amy rushed out by car to get some, while I was recruited to help with the salad, leaving Wintermoots alone in the drawing room to ponder his find. While Mrs. Wintermoots attended to her simmering sauce and peeled a few tomatoes for salad, she asked me to wash the lettuce leaves like an angel, leaf by leaf, and dry them in one of those wire-cage-like baskets, the two hinged halves of which are folded shut over the contents, then to be hung on a faucet to drip-dry in the sink — or when there's no time for that, as now, to be taken outdoors and dried by centrifugal force.

"You can just step out the back door there if you will, Jim, and swing it around for a bit. I should have done this sooner."

Standing alone there, in the dooryard, I was happy. I enjoyed whirling the basket around and around, executing a variety of arcs and circles in the air, sending the water-drops spattering in every direction, *zoom*, *whoosh*, over my head and at my side, up and down, back and forth. It suddenly brought back thoughts of the boyhood fun we'd had in Wabash vacant lots with our home-made "fire cans," metal containers of all shapes and sizes in which we'd punch holes to provide a forced draft for the sticks and coals kindled within, which we'd blow to a fine blaze by swinging the can, firmly capped, around in the air on long wire loops affixed to them for the purpose. I smiled at the memory, long forgotten, now to be savored again in what charmingly unexpected circumstances! So many recollections, half defined, dimly caught, of Hoosier days swarmed into my mind. Not least of the ingredients in the mellow mood induced was the sense of my mother fondly reconsidered, not an exasperant now, but a woman of culinary standards in their way as strict as those of the "swanky" hostess within, for whom I was performing this absurd little chore, swinging lettuce leaves about instead of equally meticulously blotting them dry with a kitchen towel as I had done for Mother.

Oh, I felt good, alone out there. Such was my secret exhilaration that swinging the greens around became almost a kind of poetry, a transport of the sort that sets ablaze the questing hearts of young men — especially one for whom all doors seem suddenly to have flown open. I cherished even the origins I seemed to be soaring above in the romantic headway I was making with Amy, as certifying how far I had come. "Oh, those Wabash Blues," I sang as I whirled the basket. "I know I got my dues . . ."

It was then that calamity struck.

In my abandon at making a ballet of my task, I had been weaving ever more complex and intricate patterns in the evening air, rhythmically to the song I was singing, or humming to tide myself over gaps in my knowledge of the lyrics. The basket in question being the double one described, the wire handle is also double when the basket is folded shut. Well, midway a sequence of some very fluid arabesques which involved passing the basket from one hand to the other with no interruption of the cadence, like the fancy work of a Harlem Globetrotter with a basketball, I lost my grip. Or rather the handle simply slipped out of my fingers. With a result that can be imagined. The basket went spinning end-over-end through the yard a distance of some thirty or forty feet, flying open, of course, and spilling greens in every direction before itself disappearing over a fence into a neighbor's yard.

My panic was one of sheer horror — but not so paralyzing to the faculties as to fog my realization that number one on the program was the immediate recovery of the basket. I tore across the intervening grounds and scaled the fence in one vaulting leap (itself replete with

memories of Hoosier schooldays, of Hoosier derring-do).
I found the basket quickly enough, caught in some kind of
flowering bush, tossed it back into the Wintermootses'
yard, jumped back over myself, picked it up and got
cracking on the retrieval of the greens themselves.

They were widely distributed. I scrambled about in
every direction snatching them up wherever they could
be found, in the grass, the dirt, among dead leaves, fragments of gravel from the nearby driveway, and in a
flower bed seen to be top-dressed with something ominously resembling the most honored and effective of fer-
tilizers. "No," I said, absolutely rejecting any speculation
but that it be mulch, or at worst peat moss, as I hastily
wiped the individual leaves on my sleeve or the side of
my coat before stuffing them back into the basket.

When I had recovered all I could — and some were to
be spotted among the branches of trees overhead, one
floating in a bird bath — my basket was no more than
three-quarters full, and that with no certainty that the
contents didn't now include incidental foliage other than
lettuce. Something must be done to plump them out, and
quickly. I suddenly seemed to remember talk of Mrs.
Wintermoots growing her own vegetables. I ran wildly
down a slope to the bottom of the property, and there in a
garden, sure enough, was a fine stand of just what I
needed. Romaine I think it was. I tore up a few handfuls
and crammed them into the basket before charging back
up the slope to where, on the driveway, I had seen a
watering hose. For what was needed now was certainly
another good wash. *And* dry. Luck was with me again.
The hose was attached, in addition to being equipped
with a nozzle affording a fine jet to be trained on the
basket (this time clutched in a death grip with the left

hand) from which fragments of soil, twigs, pebbles and other unidentifiable debris could be seen to be forcefully driven.

A sound audible above the hiss of the hose made me raise my head. This was a hell of a time for Amy to be returning from the delicatessen with her Parmesan. "Damn!" Also, Mrs. Wintermoots could be heard calling from the kitchen. Something about Amy's being back and if I was through out there would I again be an angel and grate the cheese, we didn't want to wait much longer. There was nothing to do but shut off the hose, give the basket a last vehement spin-dry or two, and go inside with Amy, hoping for the best.

I was not the boy at dinner I had been during the cock-tail hour. Jitters over the impending salad kept me pretty much tongue-tied during the Senegalese soup with which we began and the main course to which it led. Not glass after glass of Wintermoots's Chablis, greedily guzzled, could seem to prime my pump. I sat there with a mouth-ful of teeth. I fancied suspicions taking root in the minds at least of my elder hosts, as I failed to pick up on con-versational cues fed me from every direction. I was a manic-depressive, swinging from articulate gaiety to glum silence in a matter of minutes. I was a party poop after all, not living up to his billing from the daughter (assumed sanguine enough to have prompted the invita-tion). I was a one-shot, a flash in the pan. Worse, a thief; I had stolen the name for the weiner committed to Win-termoots's care, having glimpsed it somewhere in a super-market freezer and palmed it off as my own, and that with a pretense of extemporaneous brilliance, as a way of singing for my supper with no regard for the dire

consequences to others. A plagiarism suit would be insti-
tuted against Wholesome Brands, with a judgment also
bringing the firm of Wintermoots and Hale down in
ruins. This place would be foreclosed, the three cars
presently choking the driveway sold. Amy would have to
look for work now needed to support the family, in three
or four rooms back in the city where the homes once
again gave way to houses, not as a *jeunesse dorée* prov-
ing she had her roots in reality . . .

"I understand you breed bulldogs."

"No, Mother, that's Hop Kirwood."

This exchange, meant to fill a silence longer than
most, hardly restored our spirits. On the contrary they
seemed more hopelessly sunk in depression than ever.
When the salad at last appeared, my mind was like the
runny Brie with which it was served.

I fixed my gaze steadfastly on my plate, keeping a
sharp lookout for foreign matter — indeed, God only
knew what abominations. At the same time, I tried to do
this with an offhand air, like a man "toying with a little
cheese and salad." That sort of thing. One was, after all,
come what may, *dining.* But I was aware of people puz-
zling over the contents of their own portions, picking out
unmistakable detritus and setting it aside on the rims of
their plates, with an occasional glance at me from Mrs.
Wintermoots, caught on sidelong glances of my own. Oh,
it was touch-and-go. One might not come out of this with
a whole hide. One should have confessed the mishap
straight out; we could have done with tomatoes and
cucumbers, copious amounts of which Mrs. Wintermoots
had put into the salad. Now it was too late. One would
have to tough it through. But swigging back the Chablis I
wondered why there was no life in it, bejees, like Harry

Hope with his whiskey in a particularly despairing moment of *The Iceman Cometh*. The Iceman speaketh.

"Darling," Wintermoots said, "whatever is it you used in the salad this time? Nasturtium leaves?"

Then assorted summer foliage had got into our mess of greens, and mess was good. Poplar? Forsythia? Lilac? No matter. Pretty ornaments all. More intrepid use should be made of nature's bounties than was the case, wouldn't you say? And not stopping at vegetable matter either. Didn't the ancients eat birds' nests, grasshoppers, lice? So why boggle at the sight of something moving on your plate, what? Nonsense, nothing but a tomato seed barely glimpsed before being shoved aside under a clump of cucumber.

"Of course there aren't any nasturtium leaves, Jake," said Mrs. Wintermoots, picking a speck of something daintily from the tip of her tongue. "But it does seem to me —"

"Speaking of leaves," I said, "I've been admiring that plant over there." I pointed to something in a window planter, with exquisitely variegated foliage, mostly pink and green, of a kind I had in fact often wondered about. "What's it called?"

"Coleus."

"Oh, yes, Coleus. I must remember that. Doesn't one of Shakespeare's heroines wish another's frowns would teach her smiles? Yes, Helena says it to Hermia in *A Midsummer-Night's Dream*. Well, that plant always makes me want to say, 'Thy leaf can teach her flower.' "

Was I back in business? No longer a wet firecracker? It was too early to tell. I was now brooding heavily about the accident in terms of wondering whether it hadn't been subcutaneously willed, a consideration that darkened my mood the more. My feelings about my family were a murky mess indeed, with remorse perpetually qualifying disrelish, and vice versa. Alternatively, resentment constantly intruded upon my awe of those representing the "something better" to which by contrast I aspired. Who were these people making my own look even cornier and chintzier than they were? That line of feeling could have been the motivation behind such a purposeful mischance; a need subtly to shift the guilt over onto the Wintermootses, comparison with whom inspired the embarrassment, even mortification, of which I was ashamed. I had punished the Wintermootses by "letting go" with the lettuce, as with a round of ammunition, an act also achieving thereby psychic catharsis. This was what they "got" for thinking (as they would have) that my family were strictly from hunger, absolutely meat-and-potatoes. Just too hairy. Did I think it myself? All the more reason for pinning it on the Wintermootses. It's probably not too baroque to say that I was ashamed of being ashamed. Of hating to go home, ducking it whenever possible, even at Christmas time, hating to write, even to get mail. That had to be purged — at the risk to myself of jeopardizing my welcome in quarters of the very kind I wanted above all to graduate into, leaving my Wabash shell behind me by life's unresting sea. We all have household gods to appease.

One of Mother's maxims swam into mind. "We must all eat our peck of dirt, you know." Well, we had all tucked in a good bit of that preordained quota tonight I thought, as the table was blessedly cleared for dessert.

One's batting average left in grave doubt whether one could keep afloat in Mrs. Wintermoots's salon, let alone be a credit to it. It commanded the cream of Chicago and North Shore Gold Coast society, articulate spirits who foregathered there at her open-house "Sundays," always the first one of the month. The next loomed ten days off, and my invitation to it ("Save the fifth.") was half revoked as the parting guest was sped.

"I mean come if you can," Mrs. Wintermoots said at the door, rather tepidly.

"Yes, it's free and easy," Wintermoots put in, pointlessly consulting a barometer hanging in the vestibule. "People just wander in and out. Don't reach for it."

They need not have worried. Amy and I went for a late-night spin along the lake front in the course of which I grilled her on the guests generally expected at these do's, so that when I arrived that Sunday I had in pocket the dope on almost anyone I might find myself pitted against there — his interests, his hobbies, in fine his line of country — to be used as grist for the conversational mill. And not grist either; one had pre-ground a lot of verbal flour, now stacked in readiness for social circulation. The cook was on duty of course, more than augmented by a catering service regularly retained, so one was not asked to pitch in with preparations where one was likely to send buffet provisions into orbit. One had popped back a Dexamyl ere setting forth — unneeded, for one's system was clearly in its upward swing, the "flow" phase of the endocrinological tide said to rule, in intervals of seventeen days or some such, one's mental rhythms and resulting alacrity of speech (or want of it, were one caught in ebb). "Good luck with your mouth," was one's parting send-off to oneself as one sailed across the threshold, to see whether any Hoosier lad so conceived and so dedicated could be counted at last among those who glittered with the glory of the hummingbird.

The first couple to whom I was introduced were the Baileys, boned up on as railroad buffs. Fanatics on the subject. To tick off aviation was therefore indicated. Prime order of business.

"I find that there is no true sense of the Journey, aboard a plane," I chatted, punch cup in hand. "Don't you agree? Flying — how shall I put it?" I groped for the aphorism already honed to a razor-edge. "It is not a form of travel, it is merely a form of transportation."

"Right!" said the Baileys, a look-alike couple if you ever saw one, who now bobbed their heads together in a manner that made their resemblance phantasmagorical. As though one had already drunk too much and was seeing double.

There followed twenty minutes of monologue — or duologue — on the best remaining trains, to which one listened in a manner leaving no doubt that one would be reported later a brilliant conversationalist. The only one I recognized was the one famed, in song and story, as the Wabash Cannonball (now, alas, no more).

A middle-aged woman with dark hair, in a long silk gown of ice blue, was the center of an adjoining group, into which I slipped after refilling my punch cup at the buffet table. I knew her to be a musicologist who taught at the university, an authority on Charles Ives. She was expatiating on the late composer as a man fond of weaving endemic American motifs, often chauvinistically New England ones, into a variety of forms. I nodded, cup at lip. "He's a Yankee Doodle D'Indy," I said.

What promised to be an intelligent discussion was cut short by an intruder, albeit a welcome one.

Judge Barsley was then in the public eye owing to a landmark decision he had recently handed down on a pornographic movie. He was even, for a bit, a kind of celebrity, and made no secret of enjoying his hour as such. Everyone naturally was eager to hear him talk about his judgment, which had banned the film as "hopelessly and irredeemably obscene. A pot of filth."

"Of course I had to sit through the whole thing," he related, licking his thin, ascetic lips. "You can imagine what it was like, all alone, there in the dark. I felt a perfect ass."

"Like the man fishing for the pearls that slipped down the back of the lady's gown," I said from the edge of the group.

"What?"

"I feel the thing about porno isn't so much what goes on on the screen, as what occurs in the audience. We are voyeurs." I smiled about in emphasis of the point. "That is what we become, what we are for the duration. And that's bad. We are becoming a nation of viewers rather than doers. And what are we watching? Well, I find myself furtively turning to steal glances at people around me — you know, their expressions, their faces, as the action unfolds. So I quit going to such pictures before I develop an oddity of my own. I mean a voyeur watcher is not one of the more edifying of the sexual specialties, is it now?"

Later I reversed my decision on *What's Got Into Daisy* when I found myself talking to a very toothsome woman in early middle age, one of those who give quick notice, almost helplessly instantaneous, of an irrepressible need to talk sex. We stood alone together in a corner of the room, sipping our third or fourth glass of the very excellent punch the caterers were ladling out from a crystal bowl the size of Soldiers Field. Her name was Mrs. Flamsteed. Perhaps I wasn't reversing my decision as much as amplifying it beyond recognition.

"I'm not one for spectator sports, you see," I said, facing her close up with the flat of one hand against a wall, one foot crossed over the other, and breathing deeply of her perfume. "I always feel I could do so much better myself, given the bare essentials."

One went from strength to strength. One's chemical clock was striking twelve. One was hitting on all sixteen cylinders. That seemed to be the consensus of everyone who got a load of me. "Who is that?" they would whisper, hushing their own prattle when I drew near. "Oh, Amy's friend. What does he do? Let's ask him to the barbecue . . ."

"They all loved you," said Mrs. Wintermoots as again we sat *en famille* at midnight, the last guests gone and the caterers at their Herculean job of cleaning up. We had our shoes off, so to speak, hashing over a party that had been a smasher.

"Especially Mrs. Flamsteed," Amy threw in with a laugh. "Better watch out, Jim. She's famous for her heels. They're round as billiard balls."

"Not to worry, Amy. It's only your hands I'm putty in." I looked apologetically into my nightcap brandy. "Silly putty I'm afraid." The fishing for flattery was not in vain. "Nonsense, you were the hit of the bash," Wintermoots put in from the depths of his easy chair.

He had again been eyeing me speculatively for much of the evening. Now he seemed impatient to have a moment alone with me, and the women, no doubt cannily sensing as much, excused themselves to help with what must be a voluminous evening's debris in the kitchen, as well as to see the caterers off when the time came.

"Look," he said, dressing a cigar, "I don't want to pry or get personal, but here you are a college graduate obviously marking time. I mean I surely don't imagine you want to make a life in the turpentine business."

"No, sir."

"Oh, good God, I wish you'd stop saying sir. I'm not a commissioned officer. Call me Jake. Anyway. Why don't you take a shot at working in my office. You youthful idealists probably think marketing counselors are some form of prostitute — or at best pimps. No, hear me out. But it's not at all like that, it's not all I do, and there *are* rewards, unexpected satisfactions — Oh, by the way, I tried your Hot Diggety Dog on Wholesome Brands and they went for it like cobras. That'll be the name of the weiner, it's been baptized. Of course there's a bonus in it for you —"

"Pshah!" I said, flinging the very thought away with a wave of the hand. "But go on. You say it's not all you do. What do you mean?"

"I do a lot of public speaking. Kiwanis lunches, conventions, business seminars. Even spout at schools of business administration now and then. Love it. Little ham in all of us. But I hate writing the damn speeches. Tried a guy out at the agency but he's no good. Everything he turns out for me sounds like a speech, if you know what I mean. Now you, you seem versed in a whole hell of a lot of subjects, and you can turn a phrase. Hop things up a little. For instance, something you said tonight about Judge Barsley — thank God after he was gone! — about a roué like that sitting in judgment on a piece of porno.

That would fit in beautifully in a speech I'm trying to write now on the vagaries of the courts, inconsistencies and inequalities in law enforcement."

"Oh? What was that?" I asked indifferently, hoping he'd get it right. One's mots are so often garbled in the repeating.

" 'Justice may be seldom blind but it is often cockeyed.' "

"Oh, did I say that?" Again the negligent wave of the hand. "Help yourself, of course. If it's any use."

"Got to lighten things up now and again. Use a joke, or a well-timed story."

"Of course."

"Otherwise they'll fall asleep on you. Or walk out."

"Or both," I thought, thinking of Oompah at divine worship. I must have mused aloud, because Wintermoots said, "What?"

"Nothing." The day must come to speak of my family, but as St. Augustine added after beseeching God to make him chaste, "Not yet!"

"Why, you're probably a hell of a good public speaker — Amy says you are — and I mean . . . well, if you think I could be of help I'd be glad to —"

"I don't mean just ghost writing the speeches. I have in mind the office too. No particular niche, just a sort of, well, at-large job. You'd probably be full of ideas for our clients. So you'd be in the think tank. I mean what can you lose by giving it a whirl. You keep living in the same digs you had as a student, so I gather you don't want to go back to Wabash."

Again the reminder of one's family, driving over with some people rather than motoring down with friends, causing one's spirits to plummet like shot fowl. With the next heartbeat sensing oneself determinedly on the wing again, soaring above the vulgarity of one's origins.

"So O.K. Come to the office as soon as you can make it, and meet Hale, and then we can talk salary and other arrangements . . ." Wintermoots heaved himself to his feet, from which he had by this time in fact shucked his shoes, and padded in his socks toward what was presumably his den. "I'll get what I've got of a draft of that speech. You can take it home with you. Maybe subtle it up a little."

6

"GOOD FENCES MAKE GOOD NEIGHBORS — especially if you happen to be a thief."

Wintermoots was going over a speech I had just written for him. The above line, among others, gave him trouble, and as a consequence, pause. He seemed unhappy, even wretched; still masticating what should have already been digested and assimilated — for he had been given the draft two days ago for leisurely perusal in the interval between then and now. Or so it struck me, as I sat watching him across a desk the size of Rhode Island.

He broke down.

"What the hell does that mean?"

"There's a line of Robert Frost's, 'Good fences make good neighbors.' You remember it now." He gave the vague equivocal grunt of someone whose face is being saved and hates you for it. "Perhaps his most famous, except for the poem about stopping by woods on a snowy evening, of course." He nodded again. "Well, I thought there might be a laugh for you in there, some much-needed comedy relief from your statistics on the rise in crime. After all, your address is about law and order, part and parcel of the need for a return to moral values in general. The idea is that a crook has got it made if he has a friend next door on whom he can conveniently rely to unload boodle realized on second-story heists —"

"Yes, yes, I understand," Wintermoots said, resenting even more than he had the obscurity of the bon mot, the assumption that he required all that amount of exegesis to clear it up for him. He seemed to be getting more miserable by the minute, as he progressively lost his grasp of what he was reading, slipping rapidly from paragraph to paragraph of "his speech," like a mountain climber clutching vainly at limbs and rock ledges in his descent along an escarpment he had too optimistically attempted. He had stopped asking me to call him Jake, I noticed. Thus now might be the time to break the ice by doing so. Perhaps he was more than a little weary. Needed bucking up. So I said: "With your timing, you'll collect on it, I feel certain, Jake." There, it was out, like a drawn tooth, and like a dentist I wanted to say, "There, that wasn't so bad, was it?" I drew a deep breath. "You may even get a boff on it. Then, I see you pausing, with that Jack Benny timing you have, Jake, bleeding 'em slowly, don't you know, and saying, 'But that isn't the kind of fences we want, is it, or neighbors?' After the laugh subsides."

"I'll get a laugh?"

"I just laughed, the way you read it. I mean let's not worry about being too literate, and in a college homecoming address for God's sake. And *your* college, Jake."

I shouldn't have added that. His college wasn't much account, Yuppa Prairie College in North Dakota? There was no call to rub it in, even though praise had been intended, at least a sort of grace note. To which misgivings must be added the realization that they wouldn't have invited Wintermoots to deliver this speech, or perhaps any speech, if it didn't ginger up their chances of getting a really fat contribution from someone who was after all their best known alumnus, at least in marketing circles. Educational institutions have to resort to that sort of thing to keep afloat these days; even honorary Ph.D.'s are dished out in frank courtship of financial support. We've all noticed the ever more sizeable sprinkling of industrialists among the artists and scholars so laurelled at spring commencement exercises. In fact it's getting to be the other way around, a sprinkling of intellectuals among the tycoons. The president of one of our most famous bastions of learning has freely admitted that he "built the university by degrees." Can't be helped. So a doctorate in humane letters was quite in the cards for Jacob Wintermoots, somewhere along the line, some time, provided he let somebody else write his material for him. That he needed reconstruction even more fundamental than that was evidenced by what he next said.

"I'm not sure many will get it. The English department isn't their *forté*."

I winced for the third time since the beginning of our acquaintance at his pronunciation of that word, as for the third time I made a mental note to utter it correctly, and with emphasis, in his presence. No, I would do it right now, and obviously, damn whether it hurt.

"No, it may not be their fort," I said, looking away. He was straightening out paper clips, always a bad sign;

several metal squiggles lay strewn about his desk. I revolved within myself the homework I'd been able to do on his alma mater with the aid of catalogues and other materials. Their strong section was livestock agriculture, Yuppa's, not to make any bones about it, although they did have a slap-up history branch on the Plains Indians. A sizeable proportion of the faculty probably said "*forté*" as a means of displaying their linguistic polish.

"So you can throw in something like 'with apologies to Robert Frost,' or 'as Frost certainly wouldn't want us to add' . . ." Feeling this was getting ridiculous, a simple throwaway threatening to put everything out of kilter, I proposed that we skip the point for the moment and go on to his next query.

He drew a deep breath, as one inflating himself for action.

"In the section about the new morality — which you say to oldsters seems a new immorality, I like that all right — you have me say . . . where is it? Oh, yes, here. That 'I recently saw three people go by on a tandem bicycle, a second woman sitting side-saddle on the crossbar in front of the man who was pumping away on the forward seat, and I thought to myself, Ah, must be a *ménage-à-trois*. How charming!' " He removed his horn-rim glasses and dropped them on the desk. "I never saw any such thing and neither did you, except maybe in the same cartoon I did, now that it seems to ring a bell. It's not even possible. It can't be done, the way they're built."

I smiled patiently. "It's only a bit of interjected whimsy, Jake, concerning the credibility of which I can only recall what Turner replied to the woman who complained she had never seen sunsets like those he painted. You remember Turner's retort." Wintermoots growled dejectedly. " 'No, madame, but wouldn't you like to,' " I finished, with that look of pained omniscience with which Eric Sevareid, having delivered his closing snapper, brings to an end the pundit portion of the C.B.S. Evening News.

The phone rang and Wintermoots listened to somebody without really suspending his attention to the speech draft, which he continued to page through as he held the receiver wedged against his ear with his shoulder. It was evidently a consultation with his partner Hale, which he suddenly broke off saying, "He's here now. I'll ask him."

Wintermoots lowered the phone and said, "Have you thought of a name yet for that line of frozen cakes and pastries Wholesome Brands wants to put out?"

"Yes."

"What is it?"

"Just Desserts."

"What?"

"Isn't it to be a line of frozen pastries only? *Nothing else?*"

"Right."

"So it's Just Desserts. Which will also give them a built-in advertising gimmick aimed at the housewife. She's trying to give her family what they deserve, with the easily prepared sweet she herself deserves, you see, simply pop it into the oven —"

"Love it." He relayed the suggestions to Hale, whose pleasure in them could be read in Wintermoots's beaming face, and even overheard. It was now lunchtime, and he proposed we break for an hour or two and resume our huddle over the speech then.

Leaving the executive lair and strolling through the knee-high swinging gate into the large outer office where

87

the lesser employes sat, I was aware of gazes raking me from all sides, as at the firm's new fair-haired boy. There he goes, hot as a pepper and cool as Canada. Drawing urbanely on a cigarette, he runs the long, sweet gamut toward his own private office, where he is to be left strictly alone as idea-man-at-large, pampered, let sit in the park if it suits him there to await his muse. He returns a smile here, a wave there, again earmarking a toothsome typist as lunch target. Pauses to offer a word of encouragement to a man who once had a private office, in balmy days as favored as himself, now demoted to clerical chores after fizzling out at higher. "Hang tough, fella," he says, pressing the wretch's shoulder. Oh, these actors! He knows he could join the crestfallen toiler in a twinkling out here in Siberia, if he turns out to be a nine-day wonder himself. He may glitter with the glory of the hummingbird now, he warns himself, but then overnight his house will be left unto him desolate, and his bishoprick will another take.

I went with Wintermoots to Yuppa Prairie. He wanted me along not just to give the agreed-on speech a last-minute rub here and there, but also to discuss business matters that might take his mind off of it. For like all good public performers he was miserable beforehand. In fact his nerves were a can of worms — like Rubinstein's before a concert, I reminded him, Dylan Thomas's before a reading. I bucked him up with comparisons such as these, and before we knew it, there we were in a packed auditorium, I sitting in the audience, Wintermoots being introduced by the president as "perhaps our most distinguished alumni." I thought he said "alumni" though maybe I should give him the benefit of the doubt. Anyway, there he was, taking his place on the rostrum to a patter of courteous applause.

He started with an opening we had polished up on the train coming over, based on something that had happened to me once. "I hope I fare better, my young friends, than I did this afternoon," he said, keeping the horn rims out of sight till needed, as I had instructed him to do when we rehearsed the speech in the Pullman. "I had coffee with some old friends I hadn't seen in years, an interval during which their union had been blessed with issue. This in the form of a nine-year-old who sat at my feet — trying to pull my shoelaces loose." A faint titter went over the audience, like a breeze rippling dry grass —- just. I anted up a cackle of my own, out of all proportion. Watch it, I told myself. My heart was hammering, in contrast to Wintermoots's platform assurance, which I now, seeing him in action for the first time, saw was a definite asset. I don't know whether you've ever written speeches for anyone, but the phenomenon of relaxation experienced by a public performer once he steps onstage (attested to by Rubinstein as sensed the instant his fingers hit the keys) is reversed in the case of the author sitting in the audience: relatively calm beforehand, he becomes a nervous wreck the second his merchandise is up for the acid test. My pulse must have been a hundred and ten as Wintermoots continued:

"Well, I had a great time with my old friends, telling story after story. I had picked up quite a repertory in the intervening years. But the kid was a disturbance. He was obviously bucking to go look at television. Finally his mother said 'Gary, can't you sit still and listen to Mr. Wintermoots for ten minutes? Why must you always be amused?' "

We collected what we had expected on it. Not a boff, nothing to be picked up on the Richter scale, just a respectable laugh. I mean honest, not a courtesy thing. My heart sank back down out of my throat. He was going to be all right. That was confirmed by Wintermoots's pause, during which he swept the audience with a slow, comprehensive glance, and the way he said, "So it's been slow, kids. It's been tough, you guys." Just a touch of Bob Hope in the timing, the arch glance, a faint echo of Edward G. Robinson in the "you guys." We were going to be O.K. I sat back and relaxed.

"I recently attended a party where there was a high government official," he resumed, taking the cheaters out of his pocket at a point in his introductory material where we were still playing it loose, not to suggest sudden transition into the Dullsville of a speech read from a prepared text. In fact everything stopped for tea while he held up his glasses to the light, breathed on the lenses individually and wiped them with his handkerchief. He took his damn time beautifully, with that absolute leisure entertainment requires (W. C. Fields's *bête noire* was the fear that he would speak his lines too fast). My heart raced again as I waited for the next line, an interpolation that had to get a boff or we were dead. Wintermoots put the glasses on. "Well, maybe it's an exaggeration to say he was high, but he'd certainly had a few."

The result was good. We were in the groove. They were with us. I knew where all the laughs lay, and so listening with only half an ear to the serious parts of our address on "Moral Values in a Changing World," I stole furtive glances around me. My eye picked out a wide assortment: a shaggy man in a pepper-and-salt suit instinct made a professor; a woman in a bright red coat with hair piled in a great bale on top of her head; students in blue shirts and leather jackets; an Indian brave in full tribal regalia, seated next to a very plump squaw, and taking assiduous notes on what the speaker was saying. I had an uneasy intuition about him, I couldn't have said why. Just a bad vibe.

The high government official had spilled some beans about crime statistics falsified to make a government look good which had been boasting about a drop in lawlessness attributable to its efforts. Serious crimes were on the rise — was there a link between that and the general "secularization of values?" I thought we'd coined a neat phrase there. Was there just too much sexual freedom? Had the reaction to two hundred years of Puritanism, one in which instead of talking about our duties we were now talking about our rights, been so violent as to produce anarchy? Was it time for a return to principles of . . . ?

There was a cough or two, always a bad sign. A man in the row ahead of me began to nod. One of the denim-shirted cats rolled a catalogue or something into a telescope and, holding it to one eye, squinted around the house. I tensed, knowing the Robert Frost gag was imminent. We would need it. It must come through, or it was all the sandman's.

Wintermoots changed it. He wasn't taking any chances. I could sense that the instant he began to dish it out in a completely unfamiliar form, in the middle of a passage about everyone being on the take, corruption everywhere.

"You know the great American poet Robert Frost said . . ." Oh, Christ, I thought, hanging my head. This really is the boondocks. He has to explain who he is.

"Frost said that good fences make good neighbors. Well I have a neighbor who doesn't make fences — I think he *is* one . . . judging from the . . ."

The result justified him. It did quite well, and, raising my head, I saw the shaggy dog in the pepper-and-salt suit throw his head back and roar, turning to someone obviously his wife as he did.

The rest of it, I'm afraid, sounded like a speech. But then there wasn't much left. He sat down to a good round of applause. The president rose from his own platform chair, stepped up to the lectern and made a short, gracious speech of thanks. I was relieved, but emotionally exhausted — and ready for a couple of stiff ones. I had a seat on the aisle, up which I was ready to shoot the moment we were dismissed. Then I heard something that made my heart freeze.

"And now," the president said, "for our question period."

I could not reverse the impulse that had already propelled me outward. I slipped out of my seat and, bent over double like Groucho Marx, snuck away toward the door. There I stopped. I couldn't weasel out like this. I planted myself against the rear wall with my arms folded, and faced the stage. Wintermoots, catching sight of me, threw me a stricken look, almost one of accusation, as though a question period, so far from being a pop-up, was something I should have known about and drilled him for, trying out an assortment of things such as he might be asked . . .

Several students were on their feet, their hands raised. It was going to be brisk. The president pointed to one of them, a chick in a purple poncho. "Yes?"

"I would like to ask the speaker this concerning what he calls sexual license. Authorities differ on whether man is, or is not, instinctively monogamous. Some say he is. Some say he is not. What is your position on that?"

Wintermoots gulped from a tumbler of water that had been supplied him, his eye rolling reproachfully at me again. I lowered my head, not in shame, but in prayer, beseeching Almighty God that he would say something about the marriage license still being the proper kind, or something like it, so the girl could be sat down with the joke the question deserved. I concentrated, hoping to send him the message telepathically. But instead he hemmed and hawed and said something about there being two sides to everything, and what was good for one might not be good for another, that our lives needed a formal framework, like a trellis for our flowers to bloom on, and so on. It was pretty skinny.

The president recognized the Indian brave in full regalia. When he rose, his feathered headdress could be seen to extend all the way down his back.

"Is it not true," he said, and you knew you were in for one of those declarative counter-speeches masquerading in the interrogative form, "that child-bearing is not a matter of nine months but of sixteen or eighteen, if you allow for the period of lactation, and that this is too long a span for a husband to be abstemious in, if the situation requires it, and that then he should be allowed a certain latitude for sexual fulfillment elsewhere."

Wintermoots's trouble with the question may have been accounted for in part by his not understanding the meaning of the word lactation. So to define it for him as best it could be done from this distance, and by panto-mime, I reached inside my coat and drew out an imagi-nary breast, sort of cupping it in one palm, hefting it slightly you know, even held it forward like a mother

93

giving suck. He seemed to get the drift, because he gave a slight nod in return. Then he turned to the brave. "Well, marriage is a give-and-take . . ." he began, and that was when I went out.

Still, in the empty foyer, I felt guilty, like someone copping out. So I turned from the outer door through which I had been on the point of gaining the refuge of the street, and went back to the one leading to the auditorium. I stood there with my ear to the crack. I don't know what else he said to the redskin, because the answer was finished and the next question was being asked.

"You remarked," said a man's voice older than a student's would have been, coming from a point in the house that made me link it with the pepper-and-salt party, "you remarked, 'We all wash our hands of Pontius Pilate.' Precisely what do you mean by that?"

Good question. What, indeed. I had slipped the aphorism into the speech at the last minute, and we'd had no time to discuss what it meant, if anything. It just sounded profound. It had a deep ring. Plenty of *timbre*. Now I must listen closely to Wintermoots's exegesis. My ear pressed hard to the door, I heard him say something about moral irresponsibility, mankind refusing to realize that we are *all* as guilty of connivance or even betrayal as the figure we have down the centuries condemned as a symbol of it, namely P.P. Yes, I thought, nodding, that might be what it means. Yes, yes, indeed. Sounds right. Then something about moral cowardice, buck passing, a scapegoat for our own guilt in that area. Yes, that too. Could be. Right. Uh-huh. Fine.

"The young lady over there."

"You referred a number of times to the necessity of

94

evolving an Existentialist morality in the post-Christian era. What is Existentialism?"

That was when I beat it. I turned and ran out of the lobby through the outer door, not stopping there either, but continuing on across the porch to the long flight of stone stairs, down which I hurried two at a time, and sideways, like a milkman. I had thought that just before hightailing it I'd heard Wintermoots say "Duh . . ." by way of preface to whatever his elucidation was to be on the subject of Existentialism, but I wasn't sure, and anyway I didn't want to think about it now. I headed for the nearest bar and had that double.

7

WINTERMOOTS MADE GREAT STRIDES. Daily exposure to me, with what that inevitably entailed in the way of deepened knowledge, sharpened perceptions and broadened horizons made that perfectly natural. Much was bound to rub off. Still, he was to be credited with more than a modicum of personal potential, far greater than that to be normally encountered in an executive type with your standard ambitions. He was hot for learning, and that not merely in the limited sense of mechanically assimilated facts, but for expansion in the larger, and at the same time finer, sense, to be realized by faithful contact with a mind of a certain, oh, iridescence, a certain luminosity: subtle, pervasive, infectious. Given time, he might well glitter with the glory of the hummingbird himself.

Progress on the romantic front was not so sensational. I mean my progress of course. I had originally wanted to make a hit with the family because of my interest in the daughter. Now it was reversed. I was worried about a stymied affair with a girl with whose parents I was getting on swimmingly. It reached crisis proportions when we drew a blank on our first night abed together.

Amy had consistently resisted "sealing our passion" in the front seat of an automobile, under cover of park shrubbery, or on a couch in the house. Even on the sands of the beach with a youth moaning with outflung arms about "the mad, naked summer night. Take it!" Moment-seizing was stoutly averted by fighting off a lover threatening to gore her then and there thanks to an excitement brought on in part by her own amorous expertise. Expert tease? No, not a bit of it, not that at all. Our loins would in time be "sweetly hyphenated," as I put it. That was all in the cards. She just wanted our first night together to be gloriously that — with a blazing enough, but traditional, splendor. "I don't stand on ceremony, Jim, you know that but — Well, yes, I guess I do. That's just it. I want it to be beautiful, an Initiation in the most wonderful sense. In a motel room at least. With all the ceremonial feasting. Make it the classic seduction supper, if you must."

"What might that be?" I asked, looking at her narrowly.

"Lobster Newburg and champagne. It would be as though we're married. My Bridal Night."

"Okie doke."

We even fixed a "wedding date," a Friday when her parents were to set off on a weekend holiday (at French Lick, of all places! the resort for which Oompah had packed a bag in his sleep?). Amy resisted our going to bed together in her own house with a maid about, much more the plebian digs I shared with the roommate at last confessed as owner of the MG. So we checked into a

Chicago hotel, entering with light luggage not into the main lobby but through a revolving door leading into a sort of side foyer by way of an arcade in an office building, for some reason known to Amy. She also practically guaranteed the lobster Newburg as a staple specialty of the dining room, to which she said her parents had often taken her. I signed the register as Mr. and Mrs. James Tickler, of Wabash.

That was when everything went downhill. To begin with, I discovered that the quarters I had reserved ("Give me your best.") were called the William Jennings Bryan Suite, anti-aphrodisiac enough in itself. Then all the preparations — ablutionary, sartorial, cosmetic — tended to flatten my emotions some. The waiter trundling in our meal wore a sly look, and on leaving popped into his mouth an olive from the relish tray — which is all right if you like middle Evelyn Waugh.

The lobster Newburg left me rather bloated, and the champagne further dulled rather than sharpened my senses. And when at last we lay down together, all this seeming like a lot of red tape, a curiously dead, numb sort of sensation overtook me. A feeling of deflation. It was — how shall I put it? — it was as though we had already *made* love, and I was undergoing the fatigue classically the lot of both man and beast following possession.

"Whassa mah?" Amy said, flicking my nose as she bent over me, propped on one elbow.

"Post-coital *tristesse*."

"Already?"

"Yes." I nodded. "It's set in."

"You're a fast worker."

This remark was so time-honored a response to precisely the reverse of our trouble, namely *ejaculatio praecox*, as to send my spirits plummeting even further, if such were possible. There seemed little hope of getting us airborne this night. At best we were necking in bed; at worst, the bride was being sexually molested. I watched her spring gaily out of bed as though nothing were amiss and empty the last of the champagne into our two glasses, rhapsodically dribbling the contents as she returned to the bed and handed me mine. Some spilled onto the pillow, as if in a bacchanal to whose riot there were no limits.

That I had the post-congressional blahs was not clearer to me than why I had them. At least speculation could move along very credible lines.

This was a dress rehearsal — or undress rehearsal if you will — for a real Wedding Night to come, one to which possessing Amy must irrevocably commit me. What had phantasmagorically swept over my mind was the thought of the reception to which would be invited the cream of Gold Coast society — and my family. The thought had bombed into non-existence any hope of consummation. She should have let me take her on the beach, in the park, anywhere. The result would have been a *fait accompli*, and only mental breakdown, with hospitalization, would have been open to me as a means of avoiding marriage and the materialization of the specter that now haunted me. Mencken once said everyone thinks of his relatives, especially his cousins, as grotesque caricatures of himself. And no one likes it a little bit. I took exception to the fact that my oldest brother Tom and I would be dead ringers for each other if I but tilted my hat forward over one eye (or he put his on straight) or I took to chewing kitchen matches (or he abandoned the habit). My features were an even closer match for Nick's, who when eating out always spoke of "having my mouth set for" something (such as lobster), or my sister Clara's, whom I could imagine saying to Amy, if they were to meet now as prospective sisters-in-law, "Chance of showers?" Oh, my God, I thought, shaking my head as all too clearly I could see her cocking hers archly as she did when getting off such corkers.

"What's the matter, Jim?"

"Nothing. Why?"

"You have this habit of jerking your head, as though you have some kind of nervous tic."

"Do you mean something congenital, making it unfair of me to marry?"

"And you sometimes emit a sort of faint groan when you do."

"It goes with this wasting disease."

"Would you like some more to drink?"

"I have an uncle who drinks cold coffee straight out of the percolator spout. He never misses a wedding."

"Sounds jolly. Phone down for another bottle of champagne. We'll get a little drunker, and I'll see if I can get some dance music on this radio. Have you ever danced naked? I'll bet you have, you beast. You cad, you rotter, you reprobate. You despoiler of women, afterward speaking lightly of their names."

I saw a contingent of kin descending upon the country club, one or two in mackinaws, then filing down the reception line toward the table on which their presents were all laid out: to wit, one banjo clock; one globe of the world turning out on closer scrutiny to be divided into two halves which when opened revealed an insulated ice bucket; one cocktail shaker bearing the legend "You don't have to be crazy to get along with us but it helps," with possibly a dozen concomitant glasses similarly embellished; one dozen lace doilies; an original oil painting; a modernistic lamp in the shape of a ceramic black cat internally wired with an alternator which made its eyes blink when turned on; one case of Scotch . . . treasures the other guests, having gaped at them in wonder, unable to believe the testimony of their senses, would recognize as given by the celebrants who said, "Pleased to meet you," when introduced. It would be a horror story: "The Creatures From Out of Town."

The psychic mechanism behind the sexual immobilization to which these ruminations led may now be seen as similar to those speculated on as possibly basic to the lettuce mess. I was "pinning on" Amy, and by extension the entire Wintermoots family, embarrassment with my own that resulted from seeing them through their suburban eyes: it was only from such a viewpoint that my loved ones would be regarded as Creatures From Out of Town. I could not let this *snobisme* pass. We were putting on airs, were we, Evanston people? We thought ourselves better than others — than just plain folks from the hinterland? Well, I would see about that. I would "fix" them, for "harboring under the delusion," as my poor dear mother put it, that they were so superior to plain God-fearing people. Yes, for all this they must be punished, the Wintermootses, and thus they were being punished, through Amy, by a malfunction (ignition, rather than motor, trouble) certain to throw a monkey wrench into the works and knock all thought of wedding plans into a cocked hat.

Amy gave off fiddling with a bedside radio over which

she was bent, unable to find any dance music. "I'm sorry. The whole thing is my fault. Making such a big deal of it. Let's do call down for another bottle."

"It's not a stimulant, you know. Alcohol is a depressant."

"Forget that. We'll go to sleep and tomorrow morning you'll wake up all randy, we girls understand you come to that way, and then you'll gather me in and it'll be slam-bam-thank-you-ma'am. Just forget it now."

I sat up.

"No, I'll tell you, Amy. It's something I'm really ashamed of, but it's this. If we get married, you and your family will want a big wedding and a fancy reception, and then when we-uns meet with you-uns . . ." I broke down and told her precisely what had me in this funk, the specter that haunted me.

"I'll begin with my mother. Do you know how she thinks aphrodisiac is spelled? A-f-r-odisiac. Like in Afro-American. Because she thinks it has something to do with colored people being so highly sexed."

"I can't wait to meet her. Who else? One at a time."

And this was to correct nuptial malfunction! Yet it gave me an idea.

"I know you'd want to *meet* my family. That's only right. But could we do it — like you say, one at a time? A visit here, there, over the years? And would you agree to. . . . No, you wouldn't. You'd want a wedding. Not just go off somewhere and get married."

"Why not?" she said, strolling naked to the telephone. She leaned over it, looking for the room-service number on the dial. "What made you think I'd want a church wedding and all that? My parents would, especially my mother, but I don't set any store by such a waste of money. It means nothing to me."

"Really, darling? Why, that's wonderful," I said, coming toward her. "That's how we'll do it then. One at a time." I laughed, ecstatic with relief. "Because we'd be too rich for your blood, all at once! I think you'll like us. I've already told you a little about Mother. Then there's my brother Tom. He does this lobster imitation? Where he comes out with an old pair of boxing gloves on and, edging slowly toward you, threatens to pinch you with his 'claws.' A real blast. Then my sister Clara has an even dryer sense of humor — But I'll tell you about them all later. And never mind the wine now. Come to bed."

Gone was post-congressional *tristesse* — so clean gone as to be speedily acquired! Then a second time, and a third. Thus gave he nightlong proof of his love, ere yet again the cock made salutation to the morn.

8

I AWOKE SOME TIME TOWARD EIGHT O'CLOCK, in the lobby of the hotel. I was fully clothed, though haphazardly, in the disheveled condition naturally resulting from having dressed in my sleep, hastily packed my overnight bag, and descended in the elevator. The sleeve of a shirt and a necktie-end protruded from the valise, as did a tendril of garter from under one trouser-cuff. Amy was with me, also dressed in whatever she could snatch from the closet and wriggle into on awakening to realize what was going on, deciding it best to do so and accompany me on whatever course I had undertaken, or was improvising. She had shaken me once or twice, without result. Familiar with the history of somnambulism in my family, she had instinctively sensed what was up and what must be done.

I came to as I was being whirled through the revolving door by an incoming carouser of great bulk and energy, reeling noticeably under the influence. He whirled straight around back into the street again, as though in a slapstick film, landing me back inside the lobby once more, quite awake now to the sight of Amy trying to set at rest a clerk who had bustled around from behind the desk to dither about the bill. All this, together with protestations about the kind of hotel they were trying to run, by way of obligato to the main theme of the extent of our obligations, she managed to quiet down. She then led me back to the automatic elevator, otherwise blessedly empty. The door slid shut.

"Jesus Christ," I said as we shot upward. "What the hell is this all about?"

"Is it the first time with you?"

"Yes." That was not true, only true insofar as I knew. My mother, later consulted, recalled one or two minor instances dating back to my early childhood, which she had thought it best not to mention as I had apparently forgotten them.

A decidedly pale face met my gaze in a wall mirror. My breathing was rapid but not difficult; nothing more than the shallow respiration common to the somnambulist.

"It must have scared hell out of you."

"No!" Amy laid a hand to her breast with a gasp of laughter.

"What did I do all?"

"Went to the desk and asked when the next train to Wabash was."

"Ah."

"The clerk said he'd look it up. Of course all this time I was trying to get you back upstairs, but then you broke away and said you'd just flag a cab and wait at the station."

Back in the room, Amy demonstrated a marked capacity for taking charge in an emergency.

"The first thing we're going to do is get some breakfast into us. You look like death warmed over. Then we'll talk."

"Of course you're released from the engagement, if that's what it is. I couldn't have you saddled with that."

"Take a shower and shave. By that time the food should be here."

She stepped resolutely to the phone and I began to peel off my clothes. After a trencherman's breakfast — ham and eggs for me and pancakes and sausages for Amy — we settled back and tried to discuss the turn of events calmly. Though she seemed as much excited as anxious, with the keenly piqued curiosity of the psychology student present in all of us these days.

"It's more common than people realize. I had a college roommate I'd often find getting out of bed in her sleep and fooling around the room. Once I was awakened by the sound of her beating the closet pole with her fist. And everybody talks in his sleep some."

"Because of my father — who by the way doesn't do it any more — I naturally read up on it. The general theory is that the sleepwalker's actions embody or are the expression of some deep-seated subconscious wish."

"You were headed back home to Wabash," she said over her coffee cup.

"Christ, I'm tired. I think I'll lie down for a while."

Amy watched as I sank back into bed. I wadded a couple of pillows under my head, propping myself up so as to keep her in view over the foot-end. She was thoughtful, sipping coffee and nibbling a last sausage, held in her fingers. At length she rose and undressed to bathe herself. "There's only one way to resolve your conflict. Get it over with once and for all, so you won't be dragging this neurotic baggage through your adult life."

I stared at the far wall.

"Invite your family. You've got to. The whole kaboodle. Every last one of them. To a great — big — fancy — North Shore wedding."

Amy stood in the bathroom doorway, wagging a toothbrush.

"Call home."

"What?"

"Telephone home. Tell Mother you're going to get married. Break the news." She laughed. Something about her manner seemed to confirm the legend that champagne once re-activated by early-morning fluids gives you a second jag. Further bearing this out was the fact that her words had found me lying on my back, snapping my fingers as I derisively sang, "Theh said you was hah-class. Oh, theh said you was hah-class!"

"Say, 'Mom, I've found the nicest little girl in all the world. I want you to meet her — right now!' Then give me the phone."

"You must be out of your mind."

Nevertheless, nothing would do but that I fall in with this program. Seize the moment, dive in, commitment, full speed ahead. Something had happened to Amy, over and above whatever rise in spirits was attributable to sparkling wine the morning after. She evidenced that keen, almost morbid stimulation to which some females are subject when confronted with crisis. I had seen it in the Mom about to be rung up: pulling herself together when faced with a child gravely ill or seriously injured, a neighbor's house burnt to the ground, the threat of another taking gas, emergencies such as made Oompah, by contrast, crumple and reach for the bottle. I was to witness this frequently in adversities to be shared and calamities to be met together, in the long road up ahead. It has been observed that women are stronger than men as Negroes are than whites: in the short burst, as against the long haul.

I was not prepared to find my mother in the midst of precisely such a revivification.

"Hello, Mom," I could but reply as instructed, when she answered the phone. "This is me. Jim. How are you? How's everything?"

"One of those at a time. I'm fine. But your father's in a bad way."

"What way?"

"Going through a terrible — what do you kids call it today? Not uptight. A funk."

"How so?"

"Oh, you know how it is. Men go through those tailspins at a certain time of life same as us women folks."

"How is he behaving? I mean . . ."

"Oh, just a depression. Down in the dumps. Claims he's finished. Won't even play in the band any more. They keep calling him for rehearsal, a big civic jamboree coming up it would do him a world of good to march in. But he says he will never play another note. The bird is silenced. It will sing no more. Not alone that, he has intuitions of approaching death. And guess what the instructions are."

Like Soames Forsyte, I never "guess." I constitutionally resist it. Something in my nature simply militates against it. "Not at this hour, Mom."

Not that she would have liked being deprived of further talebearing by a lucky stab. There was a prolonged pause in which she could be sensed relishing the suspense she had created. "He wants to be buried with his tuba."

"But they will have to dig two graves."

"He doesn't care. 'Ish kabibble', he says. 'It's no skin off my back. Let them dig two, or go down an extra three feet.'" Mother heaved a voluminous sigh. "I always wished from the beginning he'd taken up the clarinet."

Better yet the flute, I thought, visited by memories of the flautist in the Wabash marching band kidding my father, to say nothing of the bass drummer, about the logistics problems entailed by their instruments, in his case solved by simply slipping it into his coat pocket. One saw the mortician doing so in keeping with instructions given him. Such a train of thought was hard to justify, while at the same time inevitable in a conversation I now wished to hell I hadn't been so foolish as to start. We were far from those family folk of all ages depicted, in telephone advertisements aimed at stimulating long-distance business, as happily "keeping in touch."

"He's going to put it in his will."

She was clearly much keyed up.

I lugubriously watched Amy pace around the room with folded arms, perhaps not herself actually regretting this impulsive communication, but visibly sobered by a turn of events she couldn't make head or tail of, but plainly something not bargained for.

"Let me talk to him. Is he there?"

"He's just out walking the dog. We have a dog now. I think I wrote you about Diefendorfer. He's from a mixed litter, one of those double conceptions? Where two fathers are involved? But he is part pedigree. On the bitch's side."

"Bitch get away?"

Amy now rolled her eyes to the ceiling, flinging her hands upward with a loud gasp.

"Yes. So here we have a dog, after thirty-six years."

"Diefendorfer should be a comfort."

There was another sigh from the fidgeting Amy, interrupted by my promise that I would take a run home as soon as possible and get my father to see a doctor and do whatever else might be necessary to get him through this spell, which would only be a matter of time given her diagnosis of male climacteric.

"I hope so. But he says the whole clan will be going to a funeral soon."

I slid upward against the headboard against which I had been leaning, and down which I had steadily slumped. Also adjusting my grip on the phone.

"That brings me to my news. Mom, there are going to be wedding bells."

"Oh, that's wonderful! My last boy getting married." She was ecstatic, even more buoyed than by the challenge of decomposition in a mate living with whom must by this stage of the game be pretty much downhill, there in that otherwise empty house. "Have you named the day?"

"Not yet. But soon." I thought of William Jennings Bryan (after whom the suite was named) exclaiming in a Chautauqua oration concerning America's entry into the First World War, "The quickest way out of this thing is straight through it!" Or so I had heard at my grandfather's knee. I now summoned all the strength within me. "Of course you're all invited," I said with a shudder. "Hear?"

"Well, I can't guarantee your father, in this state, or some of the other children. They're so scattered. But I'll be there, irregardless."

"Of course. You'll be there *regardless*," I said, with the tutorial emphasis reminiscent of my work with Wintermoots. The reminder that his solecisms — of which his *forté* was by no means the only one — narrowed by that much the difference allowing him to upstage Mom, or any of us, raised my spirits. It made this chore the lighter. I smiled as I said: "And now I want you to meet Amy. Amy, this is my mother. Say hello."

Amy had observably less stomach for this lark than when she'd first proposed it. But she took the extended phone and carried on from there.

"Hello, Mrs. Tickler. I . . . Yes, it's true . . . Dying to meet you too . . . Let you know about that. . . . Yes. Right. Goodbye."

She cradled the phone.

"What the hell was all that about? Bitches and graves and what not. Getting one end of a conversation like that is like being caught up in some kind of surrealist fantasy."

"What makes you think you aren't?" I answered with rather a long and peculiar laugh.

9

"GUESS WHOSE APPENDIX RUPTURED."

"Whose?"

"Guess."

"I wouldn't have the faintest idea, Mother."

"Oh, Mother, tell him," said sister Josie.

"Reverend Slosch. But they caught it in time. No complications."

"I'm glad of that. Now let me take Josie over to where Amy is. They haven't had much chance to get acquainted yet. And you might step over and have a chat with Mrs. Wintermoots. But don't monopolize her. She has a lot of circulating to do."

"The circulation manager again. Always the social director. Next stop, chief of protocol at the White House. That's this one for you."

Mother's prediction that "this one" would one day walk among the swanky had hardly been issued with any expectation of doing so herself, as a consequence. Yet here we all were at the Hilltree Country Club. My walking was brisk and continuous, much of it long roundabout circumventions aimed at giving Mom a wide enough berth to avoid hearing what she might be saying to the natives. This one's nerves, already a mess of noodles, must be spared further strain. The taxing crescendo of preparations — hashing over invitations, putting up kin descending from everywhere by plane, train and car, church rehearsal, remembering gratuities, the fussing over the menu and the logistics with bought and rented clothes — all this was now seen as a form of lunacy comparable to Christmas time, half chosen by the principals, half thrust upon them by custom: a sacrifice to the tribe. But here we were, the church ceremony behind us, the social rapids of the reception half-shot; oneself half-shot, of course, exhaustion threatening, but deliverance in sight. Up ahead was only the marriage feast itself, to be got through as near stinko as permissible, and then we would be home and dry. Not home at all, that is, but speeding toward O'Hare airport and Paris. Self-immolation accomplished, yet, miraculously, survived.

End runs executed to keep Mom out of earshot alternated with counterimpulses, not altogether punitive or penitential, to spare myself nothing in that regard. There was an awful curiosity, against which I was helpless. Some dreadful fascination drove me to catch at least snatches of the conversation the very thought of which had made my flesh creep. So that, torn between such warring needs, this one suddenly paused in mid-dash as he was executing a wide flanking movement around her admittedly swelling circle of listeners, and sidled over toward its outer edge. Imagined disquisitions on Diefendorfer's family escutcheon were only one possibility of the many that raised their thematic heads. Champagne glass in hand, pretending to ponder the company to which in part he must of course play host, this one stood sideways to the group, his head averted but his ear cocked. Mom was relating a battle she'd been waging with neighbors stuffily resisting integration.

"What the Sam Hill do you *care*? I says. I says what's the *diff*? Just think of them as dark-complected. That's what I do."

I shuddered, proud of Mom as I shot away again, this time veering toward the bar. Why did she never miss? What was her secret? I remembered her describing how she'd had one of the incoming housewives to tea, "a well-spoken young Negress mother of three, in a handsome flesh-colored dress I'd have given my eyeteeth for." What in God's name did that mean? What color was that? Behind me, she was probably dishing out some variant of the story to her growing audience, a solid hit in a privately perfected idiom unique in the experience of sophisticates for once, themselves, gaping like yokels at what they saw and heard. I chuckled unstably, and, after refilling my glass, struck off toward a corner of the room where Wintermoots could be glimpsed talking to my father and my sister Clara.

Clara was looking her best in a handsome suit toward which I intend no disrespect by calling it the color of salami; it blended perfectly with her high skin tones, in turn adroitly matched with hair tinted a soft auburn. What an appealing woman Clara would have made were it not for a habit of seeing human relations as a challenge to her skill at getting from one witticism to the next. It was like having chewing gum continually popped in your ear. Such a compulsion, which sabotages conversation oftener than it moves it along, probably springs from some deep-seated maladjustment in the jokester, perhaps inner misery, with which one must be patient and understanding, however irksome the end-product endured as a string of wisecracks. A need to evade reality may motivate such people, to fend off life's slings and arrows with a protective mechanism at once shield and weapon. More drastic psychological explanation holds the word-play and language mangling often entailed by it as fundamentally infantile, a way of deflating the communication of other people (seen as threats) to nursery gibberish. At the same time, the power momentarily so wielded enables the arrested juvenile to play-act as king of the castle, you the dirty rascal. Lord of the Punjab, so to speak.

The trio were pumping out small talk. The subject turned out to be crossword puzzles, which my father was just saying he found best for calming the nerves in his present psychic disarray (one facet of which was the tendency to advertise it at the drop of a hat). Wintermoots professed addiction himself.

"They certainly broaden your vocabulary," he said. "The other day I came across what was a new one on me, all right. Siffleur, the word for whistler, of all things. I learned it even has a feminine form. Siffleuse. That's the term for a woman who whistles."

"What does that make a woman who's whistled at?" said Clara. "A siffleusie?"

Wintermoots looked at her a moment, then smiled, as though on a decision taken to do so. I resented this. Clara's quip had been pretty nifty. Why was he being so skinny about it, instead of laughing along with the rest of us? Perhaps he was thinking of the hideous bill for all this.

"That's neat, Sis," I said loyally.

I then turned to my father, laying a hand on his shoulder.

"We're all glad you decided to come after all, Oompah."

"Why do you call him Oompah?" Wintermoots asked.

"He plays the tuba."

"Used to," said my father, casting his eyes to the floor. This continual mooching for sympathy, absolutely wherever obtainable, recruiting new sources when old dried up by reason of boredom or impatience, was definitely part of the state he was going through.

"There's another reason," Clara said. "We Dutch call our grandmothers and grandfathers Oma and Opa, so it isn't much from there to calling your father Oompah. It rolls naturally off the tongue."

"I'll never blow another note. Why should I?"

"You'll think of a reason."

"Now you know this is all baloney," I said, giving my father's shoulder another filial squeeze. "You're just going through a phase."

"Like Gary Cooper in *Mr. Deeds Goes to Town*," Clara put in. "I caught that on the Late Show the other night, but you must have seen it originally. *He* played the tuba, if you remember, and it was a great comfort to him in moments of depression. Why can't it be to you?"

"I wasn't hurt by Jean Arthur."

This was rather a sticker put forward by Oompah in his determination to offer a difficulty for every solution, to give encouragement no house room. He shuffled off to refill his glass, after muttering something about having in remotest boyhood (before we were "a beam in his eye"; he had that wrong, more a Motherism) seen a movie with Richard Barthelmess called *Weary River*, the title of which had been based on a verse of Swinburne's about even the weariest river winding somewhere safe to sea. He knew we would talk about him, having left this doleful implication in the air.

"How old is your father?" Wintermoots asked.

"Not all that old. Barely into his sixties," I said.

"I had it with my mother. It's called involutional melancholia in women. She was Scotch, and for some reason it has its highest incidence among women in rural Scotland. Or maybe for good reason. A beautiful country, but that eternal drizzle."

Familiarity with Freud's theory of male despondency in these years representing a species of mourning for lost libido had driven me to make queasy inquiries of Ooma, as my mother might be called to make a clean sweep of it. I need not have walked on eggs. She was shatteringly frank in assurances that no such explanation need be put forward for Oompah's doldrums. Sex, on the contrary, supplied his one release from them. "His natural vigor is unabated, as the Bible says about Moses when he died," she volunteered.

My brother Tom joined us, grinning as though in happy anticipation of what he was going to say.

"Well, Mr. Wintermoots, you certainly gave the bride away with style. I really dug the way you did that. It had class. It was real elegant."

"Thank you."

Tom directed their collective gaze to me. "We won't give the groom away, though God knows we've got plenty on him," he said, and gave me one of those elbow nudges that made me wish I was wearing my bullet-proof vest.

"You look as though married life agrees with you, Tom," I said, resisting visual recourse to his tummy. As my best man he had been in full fig, but had climbed back into mufti as soon as possible.

"Marry a good cook, like I did. Make sure she's O.K. in the kitchen."

"Don't propose till you see the whites of her eggs, that it?" said Clara, with something of her satiric feminist edge.

I looked gravely at Jake Wintermoots. "Might work that in somewhere in that speech to the Women's Club."

He nodded, glancing at Clara — who was craning her neck in a constant lookout for Amy. Seeing her new sister-in-law free, she excused herself and darted off in her direction for a chat. That was O.K. There was every sign the two were going to hit it off. Emergency brewed in another quarter.

My mother-in-law seemed threatened by the joint camaraderie of my brother Jack and Josie's husband, Cliff Parks, always hard to take on short notice, except for those with similarly rudimentary nervous systems. I excused myself and left Wintermoots to Tom. Happily there were no boxing gloves available for Tom to don, preparatory to going around pinching the ladies in his lobster act. One could be grateful for that. The need to rescue Mrs. Wintermoots arose from the fact that Jack's and Cliff's rousing get-togethers consisted largely in swapping stories independently acquired since last met. Their combined repertory was absolutely definitive, and a few drinks made them rather bold in trying to see just how much off-color a woman would stand for. I had already done my hostly duty by the Happiness Boys, not that a spate of smoker stories had been my sole reward for stopping. A guest named Cyril Marney had come over briefly in the course of our chat to shake my hand

and wish me well. After he'd moved along, I had identified him as a professional wine taster. That had prompted Cliff to wonder how that line of work left the practitioner on his feet at the end of a work day. "I should think he'd be pie-eyed."

"Oh, wine tasters don't swallow what they sample," I'd explained. "They ejaculate."

"Wherever you get your hacks."

I staggered on toward them now with shut eyes and gritted teeth. At this point I had come to think of the whole reception as "a tough course," like the links rolling away beyond the Regency windows, famous for their doglegs and their sand bunkers, social versions of which I was now delicately rounding or furiously slashing my way out of, as the case might be. Very little green and fairway, anyway.

The blessed sight of Rose Wintermoots being plucked away by another celebrant, leaving no immediate danger of regalement by the Happiness Boys, made me change my course. At a farther end of the long room Carter Pippin, an office colleague of some importance in the hierarchy there, could be seen, with his eye on me. I swam slowly toward him through the crowd. It would be a long journey, with cross-currents bearing one or another of us this way or that. Now I was aware of Mom again on the edge of my vision. Again the temptation to overhear what she might have to say for herself won out over the wish to keep out of earshot. I drifted, helplessly, toward the group to which she was holding court, now again visibly expanded. She seemed to be dwelling on another of her pet subjects, that of regarding retirement age as precisely the time to start living and get going.

"Not that I'm a senior citizen yet, I'll have you know.

But the older I get the more I take on." Here she ran off a string of activities, social, charitable, part-time and seasonal department-store clerking, with which she occupied herself throughout the year.

"That must keep you busy," someone said.

"As a one-armed paperhanger on a hot tin roof."

So one slunk on by, hangdog, slaying his hundreds while Mom slew her thousands. "— bored to destruction —" Still far ahead lay Carter Pippin, borne slightly off course to one's right by the shifting tides, while to the left loomed Brother Bill, with whom one must also have a word.

This blowing of hot and cold, this intermingled taste of sweet and sour, the whole dizzying oscillation between funk and exhilaration was nowhere more crazily experienced than in the guest with whom I was now squarely confronted even as Bill drew near and Pippin himself hove ever closer.

One of Mother's "tall, statutory blondes," Mrs. Flamsteed was for a split second unplaced in the whirling spectrum of impressions, in the next recalled as the woman with whom I'd had a brief but titillating passage in the course of my first evening at the salon. A bit of addenda to Judge Barsley's obiter dicta on the film he'd just banned as obscene. Even that short conversation had suggested a woman of strongly erotic temperament, if you'll remember. The impression had had nothing to do with the topic of conversation itself; she seemed to exude a sense of carnal predilection just talking about the weather; something conveyed in the throaty voice, the loitering gaze of the large blue eyes, the ceaseless play of the hands. Along with all this went sudden descents into vagueness, intermittent vacant stares a moment before incisive, that hinted at someone whose wits might be wandering, and not merely her attention. In any case, here was a groom salivating over a guest at least twice his bride's twenty-two years.

"Of course. Mrs. Flamsteed. I haven't seen you among those present at Rose's Sundays lately. Not since that first time when we met."

"I've been busy. My husband died, you know — well, my ex-husband, not that that made any difference in our feelings for each other. We remained close, and I've been devoting all my time to the business he left." I waited politely for what I knew would be vouchsafed, given such a taste for spilling intimate detail on short notice. "*Consumer Review*, you know. The service we put out."

"Of course. That huge new testing plant he built out south there. I've always wanted to see it."

"I'll bet. The Devil sightseeing a cathedral," she said with a rather teasing smile. On the surface courteously playful, but with an unmistakable edge. The thrust of the uncompromising liberal.

"I see what you mean. Yes, I am on the other side of the fence, ain't I, from your point of view. Prostituting ourselves for any corporation that wants to buy our brains — most of them manufacturing products you condemn, no doubt."

"No doubt. Well, if you ever repent. I understand you're very clever. Lots of brains to sell. Ralph Nader was out to look us over last week." She looked me over rather critically herself, as she sipped her champagne. "I would have figured you on the side of the angels."

The theme of my moral rehabilitation was dropped as we were joined by brother Bill, shouldering his way forward in a pea-green suit of snug construction, between the wide lapels of which was a bowtie I was afraid would light up at the touch of a switch concealed in a pocket. The simultaneous arrival of Pippin made me doubly uncomfortable — till I saw a way of turning that to account.

"I believe you two know each other. This is my brother Bill. Mrs. Flamsteed and Mr. Pippin. Look, I must ask Bill something — something private — so why don't you two chat and I'll be right back."

I seized Bill's arm and drew him aside.

"How's the garbage business?" I asked *sotto voce*.

"Picking up," he said, and by God if *he* didn't give me one in the briskets with his elbow a la Tom. Now was the time for the bowtie to light up, if such was in store. However, the moment passed, and I tried to make clear my sincere interest in how he was doing in the business he had pursued from the start, though continuing to talk in low tones out of the side of my mouth.

"Everything is Jake," he said. "I got six routs in all now."

"Oh, you got six routs in all?" I said, an expiatory descent to his level being safe with the other two now quite engrossed in their own conversation. "What do you think of Pop?"

"Oh, he'll snap out of it. Middle-age heebie-jeebies. Oma went through it with Opa when Oompah was our age. I'm more worried about Nick." This was a brother who had begged off, being deep in marital troubles with a wife who had herself insisted she was "too tired to make the trip" after some surgery about as serious as a manicure. "It was just a try at getting some free time with that lover boy she's fooling around with. I don't blame Nick for not coming alone. All he'd be thinking of was the two of them rolling around in his own sack. I think he should get rid of her."

We hashed over some more family gossip, the bulk of it more palatable. Then I saw that Carter Pippin was free and again gazing in my direction.

"Well, you fell in the butter," Bill said, looking around approvingly.

"Yes. Look, I have some business to discuss with this guy. Why don't you snag that waiter over there and get yourself another drink."

"That's something that's never been known to be refused by we Ticklers," he said, and shoved urbanely off.

There was no business I wanted to discuss with Pippin. But he had something he couldn't wait to dish out in that line himself.

Pippin had at one time briefly dated Amy. Whether that meant he had himself harbored aspirations to marry the boss's daughter I didn't know, but I seriously doubted it, from Amy's accounts. That had been some few years ago, when Amy had been nineteen and Pippin probably twenty-five. He was married now in any case. Frustrated romantic claims put forth in the Wintermoots quarter were not the reason he had taken a scunner to me the instant I had joined the firm. What had soured him on me from the start, and understandably, had been Jake's replacing him with me as his ghost writer. His had been the speeches deplored by Jake as sounding like speeches, being replete with phrases like "pursuant thereto" and "re-ordering our priorities." No, his skills lay more in the administrative line, and it was in such light that, con-gratulations out of the way, he struck up a little shop.

"They've deep-sixed our advertising proposal for Hamill Products."

That was disingenuous. It hadn't been "our" plan at all, but mine. But it enabled him to get in a dig no gentler for being muffled in hypocritical velvet. Too, that agency slang for committing something to obliteration uneasily recalled Oompah's threatened orders to be buried with his tuba — which I hadn't had the heart to bring up.

"And that name you suggested for that new bath gismo Timken Toiletries wants to market." It was a combination massage and soaping loofah, worn as a mitt and constructed of vegetable bristles, with which the bather gave himself a tactile tonic while lathering himself. "What was it again?"

He was only making me say it, was my suspicion. But I buckled in with a bit of a grin and said it. "The Rub-a-Dub Tub Glove."

"Yes. Can't be used. The name's already patented. English trade mark."

"I'll think of something else."

"I know you will."

By now I didn't give a good goddamn whether I ever cooked up any more cuteys for corporations big or small, soulless or otherwise, or what anybody thought of anything I did. I just wanted this over with. And also I had been touched to the quick by an exquisite memory of my childhood. Mom "getting at" our feet with a vegetable brush on Saturday nights, those bristles being the ticket for scrubbing and scouring away the crust, the veritable hoof, that collected on the soles and heels of barefoot boys in the state of James Whitcomb Riley. "Oh, those Wabash blues," I inwardly sang again, mentally throwing my head back and baying the words straight at Carter Pippin. From whose own lips came at last:

"Well, time to forget business matters for a while."

"That's right."

"Have a good flight."

Flight was good — from everything. Amy and I were in ecstasies at getting away, as we did soon enough. The bell rang for dinner. A toast from Wintermoots, a response from the groom, the cutting of the cake, and then a brief single entertainment, a magician, of all things. I had thought the Wintermootses out of their minds — as though this were a children's birthday party. But I had been wrong. We were all amazed. The Great Baldridge's shtick was to flub everything, every trick going awry and then miraculously snatched from disaster with a split-second timing that was a dazzling inversion of skill. The effect was hilarious, and wildly applauded.

"I've never seen anything like it," a guest remarked as we broke up.

"He's the best since Houdini," chimed in another.

"Ah, in my day, that was a name to conjure with," said Mother, bringing the event to a triumphal close.

It was over, thank God. We had come through. It had been an ordeal, as a glance in a washroom mirror attested. This one was light-complected with fatigue and strain, his cheeks hollow, his eyes like bad grapes. But a fling in Paris and then a fortnight in the south of France would no doubt erase the lines and bring the roses back. Anyway, honor had been satisfied, the lares and penates, one trusted, appeased. The Ticklers had survived the salon — and vice versa.

10

JAKE WINTERMOOTS LITTLE REALIZED how bad he made me feel every time he said he felt badly, or indulged in the bastard "hopefully," or spoke of "those kind of people." Such barbarisms, of which I seemed powerless to disinfect him by example, and hardly to be purged by open correction, dampened my first flush of expectation for him, in sober reappraisal now seen as having been too sanguine. There were times when I despaired of successfully discharging the Pygmalion sort of undertaking into which I had permitted myself to be drawn. Then suddenly the problem of grooming became overshadowed by suspicions about what he might be wanting to groom himself for. It began to dawn on some of us that his ambitions might be political, in which case of course a faultless English style was not of the essence.

A rapid series of speaking engagements at Republican organizations and none other; glimpsed calendar notations of lunches with party moguls; dropped hints and buzzing speculation all left little doubt. He had taken it into his head that he might become a congressman or senator, or even governor.

He became careful about what he said. He must offend nobody, least of all the conventional sensibilities of Middle America. He was no longer seen wearing shirts that were statements or neckties that hit out at life, such as were then in vogue, the battle-axe sideburns were edited away. He began laying his groundwork during the first Nixon administration, when Vice President Agnew was going about as a Savonarola rallying the country to a sense of its moral obligations, preaching the old-fashioned virtues of duty and decency, self-discipline and honor and patriotism. One morning Jake called me into his office to discuss a draft of a speech I had just hammered out, for delivery to a state convention of women voters. He frowned dubiously at the copy on his desk.

"You say something here about 'the prattling pundits of positivism.' "

"Parody of Agnew. You've been reading his screeds about the nattering nabobs of negativism."

"Yes, the —"

"You'll notice I don't mention him by name. We'll be sly, elliptical, in there, Jake. We use the rapier, not the cleaver. Maybe a swipe or two about that master of alliteration. Not since Swinburne, etc. Because I think, Jake, you should plain take him on. Razz him about this effete intellectual snob stuff. Effete means incapable of bearing young. All right. So you say something like, oh, you admit to being incapable in that area, you leave that to the ladies. It's an audience of women, so a good boff there —"

"No, no." He shook his head. "That kind of line would

be suicidal. You've got to cultivate all elements in the party, you can't ride roughshod over people's prejudices like that. Besides, they *like* Agnew here. The polls show it. He stands for the traditional American virtues. In addition to that, you can't quip your way into the White House."

"White House?"

"I mean state capitol. Or Congress, or whatever." He reddened a little, flinging a hand in a flustered gesture. "I said White House because of course I was thinking of Adlai Stevenson. His wit never got him anywhere."

"It got him to Springfield."

"The hell it did. Nothing to do with it. His integrity was the thing, and his intelligence of course. He was a political virgin."

"So are you. That doesn't mean that now and then you can't be a little tart. Heh-heh-heh. Oh, heh-heh-heh."

"You must be joking. Listen to this." He shuffled through the manuscript in search of another passage. "Here. 'I bow to no one in my appreciation of the value of the D.A.R. in raising alarm against all elements they consider alien. After all, Rome was once saved by the cackling of geese.' "

"Oh, you like that? I thought it rather good myself."

"Only flashing a Communist Party card could beat it as a vote-getter. No, the thing is, you've been great up to now. None better. Now I think I need another tone. And somebody familiar with the political mosaic here. *And* the creative department is falling down badly on a couple of our accounts. You're desperately needed. Put your brains to work there. Carter Pippin will brief you, he has all the dope."

"And will then go back to writing your stuff himself.

'That reminds me of a very dull story, ladies and gentlemen.' " I heaved myself out of my chair with an acquiescent sigh. "But do one thing for me. Ask him to retire 'overriding concern'? For the Gipper?"

"Do you happen to have anything else on hand you might show me? Notes, grist for the mill. Any recent material."

"Nothing I want to see the light of day just yet," I answered, as one who in his major phase reserves the right to self-veto work produced, if deemed not up to snuff. "I have some things of a possibly sensitive nature that I'm arranging to have kept in a vault until a hundred years after my death, when everyone else who might be concerned will also be gone." To show there were no hard feelings, before going out I picked up the Chicago telephone directory and threw it on his desk. "Read this and tell me what you think. I'd very much like your opinion."

While Wintermoots proceeded to build his political fences on the moralistic line taken by the Vice President, and echoed by a law-and-order administration in general, so that the republic rang with clarion calls to probity, I concentrated exclusively on agency clients. I took a lot of work home with me, but busy as I was I thought I should make an effort to catch a few of Jake's speeches, now part of a primary campaign to win his party's nomination for senator. They were pretty soporific, but suited to political purposes in a climate of moral rearmament. Amy by now had a master's degree in sociology and a job as a case worker with something called Community Services, in effect a settlement for delinquent boys, partially supported by the state but also dependent on private donations.

One night when she was working late at the office I

attended a rally apparently crucial to Jake's chances. He was to deliver what is called "a major address" in a Chicago north-side auditorium. There was a band, a fair crowd, banners, the usual placards. One of these read, "Wintermoots ain't in cahoots," another, "Everything is going to be Jake!" The blood was hardly stirred by these legends, probably also the work of Pippin, whose oratory that night was everything you would have expected. Which was what spelled disaster, as it turned out.

I was dog-tired, after a couple of grinding days with clients' problems, and should have been in bed by the time Wintermoots, preceded by a couple of other human phenobarbitals, finally rose, to some whistling and foot-stamping, hardly enough to wake the dead. It was now probably ten o'clock. He started in. He thanked those responsible for this testimony of confidence, which would soon become a mandate of the people. He was reminded of a story. He ventured to say. He reordered some options. He proposed viable alternatives and spelled out some needs till one's eyelids grew heavy. One nodded approval as one applauded along with the rest, then one was nodding without applauding. "Jesus Christ," I said to myself, like the aged Chief Justice Holmes when once he caught himself falling asleep on the bench. One came to with a start, but then dozed off again. The bromides came on, washed gently over one's drowsy spirit. At last one's head dropped to one's chest and was not raised. What in God's name was happening? You know it. Wintermoots rose to a climax as I sank into definitive slumber. I mean this was beddy-bye.

"Elements in this country," he was saying, "are disturbed by other elements admitting, nay proudly proclaiming, a swing to the right. Are we swinging to the right? Well, as to that, my fellow Americans, it's a hard question to answer. But for my part, I say without hesitation or hint of indecision, let there be a swing to the right" — here he raised a finger dramatically aloft — "*as God gives us to see the right!*"

That probably did it. Because only a later glance at the typescript together with some filling-in from friends enables me to reproduce what happened. I picked my way out of my seat toward the aisle and proceeded up that toward the exit with my arms out in front of me. The speaker — as I was later informed — paused and looked over. There was a kind of flabbergasted hush over the audience, of whom I was in full view for I had sat up front, then a scattered laugh or two, and finally gales of mirth. Both the loyal party workers and neutral observers took the figure they saw to be a plant from the opposition camp, making a sort of sardonic one-man demonstration. An alert newspaper cameraman sprang from his own seat and pattered along beside me, clicking away. I didn't see him till I came to outside in the street.

"That was quite a gag," he said. "Could I have your name? I'm from the *Trib.*"

"No gag," I said, reconstructing in a flash what had happened and trying to reassemble my wits, "and no comment." I flagged a cab, still mumbling as somnambulists do, and sped for home, where I should have stayed.

Pippin had a cow. Not that I could blame him. Except that he too thought it had been some sort of prank, which absolutely amazed me when I finally tumbled, at a point well along in our set-to at the office next morning. He dropped on my desk a copy of the *Tribune* he'd been carrying, an ominous sign. I hadn't dared even to glance at it.

"What have you got to say about this?"

"Yes, I saw that," I lied, as a pretext for not having to look at it now. The story could probably be reconstructed from strictures that would be forthcoming. This would have to be played by ear, and very, very carefully. Open generalities would be wisest at first. "The whole thing is unfortunate, and I'm sorry, but *it was no reflection on you.* I sleepwalked out on the speaker, not the speech."

"Well, there's blood on the moon in any case. Has Jake spoken to you yet? He will. Of course the *Trib* would eat it up. They're for Jarvons."

"It's nothing that can be helped. It often runs in families. It does in mine. My father has been troubled with it all his life, and I seem to have inherited it. It's congenital. Little is known about the phenomenon, but the psychological explanation is that it's expressive of some deep-seated conflict, or unresolved disturbance, or wish, in the victim. He's simply acting it out, unconsciously of course. People are fascinated by it because it's so — eerie. 'The sure touch of the sleepwalker.' That's a line from some writer I can't for the life of me place. Do you? You're so widely read, Carter."

Pippin gaped in astonishment. He had a glazed expression, like someone who has been spun around several times preparatory to pinning the tail on a donkey, and now has his blindfold removed.

"Let me get this straight. I mean I don't quite understand. You mean you actually were sleepwalking? Like Lady Macbeth, for Christ's sake?"

"Of course! For God's sake, Carter, you surely don't think I'd pull a jape like that. What the hell ails you?"

He threw his head back, running his hand through his

hair as he rolled his eyes to the ceiling. "Well, I'm a monkey's uncle."

"I was bushed, dead, and must have dropped off. My father did it in church one time, so I come by it honestly. Again, if there *was* any *arrière-pensée* about it, I mean subconsciously, it related to the speaker, not the speech. That was all that could have been expected."

This was the reverse of what I must tell Wintermoots, which would be closer to the truth of the matter, insofar as there might be anything psychically tendentious in the episode. So viewed, it would have to be seen as a kind of surreal satire aimed at a rival at whom one was getting his own back. Not a very pretty story, but then neither are our normal dreams. Low cunning carries all before it once we leave the necessary dissimulations and lubricating hypocrisies of waking life for the Walpurgisnacht of slumber. None of us is nice then. It's no wonder we spend so much of our daily life saving one another's faces. It's the least we can do.

But there was blood on the moon, I knew that full well in my dread of the confrontation with Jake that awaited me. The phone had rung twice in the course of this passage, but I hadn't answered it for fear of reporters. I must not be reached for comment. I must be kept strictly under wraps. Statements could only prolong coverage of an episode already *contretemps* enough. But it had been Jake trying to get through to me, for which purpose he finally dispatched his secretary in person.

Miss Finley thrust her gray head into the room. "Mr. Wintermoots would like to see you."

"Right."

Wintermoots was on the phone when I was shown in

by Miss Finley, who closed the door after me with lowered head, as though noting a blemish in the carpeting. He waved me to a chair while he continued a business talk, but I strode across the forty-foot room and stood before one of the oils that constituted his hobby. He was a Sunday painter. The landscape, like all his, had a certain dreamily diaphanous quality, something reminiscent of the Impressionists yet with a touch all his own. This "something different" was a kind of grainy texture, previously noted in murmured praise, quite sincere, on which I couldn't quite put my finger despite its being teasingly suggestive of a familiar element in contemporary life. Suddenly now I seemed to perceive the artist's inspiration: poor color television reception. The lake shoreline at which I gazed was Seurat's pointillism with a little extra, not infelicitous blurring — precisely a scene being watched before a set with imperfect definition.

He finished his conversation and hung up.

"I've always liked this. Strikes a mystic note." I stepped toward his desk. "Of course I'm sorry about what happened. Which of course I couldn't help. You know about all that, well, family history, just as well as Amy. I never kept anything from her, or from her family. We discussed it all openly like two intelligent people. Maybe I shouldn't marry, pass this curse on, I left the decision up to her —"

"All right, all right, there's no need to be melodramatic. Talking about curses and blots on the family escutcheon. Christ, you don't have to be hairy about it, as though you're one of the cat people." His irritation with the line I was taking probably stemmed from resentment at having the role of victim wrested from him before he had it fairly in his grasp. He picked up the morning paper and threw it down again. "I suppose you've seen this?"

"Yes," I lied again. "And frankly I think your beef is with them. They're for Jarvons, and fear your possible nomination." This was buttering him up with margarine, and diet margarine at that. For he hadn't a chance.

"You notice they report it not just as a gag, but as a novel form of heckling, or demonstration. Christ, the Jarvons forces may take it up, get whole rows of plants to somnambulate out on me. I may not be a firebrand but —"

"Shall I phone the papers and make it clear it was a bona fide thing? I'm a sickie?"

"No! Leave bad enough alone. You're to remain absolutely incommunicado. You're not to be reached for comment, head for the tall timber if you have to, hopefully so it'll all blow over." I winced again at this solecism which is spreading like a cancer through the body lingual. "Further publicity can only make it worse." He paused and eyed me across the desk. "I've read up on this — ailment of yours. I mean when Amy first told me about it. The best theory is that it's an expression of some deep-seated conflict, or hostility. Was I that bad?"

"Jake! You were great. If it was aimed at anybody, it was *at the speech, not the speaker.*"

"You resented Pippin when I replaced you. There's that."

"We're all human. I'd give anything for it not to have happened. But I was dog-tired. Up till one and two o'clock the nights before working on that contest idea for the Jeepers cocktail cracker people. They're gung-ho on it, and the pressure's been terrible. Head feels like a steam kettle. I shouldn't have gone, even out of loyalty to you."

"If it had been any other night. That crowd. And my old college English teacher was in the audience to boot. I

135

spotted him. Loftus, their far-out man, I think you met him when we went out to Yuppa Prairie. Teaches all the moderns — Galsworthy, Hardy, Arnold Bennett. Writers like that."

"Again, a thousand apologies."

"This could finish me."

"Jake. Sweetheart."

"Go out as a laughing stock. Can you imagine Jarvons not making hay of it?"

"He's a Nixon man. And they'll stoop to anything." I flapped my arms out. "It's your party."

But the cloud did have a silver lining. It gave Wintermoots an excuse for a defeat that was inevitable anyway. Alternatively, being the scapegoat for the landslide he was buried under was some salve for my own spirit, wounded enough in all conscience God knew. I mean the fact that I *saved* his face by leaving him with egg on it was some compensation, borne in suffering silence of course. He'd never have got to first base. The polls showed it. But now he could keep me forever nailed to the barn door by pointing to the slogan, cooked up by Jarvons or somebody in his camp now at the eleventh hour, by which Jarvons delivered the *coup de grâce*. "What this country needs is a stimulant, not a sedative." By a last weird twist of irony, it was one I had proposed to Jake myself.

"The sure touch of the sleepwalker."

Where *had* I read that? Odd that I couldn't remember the poem, novel, essay, considering my almost total recall, not only of every line that means something to me or for whatever reason fascinates me, but the time, place and circumstances under which it was first encountered;

indeed, often its very position on the page when originally read. For example, I can visualize the exact location, two-thirds way down the right-hand page in the Viking Portable Fitzgerald, where the disintegrating priest in the story "Absolution" says to the boy whose confession he is hearing as he is cracking up: "When a lot of people get together in the best places things go glimmering." Of course it isn't just as a "fine line" that the words embedded themselves like a quill in my memory, but as a *cri de coeur* wrung from a soul in torment whom I saw as my own mirror image, then in an admittedly frivolous or at least shallow vanity, in riper years in a more chastened sense. Racked by dreams of the worldly pleasures he has foregone for sanctity, Father Schwartz was the harried counterpart of myself, whose own life story has been rather that of sanctity renounced for the world. A sort of Pilgrim's Progress in reverse; as though our young Christian, his back turned on the City of God, sets his face like flint for the beckoning glamors of Vanity Fair.

In that light I could well sympathize with Jake Wintermoots's obliteration on a campaign trail only he imagined could ever have led anywhere, least of all to that ultimately glimmering Best Place on which he had secretly set his heart, namely the White House, revealed as such in one of those slips of the tongue about which we must be kind, kind. He simply did not bat in that league, nor ever would have even if he had Winston Churchill to write his speeches for him. Visions of political glory are certainly not mine. But like a hermit crab occupying the discarded shell of another creature, I could get into his dream qua dream. I would be invited *to* the White House, as a dazzler all hostesses sought, a hummingbird even the First Lady would deem a catch as she watched him flit from flower to gowned and scented flower, gliding in evening fig across the ballroom floor. This fantasy was actually to be fulfilled, thanks to a series of dizzying twists and turns in my career I could scarcely have foreseen a week before they began. The point is that our pipe dreams, Jake's and mine, only differed as variants of the same consuming human hunger: to be somebody. His secret ambition was now liquidated; mine — shamelessly, I admit it, to be counted one of the Beautiful People — was alive and about to catch fire.

The odd thing was that at the time I seemed to be on the skids as the firm's fair-haired boy. None of my recent marketing proposals had been turning the clients on. For example, the name I had come up with for some individual bags of dried dog food about to be tried out prior to Broadway, "Pooch Pouch," was turned down by the mfr. as "lacking in dignity." One of the firm's brass told me so over one of those three-hour lunches from which the creative fraternity stagger home to their wives at the closes of days of which even such ordeals are far from the fatiguing total. "It has negative vibes to dog lovers, who don't like to have their pets demeaned," he said. An inadvertent glance in a wall glass confirmed that I was getting pouches under my eyes and would soon look like a pooch myself if I stayed in this game much longer. A basset. At the same time, I pricked up my ears on the "vibes," as having the right ring for yet another mfr. yearning to add yet another cold breakfast cereal to the half-acre of shelves devoted to same by every supermarket. As it turned out the corporation *was* presently test-marketing the stuff eventually so christened, with the slogan, "It sets you vibrating for the day." But whether from lack of vibes in the combination itself or because the fodder in the boxes tasted like something that should rather have gone into old Dobbin's nosebag the tryout was anything but gangbusters. Concerning that fiasco I had to huddle with Carter Pippin over another of the Homeric lunches. I couldn't have endured it without three martinis, and I was feeling no pain when Pippin pressed me once again to try it for a client we were in mortal danger of losing, having struck out twice with it already. "The ingredients show up beautifully under a laboratory analysis. As nourishing as anything on the market," he said. "So what name might go well with 'The thinking man's cereal'?"

"Well, if that's the slogan they're set on, why not call it Joyce Carol Oates?"

He shot me one of his quick, not-exactly-a-glare glances of irked amusement, the envy not altogether concealing an old irritation with himself at being not quite first-rate. He took the tab from the waiter, as my immediate superior in an office no less observant than most of the pecking order.

"Three people glance at their watches," I said, in a schematized pleasantry of the kind recycled from the old salon days, regrettably no more. "Psychiatrists, prostitutes, and guests."

"How about hosts?" Pippin returned, showing hitherto untapped resources as he signed the check. "I think it's time we took you off this account. You might go back on Kruger Razor, though they don't much like 'Kruger Blades Have the Edge.'"

Was one unravelling? An imminent has-been? The poor Haverstraw, beside whose desk I had ofttimes paused to drop a word of encouragement on my strolls through the outer-office Siberia to which he had been banished from a private lair very like my own, had by now left altogether. Did the same fate await me, my vogue over? Would my house be left unto me desolate, my bishoprick another take? My services no longer seemed to be clamored for by mfrs. as once they had, if that was any augur.

Two things were still going for me. One was the contest I had cooked up as a sales-promotion device for the cocktail cracker called Jeepers, a very good one flavored with sesame seed. Boxtops were used to mail in answers to questions asked elsewhere on the package, each series of correct answers to be awarded a prize of one hundred dollars. The questions had to do with famous people in all walks of life, from athletes and jazz musicians to poets and kings. There were twenty questions in all, giving the contest its name, spread over twenty weeks, to keep that mdse. moving. Entries had to be postmarked not later than midnight of etc., etc. "Paralleled," which one had always thought the *mot juste* for the speeches Pippin ghost-wrote, admittedly also described this little stunt, but it did hypo sales. *Vroom.* That was all that mattered. It remained for the Federal Trade Commission to supply the long-missing prefix, making the contest unparalleled, unprecedented, and un-about-everything-else you could name in the history of commercial promotion.

Pippin came into my office one morning, his face ashen and sober as the skies in "Ulalume."

"There's blood on the moon."

"Not again?"

"Haven't you seen this?"

Good God, the morning *Tribune* again, folded into a square so as advantageously to display a story on the bottom of the front page — which, Pippin said, was where the New York *Times* had run it too, as an eastern associate had woke him up by long distance telephone to report.

"The Federal Trade Commission," the story began, "in a step it describes as innovative in the consumer field, is attempting to force the makers of a cocktail cracker called Jeepers to pay $100 each to thousands of unsuccessful contestants in a promotional contest called Twenty Questions.

"The FTC yesterday made known its intention to issue a complaint charging Jeepers as well as Wintermoots and Hale, the market counseling firm which developed and ran the contest, with 'false, misleading and deceptive acts' in conducting the contest earlier in the year."

My phone rang just then and Pippin grabbed my wrist as I reached to answer it. "You're not available for comment — as you'll find when you read on," he said in a hideous whisper. I read on, the inside of my mouth feeling like a piece of rotted fabric.

"The FTC has filed a proposed cease-and-desist order, calling for the payment of prizes to contestants said to have been misled by the wording of the contest rules. The order would prohibit the defendants from 'wrongfully withholding the earned prizes of $100 from contest entrants who mailed in boxtops that were complete and correct under reasonable interpretation of the contest rules — that is, boxtops which contained at least one correct 'answer' to each question which could be correctly answered.'

"The game involved famous people in various fields of achievement. The FTC claims that the published directions and rules misled persons of 'average sophistication and intelligence in semantics' to believe that a $100 prize would be awarded to anyone sending in a correct answer to each question, whereas an undisclosed rule required that most if not all the questions called for more than one correct answer. Thus the multiple-answer requirement was the condition on which the deception hinged — the gimmick in the competition. 'Many if not all the 1.5 million who participated submitted at least one correct answer to each question,' the FTC went on to point out. 'Thus the Jeepers corporation and Wintermoots and Hale would be obligated under the proposed preliminary judgment to shell out an additional $150 million in prizes.' The only Jeepers executive who could be reached for comment said quite pithily: 'It would ruin us. We would go to the cleaners.' "

The newspaper seemed to be cackling in my hand as, unable to turn to where the story was continued on page 61, column 3, I set it down beside the again ringing telephone.

Carter Pippin stood at the window, gazing down the twenty-two floors at this northern limit of Chicago's famed Magnificent Mile in a manner that struck a most disturbingly suggestive tableau. My tongue had apparently become thoroughly mired in some substance such as peanut butter, so that it could not be bent, cajoled or otherwise manipulated in the manner normally required for conventional speech.

"And to think we came within an inch of deep-sixing the idea," he said when the phone had stopped its screaming.

"Would to God I were deep-sixed myself." This was of course a hypocritically melodramatic overstatement of a condition of mind quite honestly, however, to be scaled down to the wish that I were still "in turpentine," a somewhat more modest form of self-obliteration. Or probably

I should have pushed on with *Munching on Mrs. Dalrymple* . . . "It's all too ghastly for . . ." I would probably not have finished the comment even had Wintermoots himself not just then have burst through the door.

He had been doing a spot of jet-setting and was now freshly returned from ten days in the Caribbean. Hale, semi-retired, hadn't been in the office for weeks, and Wintermoots had left his affairs in the hands of trusted lieutenants. He was tanned the color of pumpernickel, so that whether he too was ashen beneath the semi-tropical veneer was a matter of speculation. He had developed a sort of jowly lugubriousness, principally the result of a deepening of the laugh lines running from the corners of his nostrils to his mouth, at the moment markedly amplified.

"What the hell is this all about? What is all this about undisclosed rules and multiple answers and Christ knows what all? Will somebody fill me in? Can you give me some for-instances?"

"Well," said the author of Twenty Questions, "there was one about 'Who ran the mile in under four minutes in the 1954 International Amateur track competition?' We would all instinctively say Roger Bannister whom we remember first cracking it then. But there was another miler who did it too. Landy I think his name is. Again in sports, who hit four home runs in one game? Most of us would say Willie Mays right off as the most recent, but the record is shared by eight other ball players. Any one answer would be correct according to the FTC, but incomplete as far as the rules went. Apparently."

"*Apparently*? Wasn't that made clear in the poop, for Christ's sweet sake? Do you understand that your father-in-law is *Poor*?"

"I don't know, Jake. That wasn't my job. Our job. We only cooked the dish. It was up to Jeepers to serve it."

"Gawd," Jake said, plowing a furrow in the rug. "We're all cooked now, it looks like. This could ruin us. A hundred and fifty million smackers! We're through. Fini. Kaput. The poorhouse. That's it. Selling apples in the street. An apple vendor. Maybe chestnuts. But a vendor. In the streets. *Down there.*" I saw him picking up cigar butts on Michigan Boulevard, cadging drinks in North Clark Street bars.

"Jake. Sweetheart."

"Yes, let's not holler till we're hurt," Pippin said. "A hundred questions come tumbling into mind. Who would be liable? Jeepers first, of course —"

"Who would then turn around and sue us for the recovery of funds the loss of which would be our responsibility as sponsors of the contest," Wintermoots said.

"But to whom would Jeepers be accountable? The FTC? I very much doubt they have the authority for court prosecution."

"That's what I'm trying to get a reading from Wagondust on. I've got a call in to him now." Wagondust and Turley were the law firm we retained. "Whether the FTC has any jurisdictional —" The phone rang again, and Wintermoots said, "No! You're not to be reached for comment. That's flat. Nor is anybody. But of course that may be Wagondust. I've ordered him to be switched here. I'll take a chance."

Gingerly, as though it were a stick of dynamite, Wintermoots reached for the phone and raised it to his ear. "Yes?" It was Wagondust.

He was a good twenty minutes with an opinion ranging across every aspect of the matter as he knew it. Wintermoots's end of it was a listening sequence of "Uh-huhs." All three of us sat down midway the discourse, Jake sinking into my swivel chair. The gist of the opinion was to justify doubts already expressed, in a spirit of desperate wishful thinking rather than one of informed grasp. No deceptive-practices case could be cited in which the payment of money to private citizens under these precise circumstances had been successfully ordered. The commission had no actual power to order it — or at least its power to do so had not up to now been tested in the courts. It was at the time seeking a specific mandate from Congress authorizing it to impose penalties and award damages to victims judged by them to be such in this area of trade practices.

Jake seemed somewhat relieved on hanging up, a relaxation with which we were glad to be infected as we listened to the recapitulation. But we were far from out of the woods, he reminded us, and might never be home and dry. Even if a court judgment were slapped on Jeepers, requiring them to cough up, and they appealed it to near-infinity, as would W. and H. if they in turn sued us for recovery, in a litigation even more hopelessly entangled in matters of interpretation of responsibility as between agency and client, so that it would all go on and on like Jarndyce vs. Jarndyce in *Bleak House*, till we would all be generations dead before it came to an end by collapsing of its own juridical weight — even then there would be the immediate, almost certain harm the publicity would do us. That was true enough. A client we had been on the verge of landing, a soap company, cooled off that very week and went somewhere else. And the cry "We want Tickler, we'd like Tickler put on this," was no more heard in the land.

But hold it. Let's not write him off quite yet. He has an ace in the hole, one last iron in the fire. One he can turn his full attention to with a clear conscience on the Jeepers mess. For my job had been finished when I had drafted and turned over the batch of questions for the idea I had cooked up. Any ambiguity about the rules, whether deliberate or accidental, was the Jeepers people's responsibility. The reports erred in saying we "ran" the contest. Still, I had a nagging uneasiness about the whole thing, a deepening of the schizophrenic sense about this entire line of work, which Wintermoots had twittingly suggested might discommode my "youthful idealism" the night he first offered me a job. But I had seen nothing yet. My remaining project was destined, not to drop into the legal limbo where the Jeepers business reposes to this day, but to flare up into a national scandal, a *cause célèbre* on a scale making our poor "Jeepers creepers" look like a party that you think will never end.

11

LITTLE RED POOLROOM WAS A QUIZ SHOW cast in the form of "intellectual pool" being shot between two contestants answering questions of steadily graduating difficulty ranging from one to fifteen, each correct answer constituting a pocketed ball entitling the player to go on to the next, until a missed question gave the opponent the table, at that stage of the game. A scholarly version of straight pool. Whoever won the toss for the first play "broke" the set with a fairly easy question — such as "Who was our second President?" — generally regarded also as sinking the number one ball for him. The traditional jinx of the eight ball was observed by making it the first real toughie, after which the questions escalated steeply, becoming more obscure or multi-part, till the fifteen ball (on which, as in straight pool, the balls were racked up again) posed you something like, "What was the original name of the character in a famous novel who changed it to Don Quixote?" (Alonzo Quixano) or "In Greek mythology, who was Epimetheus?" (Brother of Prometheus and husband of Pandora).

Each point was worth a hundred dollars, so that running the table, which in regular pool would net you a hundred and twenty points, won you twelve thousand dollars of the sponsor's money, or nothing to sneeze at. Just as among real-life pool sharks phenomenal runs of eighty and ninety and more are no rarity, so we had contestants who seemed storehouses of facts that enabled them to go on week after week — within the categories concerned, because each game was held to a pre-established area. The winner reappeared the following week with the same or another opponent. The ideal ball for your opponent to muff was fifteen, because then you could start a fresh table-run of your own beginning with the relatively easy questions — provided you sank the fifteen of course. A ball muffed twice would come back to the first player with a different question, then another if necessary, for every ball must be sunk in rotation.

Sitting in front of my television set at home I naturally felt a keen excitement watching my brain child roll along from week to week — and also an intense envy. Two of the early performers on Little Red Poolroom seemed in particular to possess brains that are "like wax to receive and like marble to retain." One was a young woman named Angela Burwash who in the botany category was able to answer as with a snap of the fingers that Dutch elm blight is a disease caused by a fungus transmitted by bark beetles which breed in dead elms and feed on living, thereby destroying the water-conducting vessels, causing the death of the tree. "Jesus," I breathed, watching with Amy. I leaned back in my chair, shaking my head. "And

148

she's beautiful too." The other was an equally personable chap of thirty-one named Tommy Trotter, who finally "bumped" her, in the studio jargon, by nine points in a game which was to become the first in an unbroken string of seventeen in which he used sixteen opponents and racked up total winnings of well over a hundred thousand dollars. It seemed Tommy Trotter would go on forever, or at least till he had bankrupt or acquired control of the Langley Laboratories, who made the cosmetics advertised on the show. You'll learn presently who was hand-picked to stop him, said he simpering at his shoes.

Now like all of us watching quiz shows I would call out answers I knew, trying to beat the contestant out there in Never Never Land. "Mrs. Gummidge! Parahelion! Reciprocating engine! Dante Gabriel Rossetti!" I would bark, till Amy found more entertainment watching me than she did the show. Once, observing me, her smile faded and she said, "For God's sake, Jim, you're sweating. Look at you."

I could feel me. I shrugged. "It's my show."

"No, it's more than that. The way you identify with them. Especially that Angela Burwash. Do you realize you were sitting there licking your lips? I don't mean over her. You'd like a crack at it yourself, wouldn't you?"

It was the truth. I fantasized endlessly over Angela Burwash, the sexual flavor uppermost in such imaginary moments as, having bumped her with some almost inconceivably arcane question, I expressed my regrets in terms of the lovelorn schoolboy who tells his classroom sweetheart after spelling her down, "I'm sorry I spelled that word." It was easy enough to put myself in Tommy Trotter's shoes when he defeated her, and began his fabulous reign as quiz champ. Here, a special yeast leavened in my case what was a normal enough male woolgathering loaf.

Trotter was born to the role, as one of an Eastern family with roots deep in the Colonial American past and a pedigree loaded with scholars, judges, learned divines, poets and other intellectuals. Charming, boyish, with a most engagingly open grin, able, as one heard, to converse from scratch on any number of subjects, now wined and dined and photographed and interviewed to a fare-thee-well, sauntering into the best restaurants in clothes tailored to a gnat's eyebrow for what is known as casual elegance, he — well, glittered with the glory of the hummingbird. He was a sprig of such aristocracy as we have. While I? I was from a teeming Hoosier household more than one of whom might have referred to him as "one of them scions." Is it any wonder that I dreamed of toppling him in turn? That I should even meet him seemed unlikely, unless spotting him, as once I actually did, whirled streetward through the revolving door of a Loop hotel, I were to push my way through the mob of women around him and, extending my yokel's paw, say, "You don't know me but —" Never. I would die before thus admitting the anonymity in which I was drowned. I hadn't even met the producers of the show — in which we took local pride because, though of course it emanated from New York, it was taped before a live audience in Chicago. Why the hell wasn't anybody dying to meet me? Hadn't I concocted this moneymaking feather in our corporate and municipal caps?

Then suddenly one day the producers asked me to lunch.

Russell Falconer being also the master of ceremonies, or "referee," the bulk of the production duties fell to

Versprunk. What they wanted to do, they revealed after a cocktail or two, was pick my brains of any other ideas for possible quiz shows. There were no less than five going on the tube at the moment, day and night, which meant enough, or that they had become such a staple of television entertainment that another could readily find a sponsor — provided it were as original in concept as my School Pool, as they called it for short around the shop. I shook my head. I hadn't another notion in it. Falconer pressed the point, pulling from his pocket a tract he had just been handed on the street by one of the dispensing devout, which proved the universal validity, or at least appeal, of the quiz principle.

"Seems to be about the Bible and Biblical characters," he said. "I haven't even looked at it closely." He laughed, perusing it. "Would anybody like to be grilled?"

"Shoot," I said, feeling my religious upbringing might stand me in sufficient stead in taking on a catechism presumably elementary enough.

"O.K. Let me just see here . . ." Falconer adjusted on his fine aquiline nose (yet one set in a face reminiscent of a decadent Roman emperor) the pair of horn-rimmed glasses he had put on, and peered studiously at the leaflet. The questions were far from rudimentary. "First, where is butter mentioned in the Old Testament?"

"One of the Psalms. His words were — No, the words of his mouth were smoother than butter, but war was in his heart."

Falconer consulted the back of the leaflet where the answers were.

"I'll be damned. That's right." He shot Versprunk a glance before returning to the questions. "Sounds like a culinary quiz. Where are cucumbers mentioned?"

"One of the prophets. Isaiah or Jeremiah. I'll take Jeremiah. The line is one of those about the daughter of Zion. She is left as a something in a vineyard, as a lodge in a garden of cucumbers."

"It's Isaiah actually, and a cottage in a vineyard, but that's the line, right on the button."

They both looked at me, then at one another with a wild surmise. The quiz continued.

"What is the origin of the word shibboleth?"

"Test word used in a battle by the, wait a minute, Gileadites, yes that's it, to distinguish from their own soldiers the fleeing some other ites, I think the Ephraimites, who couldn't pronounce the *sh*. It came out sibboleth. Over forty thousand were slaughtered when they failed to get that little old sibilant right."

Unto what city was Jonah ordered to go by the Lord? Nineveh. What country did he set sail for instead, with disastrous results? Tarshish. How old was Abraham when he died? Didn't know. It was a hundred seventy-five. Whose ass talked back to him? Balaam. Who was fed by the ravens, and where? Elijah, at the brook Cherith. Shifting to the New Testament, whom did Paul give his famous advice to "use a little wine for thy stomach's sake, and thine often infirmities."? Timothy. What was Christ's first miracle? Changing water into wine at the marriage feast in Cana. What was his second? Didn't know. Name the twelve disciples. That I couldn't do either, as few could. I only got eight. What was Paul's original name, and where was he born? Saul, in Tarsus, an important seaport of ancient Cilicia. What language did Jesus speak? Aramaic.

There ended the quiz. The other two sat and stared at

me. Falconer removed his glasses and pocketed both them and the tract.

"Where in the hell did you learn all this?"

"At my mother's knee. And in church, catechism, Sunday school. I would be a devout man today," I laughed, "if it weren't for my religious upbringing. All this was dinned into my ears, shoved down my throat, and rubbed into my pores like Sloan's liniment when I had a winter backache."

Versprunk, a thickset man with a mop of hair as black as tar, had been studying me with a somewhat more portentous air, as though away ahead of his partner. "How would you like to go on the show?"

"Ah, come on," I said, with a dirt-kicking grin I'd like to have seen.

"No, seriously. You're not cross-eyed, reasonably dressed, and your ears are pasted on straight. Not any pretty-boy, but probably photogenic would be my guess, though we'd have to screen-test you of course."

"Me up against Trotter?"

This was where their expressions began to change. There was now some peculiar visual byplay between them, accompanied by throat-scraping and even chair-scraping and no little hemming and hawing.

"I'd foresee no difficulty about that," said Versprunk, much the greater smoothie of the two. The air seemed suddenly smoky with some kind of duplicity I couldn't quite put my finger on. "You're probably widely versed in as many general categories as most of our hot shots. Like what is osmosis?"

"Oh, for Pete's sake. The tendency of a fluid to pass through a membrane into a solution of lower density. I feel some kind of osmosis going on here. What gives?"

"Who wants to make your flesh creep?"

"The fat boy in Dickens."

"How often does the Halley's Comet turn up?"

"Every seventy-five years. Actually a little more like seventy-six."

"You see? A savant."

"But those are all questions that have been asked on School Pool, which you know I watch. As though you're rigging me to look good so I'll let myself be sucked into . . . into winding up with egg on my face before twenty million people."

"Not quite that many. Our Trendex slipped a few points last week. Meaning we've had it with Trotter, and he with us. He's dazzled the country for too many weeks, now they're getting a little glutted with him. He knows it too. He'd like out. Fifteen weeks has been enough. He's willing to . . . meet his match next week or the week after."

I sensed a bolt being slid halfway somewhere in my mind. "You mean he'll take a dive?"

They both shrugged as they screwed their faces up into meaningless expressions, coughing and reaching for their drinks. I watched them intently. "He'll go home with well over a hundred thousand," Falconer said. Cynicism, carefully concealed up to now, seemed to emerge in full, like worms from the woodwork, yet with a hint of worse to follow. "Wouldn't that satisfy you? Shouldn't it satisfy anybody?"

"That doesn't quite answer my question. What —?"

Falconer gave a labored laugh in Versprunk's direction as he gestured on a note of good-humored tolerance in mine. "The quizmaster here." Treading on his words, Versprunk said hastily, "We make sure his opponent is as carefully hand-picked as he was. We make sure he's trained, for the knockout and then for a run defending his crown."

I drew a deep breath and let it out slowly, as though exhaling for all of us the last remaining gasp of hypocrisy. The bolt had shot free. "You mean this whole show is fixed."

They began to swivel and twist and fidget about, as though some kind of itching powder with which the chairs had been doctored, up to now inefficacious, had at last managed to penetrate their pants' seats. Versprunk was the first to recover some of his aplomb. He grinned at me — here it is — quizzically as he said: "Would you like to take on Trotter legitimately?"

"My baby, that I should have retained control of, at least consultant on the questions, editor or something, a hoax. This is a hell of a note! This program designed to restore faith in and respect for learning among the dropout young, make them see knowledge as a dazzling thing — Trotter getting a hundred letters a day, many from children to whom he's been a hero, saying he's made them *eager* to hit the books, do their homework, not just silly women offering to marry him — praised by educators too, thanking God for the result — the whole thing is a mare's-nest!"

"Now just a minute. This is all in how you look at it."

"A pigsty is a pigsty no matter from what angle it's viewed."

"Please knock it off and listen. For one minute. The people we have on the show *are* learned, at least in their categories, some more than one. Cooley and Watson with their baseball and boxing statistics, well that's one thing. But Angela Burwash is a very highly educated woman, with a doctor's degree in history. Ditto for Trotter in literature. People who want on the show, to strut their stuff, why not, applicants, are put through a rigid examination, as stiff as any college boards. We just make sure, a, the quizzing is arranged to make the battle of wits entertaining — that this learning for which we want to and do engender a respect is *exciting* — and, b, it makes for a week-to-week cliffhanger."

Falconer was leaning forward, wetting his lips in a manner indicating that he wanted very much to interpolate a point here. Versprunk made it. "You, for instance. You've just now passed about as tough a test in one category as could be imagined, with flying colors. Would it be such a sin to see them flapping merrily in the breeze? For a few weeks? Would it be such a sin for us to, as we prefer to call it, control the conditions under which that just due would be guaranteed you?" He let go a fork he had all this while been twirling in his fingers and leaned back. "Well?"

"Like everything is relative," Falconer dropped into the silence. "It's all relative. Like . . ."

"Pirandello," Versprunk put in for him, apparently no ignoramus himself when it came to that. "The illusion is the reality, and vice versa. Like Vaihinger." That authority, adduced here with the dexterity of a pocketed ball, came as a surprise. "You know that philosopher? Promulgated the 'As If' principle. We live *as if* something were true. Everything we think is some kind of fiction."

"Hear the guy. Should put him on the show. No, seriously, we're not a couple of sharpies would do anything for a buck. Or the sponsors either. Look what it's costing them! *But it's got to be a show.* That's why we brief contestants, coach them, even in how to act in the sweatbox. Not just toss off the answers. Bleed it a little. Fish it up out of the recesses of your memory or even the depths of your subconscious in an agony of effort, of concentration. Close your eyes, bite your lip, mop your brow over something you've got on the tip of your tongue, why not as long as the result —"

"Jesus," I whispered, "what a laugh all that seems now. I can see Trotter." I shook my head. "Maybe he's wrestling with his conscience."

"I can remember Oliver St. John Gogarty on a radio show called Information Please years ago." Versprunk again, chewing my other ear. It was like being tempted by the Devil in stereo. "You're probably too young to remember the show, but one night when Gogarty was on, it's just something that sticks in my mind, a question was in what poem do we find the line, 'Nine bean rows will I have, and a hive for the honeybee.'" He paused meaningly. I delivered.

"Yeats's 'The Lake Isle of Innisfree.'"

"He sinks the nine ball! Anyway, don't you think the question was specifically picked as one Gogarty would know? Not by prearrangement, obviously, just as a courtesy to a guest. Of course. Would you consider that immoral, or crooked? O.K. There you are."

By now our food had arrived, and we ate in silence — though not very heartily — for some few minutes. At last Falconer moved his plate back an inch or two in order to rest his forearms on the table-edge.

"Why don't we do this. I'm having this idea. It's your show, your baby that you, like, set out for adoption, and now you find it's been kidnapped by gypsies and raised to steal. You're going to snatch it back and set it on the straight and narrow. Right?"

"Meaning?" I said, lowering my eyes to a forkful of lasagna.

"Meet Trotter head-on in a joust on the Bible."

My palms were moist, and I could feel tiny rills of perspiration under my arms. I wiped my free hand on a trouser-leg.

"We'll use the questions in this tract as a basis, sort of. You've answered them honestly so there'd be no dishonesty about repeating them under conditions merely reproducing these ones today. You'll cram for the category obviously by holing yourself up in a hotel room with a Gideon Bible, reading it from end to end, with a pot of black coffee and an icebag on your head. So will Trotter. When you get to the twelve Disciples, well, we'll leave it up to your conscience whether to fill in the gaps on those you missed. And any others you muffed. We won't ask Trotter to take a dive on any particular question, which has been our format technique up to now, *if* he knows it. I can see it already. How we'll bill it. The Battle of the Series. In this corner, a boy from the Bible Belt. In the other, the Champ of the Eastern Establishment. Yipee! Absolutely the Dream Match of the year!"

12

WEDNESDAY EVENING AT TWO MINUTES TO EIGHT. The minute hand, then the second hand, crept like tarantulas across the face of the clock. The sweatbox, as they called the isolation booths in which the contestants faced each other and the announcer, was well named. I was pouring perspiration in a thermally comfortable enough temperature of sixty-eight. My ears were clammy under the headpieces through which could be heard Falconer regaling the gladiators and spectators both with some intendedly relaxing "warmup" chatter. My heart pounded like a bass drum. My head ached, my guts were a swarm of bats. However had I let myself get sucked into this — nightmare?

Trotter waved at me through his glass wall, smiling his famous "open" smile. I returned what must have been a sick grin indeed. In a few minutes I would be naked to millions of people — which was what the studio audience of five hundred before whom the show was about to be taped amounted to. Next Monday at exactly eight o'clock I would be watching myself — do what? Fall flat on my face? I would have given all I would ever own to exchange this for a simple death. Maybe I was dying. My vision seemed to mist, my brain swam. My bowels rotted within me, I could feel my very balls crawl with fear. In half an hour I would totter out of this coffin, a broken, wrung, wilted shame of a man . . .

"Good evening, ladies and gentlemen!" Falconer was chirping. "Welcome to another exciting game at the Little Red Poolroom! This time we have a new challenger. Out of our great Middle America — the Bible Belt! James Tickler of Wabash, Indiana! Facing the still undefeated Tommy Trotter on the subject *of* — The Bible!"

There was the usual longish plug for the sponsors, from whose line of cosmetics a rejuvenating face cream was tonight singled out for special encomium. Then:

"Trotter having finished with a table run last week, he breaks first with a question, good for one point, and one hundred dollars, having to do, not with the Scriptures themselves, but, by way of teeing off, what a famous young fictional character, Tom Sawyer, answered when it was put to *him* one morning in Sunday School. For a hundred dollars, Tommy Trotter, what did Tom answer when asked, 'Who were the first two disciples chosen by Jesus?'"

We were off! My knees turned to rubber, my tongue to ashes. Were they pulling a fast one on me? This had never come up in the course of our "prepping," during which they had let me ramble on about my own boyhood with tales ranging from Oompah's reluctant church-going to Mother's embarrassing Reverend Slosch with that business about Our Lord's pedigree.

Trotter was screwing his eyes up, biting his lip — the usual histrionic bit. Good God, I thought, he certainly knows the answer to this one. That I had it ready on the tip of my own tongue suddenly seemed to gather all my nervous forces together. I came to focus. I was ready for battle. I not only knew the answer, I knew how Mark Twain ended the chapter. "Let us draw the curtain of charity over the rest of the scene."

"David and Goliath," Trotter said at last.

"Correct! Now the two ball, and we begin in earnest. Who, actually, *were* the first two Disciples appointed by Jesus? In other words, what's the correct answer?"

Since this was a multiple-answer question, I was "blacked out" of Trotter's reply, in keeping with a rule safeguarding a contestant from giving an opponent the benefit of a possibly partial answer, which would make it easier for him if he got the play. But his mugging and head-scratching seemed genuine this time. I learned later that he got the first, Simon Peter, then took a wild stab that turned out to be wrong, Matthew.

"No, I'm afraid that's incorrect," Falconer said, and turned to me. "James Tickler? What should poor Tom Sawyer have answered?"

"Well, there's no absolute certainty, because of a little discrepancy among the Gospel authors, but it's the generally accepted belief that Simon Peter and his brother, Andrew, were the first to join Jesus."

"No Tom Sawyer he!" Falconer cried, flinging a hand in my direction. "So all right, Tickler has the play! Now chalk your cue for ball three. Still in the New Testament, what was St. Paul's original name and where was he born?"

"He was born Saul of Tarsus."

"Rrright! For the four ball. To what city was Jonah ordered to go, and he didn't — with results we all know!"

"To Nineveh."

"Rrright! Back to the New Testament again. Ananias's name is synonymous with lying, for having, shall we say, reported falsely on his income. But he had a partner in the deception. His wife. What was her name?"

"Sapphira."

"Rrright! For the sixth ball and six hundred dollars, what gentleman of Galilee, because of his short stature, climbed up into a tree to get a glimpse of Jesus?"

"Zacchaeus."

"Again correct! The seventh ball. Whose ass talked back to him?"

This was a bit thick, this child's play. Or perhaps not so to one unversed in Holy Writ. I thought they might have made it a little stiffer, yet not regretting they didn't. Because I was tasting victory, I was already drunk with it. I was dizzy, now with ecstasy.

There was time out for another plug, followed by an interlude of music by a rock quartet. Then came the eight ball, the traditional first toughie. I steeled myself. How far would they go with their "controlled circumstances"? I had not been fed answers to questions. They were asking me questions to which the "briefing" had shown I knew the replies. How venal was that? I had no idea. I no longer knew, or cared. I was on the wing.

But the eight ball was a brute.

"We return to the original question," Falconer was saying. "For eight hundred dollars, name the *rest* of the twelve Disciples."

Well, I had refused, in cramming for this, to stoop so low as to memorize them in a manner I could reel off by rote. I had read them through two or three times, however. But I could only get six. So the play went back to Trotter. He apparently got several, then faltered. In keeping with the rules, the play came back to me with a fresh question.

"Where, in the Old Testament, we'll give them that hint, is butter mentioned?"

"One of the Psalms. The words of his mouth were smoother than butter."

"Rrright! The nine ball. Where do we find cucumbers mentioned?"

"Isaiah. . . ."

And so on. I have no idea how carefully this was plotted. On the eleven ball, I missed again. Something about the cities visited by St. Paul on his journeys. Trotter had clearly been briefed to make a run of some sort here, because he answered it, with the customary agonizing, mopping his brow with the handkerchief that was also part of the act, then pocketed twelve and thirteen as well. That gave him, as Falconer said in a breather for another commercial, 37 points to my 54.

Shooting for the fourteenth ball, Trotter had a chance to all but close the gap between us. If he sank it, the score would be a mere 54–51 in my favor, with the last ball remaining. I began to sweat again — or rather I could again feel myself sweating. My shirt felt like a poultice on my back. Falconer was announcing it as a two-part question, of which the first part was something everybody knew so they wouldn't even bother to black me out on it. It involved someone whose name was a household word for bright raiment. I knew then what I would hear: "Who was famous for his coat of many colors?"

"Joseph," said Trotter, with the grace not to chew the scenery.

"Right you are," said Falconer. "Now for part two. He had eleven brothers, as we all also know, sons of Jacob. Here's what you have to do to sink the fourteen ball and all but tie the score, as I see by our scoreboard. Name eight of those brothers, and by extension of course eight of the twelve tribes of Israel, who were named after them."

I damn near blacked out with my earphones. I began to mutter to myself in possible preparation for a flub on Trotter's part. "Reuben, Benjamin, Judah, one that begins with a Z . . ."

I heard my earphones turn "hot" again and sensed from Trotter's face what Falconer would say.

"I'm sorry, that only gives you four, and your time's up. The play goes back to our challenger. Can he name eight of those famous brothers?"

I drew a deep breath and began.

"Well, there was Benjamin, the youngest, and Reuben, who as I recall was the eldest, Judah of course, and one that begins with a Z. Zebulun! Gad!"

"Is that last an expletive or an answer?"

"Both, but that is another of the brothers."

"Right! That gives you five. Any more? Long or short, we don't care —"

"Dan!"

"Six! Another minute to go. Two more."

"Let's see, there's another Z in there somewhere. Zilpah? No, that was one of the mothers. Oh, Simeon of course."

"One more. We're all hanging by our teeth. One more. Think of the brothers or the tribes, either one —"

"Of course! The tribe that supplied the temple servants. Levi!"

"Terrific! That gives our challenger a commanding 68, and after this brief message we'll give him a shot at the last ball left on the table."

Trotter went slack in his sweatbox, whether from exhaustion or, what was more likely, relief at last from the weeks of strain and tension that had been the gruelling price of his celebrity, seen as such now by the successor to whom it appeared he would pass on both the glory and the horror.

Falconer had finished singing the praises of Langley Laboratory's New Lease on Life facial cream.

"Now then, Jimmy Tickler, for fifteen points and what looks to be the game. A question about the genealogy of Jesus, as given in the opening chapter of "Matthew." Somewhere along the line, there was an ancestor who was not Jewish. Who was it? From whom did Our Lord receive his non-Jewish blood?"

In an almost dream-like recapitulation of a childhood scene lived long ago, the words formed themselves on a tongue no longer parched. The timing was perfect. I spotted Versprunk in the control room giving the sign to draw it out — a slow, lateral parting of the hands, palms down. Then, when the answer seemed too leisurely, the cue to speed it up, a rapid circular twirling of one finger given with his eye on the clock overhead.

"Well, there was . . . No, that couldn't be right. Let's see . . . Oh, yes, of course. There was Ruth, daughter of — no, daughter-in-law of Naomi. Ruth of whither-thou-goest-I-will-go fame. She married Boaz, in whose field she had gleaned. They had a son. I don't remember his name, but he was the father of Jesse, the father of David, who we all know was an ancestor of Jesus of Nazareth. But Ruth was a Moabitess."

"Ab — solutely correct! Amazing! And so, ladies and gentlemen — we have a new quiz champ! Jimmy Tickler! Of Wabash! Indiana!"

Thus I restored to my old show at least a measure of the honesty of which it had been defrauded by unscrupulous men. Paying for it with a bit of my own, of course. That was the delicate moral transaction on which I had embarked. The now at least partially recovered integrity was there thanks to the loan of my own. That was under lien, if you will, paid off in small weekly sums to the public purpose to which it had been mortgaged. The cost of some ethical strain to oneself was gladly borne, that this nourishment might be vouchsafed the nation with measurably less chicanery than had been hitherto the case. Those rascals were not as corrupt as they had been; I not quite as blameless as might ideally have been wished, but then — to make the world that much less a bog for decent men to slog their way through, was that not a plus? The books of this life will never balance, but they would come that miniscule mite closer to bearing scrutiny, on this paltry page, for as long as I might sustain the terrible burden of "star," that gruelling investiture dependent on such concessions as one was willing to make for the cause *and no more*. Thus the long, dedicated conversations with Falconer and Versprunk, in which everything one knew in a certain category might be teased out of one in order that questions might be tailored to match this so, so legitimate store of knowledge; now and then, the more honestly open device of consenting to be handed answers to questions that might — or then again might not — be asked. Exhaustive cramming required of one in any case! The midnight oil burned as it had not burned since those faroff schooldays when one had acquired what one knew! These balder promptings intended merely to tide one over "stumpers" between long, nationally edifying stretches in which one dished up answer after answer from the store of learning for which one had validly presented his credentials. One demonstrated one could go the whole road; what mattered it to be helped over a stile here and there?

As for the money, nothing. That would go straight to Community Services and the settlement club it ran, to which Amy now devoted her full time. It would be the ultimate and never-lost-sight-of beneficiary for which one not only willingly, as one gave alms, did not let his left hand know what his right hand was doing, but for which one subtly heeded the Master's even subtler injunction, here as relevant as ever could be: "Make to yourselves friends, therefore, of the Mammon of unrighteousness, that when ye fail, they may receive you into everlasting habitations."

What were these habitations? Hardly everlasting, indeed ephemeral enough. But for this brief tenure all for which one could have wished, all for which one had sickened, as the rustic come to the metropolis. The whole world was a salon now, in which one sparkled and shone day and night in public and private. This was Vanity Fair at last without stint or respite. Hostesses fought to have one for dinner. Autograph hounds mobbed one as one emerged from the studio, accosted him on the street, shuffled up to one's table in a restaurant, menu and pencil in hand. One was beleaguered by journalists for interviews, begged for appearances on late-night talk shows, asked for book blurbs, for wine, whiskey and after-shave testimonials (about which one was incorruptible), hit for donations to worthy causes (all such requests answered with a note explaining the money was already earmarked). One got fifty letters a day, then a hundred, many from students saying, again, to the new champion how they had been inspired to do their homework, or from parents expressing thanks for this change in their children. A news magazine that had been readying a cover story on Trotter abruptly switched their attention to his successor, and when that hit the streets it all tripled. Even reading the letters was hopeless, let alone answering them. Three movie studios offered screen tests, one a role in a forthcoming film without one. There was a letter from the office of the president of a midwestern university, offering an honorary degree. A new street on the spreading outskirts of Wabash was to be called Tickler Avenue. Could one be present at the dedication? One could, and was. So were photographers, and a researcher for the cover story being whipped into shape. That was entitled "What Makes Tickler Tick?" and it ran in part:

He wears his erudition lightly, as casually as he does the patchwork "hobo jacket" he has made the season's rage by sporting it about town as well as on the No. 1 TV quiz show where steadily swelling millions of watchers have kept their eye on him for twelve weeks now, hoping, as do the sponsors, that he will match and then beat previous champ Tommy Trotter's record of seventeen weeks. It's a little like rooting for Hank Aaron as he creeps up on Babe Ruth's home-run record. Tickler calls the jacket his "coat of many colors," after the garment worn by brother Joseph concerning whom he answered what he considers his lucky pivotal question in the Scripture bout on which he toppled Trotter from his throne, naming eight of the other eleven brothers (and thus eight of the twelve Tribes, a feat many devout Jews could not perform).

The magazine got its own flood of letters on that one. The article continued:

"What's he like personally?" is the question oftenest asked, as it is of all celebrities. He's simply a Restoration wit *de notre jour*, adapting the traditional English literate pleasantry to the American wisecrack. Hearing a notoriously rather henpecked husband described as having been on at least one occasion outspoken, he replied, "Yes — by her." An administration ceaselessly diverting attention from present crises to past accomplishments he calls "government by exhaust." He likes to be around people with the same taste for absurdity. He goes to a dentist who when making wax models for bridgework says, "And for my next impression . . ."

The far cry from his Bible-belt origins represented by this fancy for Babylonian worldliness is what makes him the complex character he is. His mother puts his hometown origins in the simplest light. "This is Middle America," she said. "This is Agnew country. We believe in the simple virtues, the homely values. We put everything on the line — including the wash. I still hang mine out in the back yard where I can see it flapping in the wind blowing off the good old Wabash River, and my neighbors can see it and I can theirs." [There was a picture of Mother in the yard, holding a wicker basket and talking through a mouthful of clothespins.] Her son's penchant for pithy statement has always stood him in good stead, she says, wryly displaying an old letter he once sent from camp when he was eight: "Dear All: Well I want to be sure this gets in the next pickup, so will close now hoping everyone is O.K."

His father is a poetry-writing travelling salesman for a pharmaceutical house, who does not share his wife's cozy religious faith. A sample of his verse:

169

If I make my bed in Sheol, behold, thou art there.
If I take the wings of the morning and fly to the
Uttermost parts of the sea, behold, thou are there.
So why is it that when I go to the Second Presbyterian
Church of Wabash, Indiana, lo, thou art not there?
Why is that the case, I would like to know, I'm only
asking. Selah.

The slightly waspish note with which Tickler's normally genial enough wit sometimes alternates might be traced to this parent. Finding himself on a recent talk show tangling with a Women's Libber whose own Brooks Brothers button-down shirts and plaid trousers have become a well-known sort of emasculating agitprop, Tickler found the exchange becoming progressively more heated. "I suppose you fancy yourself the answer to a woman's prayer," she flung at him. "No," Tickler retorted, "but I suspect you are." He does, however, consider the bruited difference between the sexes dangerously exaggerated. "They don't have one form of sex, we another. We're on different thermostats, but we're all warmed by the same old boiler, and we'd damn well better not let it blow up on us."

How long can he go on? That's itself the Big Question on Poolroom. His winnings have already crept toward the $100,000 mark. He will pocket none of it, and "the IRS will get as little of it as I can manage," the rest going in toto to a cause very close to him and his wife, the former Amy Wintermoots, a masters-degree sociologist now an officer of Community Services, a welfare organization operating out of a seedy storefront in a run-down Chicago neighborhood that, among other things, finds foster homes for boy juvenile delinquents themselves from broken, or nonexistent, homes. How close the charity is to their hearts may be gauged from the fact that the Ticklers have themselves taken in such a boy. "That's pretty close," he wryly admits. "But I'm enjoying this roller coaster ride. Every minute. And I'll take all the gravy I can get. The kids can have the meat."

A stout advocate of marriage (and growing stouter every year) he was recently asked what he considered his most cherished memory of domestic life to date. He answered unhesitatingly: "Eating TV dinners together while watching Julia Child."

13

PROFESSIONS, LIKE NATIONS, are civilized to the degree to which they can satirize themselves. England and Literature occupy, by this yardstick, their respective eminences. Sociologists tend to jabber in the double solemnities of their own profession and that of psychology too, making for trains of verbal boxcars such as ethico-socio-psychic inheritance syndromes, and sick headaches in the listener.

Amy never used any such jargon, save in an occupationally self-spoofing way. But the dossiers she regularly carried home were full of it, and these increased as her work load did. She often took the familiar Manila folders to bed, where in the early years of our marriage she spent a great deal of time upside-down in the effort to become pregnant. Remaining horizontal after love retained the male sperm, which was to be even more advantageously hoarded by lying with her legs as far up a wall corner as she could get them, at the head-end of the bed, her body jackknifed so that she was all but resting on her shoulder-blades.

As prospects for having a natural infant waned, the question of adopting one arose from time to time. But an emotional factor always complicated our thinking about it, more hers than mine, being professional in her case. Part of her job at Community Services was to find foster homes for the delinquents in one way or another under her wing. Married couples willing to perform this service were of course paid by the state, but it wasn't easy to find people willing to shoulder a responsibility that consisted, often enough, in having boys in trouble with the law paroled to their custody for probation. There was always a waiting list, always. So that every time we got ourselves revved up to apply to the Cradle for a baby, the specter raised its head: how could she "have the heart" to indulge her feelings by selecting a cherub wriggling in a pink or blue blanket when there was this eternally irreducible line of troubled boys for whom it was her job to find "residential custody." At the same time, taking any such on posed a challenge for which one's own character hardly seemed sufficiently oaken. One was torn. On the one hand, flocks of Maeterlinckian bluebirds fresh descended from heaven; on the other, a passel of pubescent near-villains queueing up for release from hell. The dilemma went unresolved as the months, the years floated by.

One evening as I was trying to repair a defectively wired electric fan, Amy read aloud to me from her homework. I sat on one bed chewing my tongue as I plied a screwdriver, she disposed on the other with her feet up the wall, in the inverted position on which she died hard though the gynecologist had long ceased to pin any hopes on it. The inevitable brown Manila folder lay beside her as she regaled me with some tidbits from Chip Griswold's dossier.

"Suspected of school vandalism at the age of nine, chronic cheater on his exams. Definitely an under-achiever. Convicted of shoplifting in a ten-cent store, given six months in a correctional institution by Judge Sayquaff. Sentence suspended because first offense, assigned to foster home from which he ran away after three weeks on grounds that the husband and wife were 'a pair of sugar cubes.' "

"What by the way —?"

"Arabian. It's an Arabian name, or an Americanization of one. Wonderful man, Judge Sayquaff, heart like a ham."

"And then the sugar cubes?"

"Square. Too much. Like nowhere. Well, never mind his record, which of course isn't official since he's still a minor. The thing that sticks out in all of this is his family life. If ever a kid was the product of a broken home this one is. Father real cute. Skipped the country to avoid alimony payments, and is now presumed living in Europe with some chick, unaware that the wife and mother has died of an overdose of drugs."

"Sounds as though the kid's due for some kind of break. Where is he now? Not with another pair of sugar cubes I trust."

"I'll come to that in a minute. Here's the interesting part, from a psychological point of view. He's obviously seething like a volcano with resentment toward his old man, who at the same time he pretends didn't desert him, covering up with a lot of stuff about what pals they always were and how he's just trying to get his bearings abroad so he can send for him. None of it parses, because during the period the kid says they went on camping trips and what not, Griswold *père* was shacked up with this sex kitten he finally took off with. Whole thing's a mare's-nest, this fiction the boy spins. To all intents and purposes he is an orphan. Would you believe we call that a *de facto* orphan?"

"I believe it. Kid sounds interesting, if a trifle kinky."

"Would you like to meet him?"

"Don't tell me it's time for another boys' club barbecue."

Amy broke down, without necessarily dismantling her position.

Mr. and Mrs. Edmondson, in whose not-quite-so-square foster home the Griswold was currently billeted, had petitioned for a break of two weeks or so in order to visit a sister in Seattle who was about to have a serious operation. Community Services had to dig up a substitute instanter.

"Have you got anybody in mind?"

The pause, at least, was pregnant. And just too long for me not to surmise what would follow.

"Why, I was thinking it might give us a sort of, you know, dry run for what we've been speculating about. I mean, to see how we'd like being parents, are we parental timber. And it'd only be for a few weeks."

"Shouldn't any change like that be cleared by the courts?"

"Oh, I can get that from Judge Sayquaff in ten minutes."

"And go through committee at the Center in any case?"

"Oh, good God, committees. Don't you know that a camel is a horse designed by a committee? Something like this has got to be done on a quick personal decision."

The instant I laid eyes on the Griswold, peering apprehensively from a window as he alighted from the car in which Amy had gone to fetch him, I knew I had seen him before, and where. He was the Dead End Kids rolled into one. All six of them. Fears that he might not make himself at home while sojourning beneath our humble roof were dispelled by the nonchalant manner in which he pitched a wad of bubble gum into the shrubbery. He dug out of the back of the car a blue canvas duffel bag and a handful of LP's, the top one discernible as an album of rock music by a group known as the Veiled Threats. I regretted we had assured him there was a portable phonograph around for use in the guest room. He was wearing a red T-shirt and the *de rigueur* blue dungarees, and barefoot.

"It's nice to see you, Chip," I said, holding the door open.

"Thank you, you're very kind."

"Give me your valise."

"Oh, would you?"

This was a surprise, not that anyone was buying it. If anything I got a firmer grip than ever on my bridgework. It was just that discourtesies consisting of a satirization of the amenities which all concerned were striving to inculcate were a twist one hadn't bargained for. Nothing in Amy's dossier had prepared me for this rather exquisite little perversity. Anyhow, the act as such didn't last long, though the ironic tone prevailed. We introduced the dog that bounded into the vestibule at the moment, a Lhasa apso named Frank about whom we delivered the customary spiel on the rarity of the Tibetan breed, the small number still to be found in the country and so on.

"You must have trouble getting parts for him," said the visitor, strolling on forward to inspect the house in general. He was shown to the guest room he was to occupy, then I hurried back downstairs to mix myself a stiff one.

What he had lacked as an autobiographical ingredient his case dossier made no bones about stating: a decent domestic example. In particular, an affectionately "supportive" father figure, the abysmal want of which was the more dramatized by this make-believe concealment. That must be rushed in by all means before it was too late. I was, for starters, glad to offer some evidence that the adult male animal wasn't all that bad by rustling up the dinner for the evening that lay ahead. That was of the essence in the example that must be set, the standards to be upheld.

"Do you like chili con carne?"

"My old man used to make it."

The "my old man" was reassuring rather than the reverse. Under ordinary circumstances it would be resisted, even mildly rebuked. But it was better than a fresh dose of the sardonic pastiches of Little Lord Fauntleroy, for a revival of which I had been rather jumpily steeling myself. They would have been a far peskier thing to field. As I saw when there was a sudden, as it were war-of-nerves, revival of that vein when at last we sat down at table. But after a spate of "Oh, thank you's" and "Yes, I believe I will have some more roar onion," as the dishes were passed around, there came:

"Look, how about a glass of that beer you're drinking?"

"Oh, I'm afraid that's out of the question. It's against the law to serve fourteen-year-olds alcoholic beverages, you know."

"My old man always gave it to me."

"That's different. Give a kid a slug of suds, long as you're having it yourself, no harm done."

"So if Mr. Tickler was your father, he'd say yes," Amy put in. There was an ill-concealed leer from the guest, as for reflections that might be secretly aroused within the juvenile breast at the thought of such a bloodline. "Mr. Tickler usually prefers wine at dinner, but for washing chili down . . . It's one of Mr. Tickler's specialties. I suppose it doesn't match up to your father's."

"Be honest. Show me no mercy."

"Well, he made it a little hotter, like the Mexicans. That's why I think the roar onion hops it up a little. Better than crackers."

"Yes, well, we have to defer to the ladies, who don't like it as hot as you and me, probably. All right. I made it with a prepared mix. I'm a fraud. You can take down my confession, officer. I used that brand that rates them two-alarm, three-alarm and four-alarm chilis, according to how much chili powder you use. What we're eating is the two-alarm. Too hot for Mrs. Tickler, not hot enough for us. Right?"

"But beer is indicated."

Where the hell did he pick up language like that? Words, phrases, fine talk no doubt absorbed from television and the movies and stored up for later acerbic use against a system, an establishment, intent on pressing him into a respectable mold. "Oh, all right," I said, "I guess one little glass —"

"Please don't get up." He went into the kitchen himself to fetch a bottle of Löwenbräu from an icebox thus also to be cased for later reference. The next day I found two empty bottles in the back recesses of his room closet.

In the few moments he was gone, I gave Amy one of

those glances that "speak volumes." In this instance, rather, a gaze that asked them. Where was the standard street tough I had been led to expect? Had we not here, so far from an archetypal Dead End Kid brought to fruition, a larval Raffles, such as might in the end insinuate himself into her very mother's society, from an evening's dalliance in which he would slip upstairs long enough to diddle the safe in which the ice was kept? Amy gave a quick shake of her head as I started to put some of this into words. The kid returned.

"Ah, beer is good," he said, tilting the tumbler brought along, as he poured half the bottle into it. We all stared at the contents as they settled, as though powerless to remove our gazes till the head had cleared. "Cheers."

"Cheers."

He licked his lips. "I love beer. I don't," he dilated urbanely, "agree with whoever said it should be poured back into the horse."

I cleared my throat, swivelling somewhat on my chair. "It's just that I think there's such a thing as taste. And at the table —"

"By the way, have you heard the one about the father telling his son about the birds and the bees?"

The circuitousness, as well as the speed, with which he was dragging things into the conversation clearly showed that he had one aim in mind: to get our corks. To see how far he could go. To shock us. It was plainly our task to steer a fine line between a square (let alone cuboid) disapproval on the one hand, and a morally irresponsible permissiveness on the other. This would be a good moment to begin, the story being a little gamey, but not raw. And in all conscience, this is the kind of game all children play with their parents; I remembered it from my own years as one of eight always trying to crack our parents up. A response putting me on the kid's "side," as man to boy, was the ticket here.

"Yes, but I don't believe Mrs. Tickler has."

He gulped back some of the beer.

"Well, there was this couple, where the mother was always telling the father it was time to tell their kid about the birds and the bees. Go on now, she says, it's time he learned about them. So all right, the father finally puts down his paper and takes the kid on his knee and says, It's time I told you about the birds and the bees. What about 'em? the boy says, and the father says, You know that time we went on that nature hike, in the woods? Yeah. And you remember that lake we came to, and we saw those girls bathing in it, naked? Yeah. And you remember how when they came out we took them in the bushes with us? Yeah. And you remember what we did to them there? Kid says yeah. And the father says, Well, that's what the birds and the bees do."

Amy managed a courteous ripple of laughter, then instantly picked up her own glass and drank, probably to exempt herself for the moment from the obligation to present any kind of facial expression.

"I know what let's do," she then said. "There's a new Jack Lemmon movie playing at the Bijou III. I think it's rated PG."

"Parental guidance suggested," Chip said, the grin this time a little more sardonic, with an edge of bitter private implication. He seemed to bristle as his dark eyes darted from one to the other of us, and he pushed back a mop of black hair. He then stared straight ahead between us.

"Is that what PG means?" I said. "I thought it meant Procter and Gamble." My own smile, sympathetic and friendly, fell on stony places. "You know, clean. Laundered for the general public. But let's go anyway. It can't be a total loss with Jack Lemmon in it."

The manager of the movie house intercepted us as we strolled up to the wicket with our charge between us. He hadn't brought any shoes at all, which had absolved me from invoking such principles of dress as might be required at table or in public appearances.

"I'm sorry, but we can't admit anyone without shoes."

"Why not, may I ask?" I said.

"Sanitary rule."

"Sanitary. This boy — this traditional American Barefoot Boy — *with* cheek of tan — has just emerged from his evening bath. I submit that there is not a pair of shoes in the house the equal of his feet for cleanliness."

"I'm sorry, sir, it's simply a law. Restaurants, stores, all —"

"Don't you see the absurdity of it? What could be less hygienic than the shoes you insist on? You might more rationally insist that customers remove those before entering, as in certain oriental —"

Amy tapped me on the shoulder and pointed to a discount house blazing with lights across the street, surmounted by a sign reading "Open 10–10." I snatched Chip by the hand, sprinted through the traffic, and inside of five minutes was back with him. Amy was standing by with the tickets, and we sauntered past the nodding manager, at whom Chip, shod in blue and white sneakers, and chewing a fresh cud of bubble gum, shot his leer as we entered.

So we vouchsafed, for two weeks, the domestic ambience our young friend had so long lacked and to the want of which his delinquency might be attributed: an atmos-

phere of grace, of finely shaded tolerance, of subtly inter-
playing temperaments, a civilized mixture of ingredients
to which the affectionately supportive father figure must
ever be held cardinal. The results were instantaneous
and dramatic: the unexplained disappearance of a car-
ton of menthol cigarettes; large, pink quids of bubble gum
disposed along the bedpost with a manifest knack for
improvisation; and twenty bucks missing from my wallet
— to say nothing of the bottles of Löwenbräu abstracted
from the fridge.

"I don't blame the Edmondsons for having a very sick
sister in Seattle," I said. "I would too."

"It's discouraging I admit," said Amy. "But damn it, we
can't *be* discouraged. Or I can't be. It's my job not to be.
It would be immoral."

"It's not discouraged I am, it's intrigued. God, I never
thought that word would cross my lips."

"We've got to give the kid time. You can't expect to
offset a dozen years of absolutely ghastly home life in a
couple of weeks."

"Oh, Mrs. Edmondson's sister is lingering? It's touch-
and-go out there, is it? No telling when they can get
back?"

"He needs endless amounts of, well, what you've been
giving him in particular. Not me so much. He knows our
taking him for a little longer has been in the wind, in case
the Edmondsons got hung up out there. It would be
cruel to scrub that, and where would I settle him?"

I suppose I was a soft touch because things had been
going so swimmingly with me personally. The quiz show
was zooming along, the fan mail piling up like snow in a
blizzard, and to cap the climax we had just received an
invitation to the White House.

"O.K. I'm game if you are."

"You'll never live to regret this, darling."

"That's what I'm afraid of. Get me a bulletproof vest for my birthday."

The White House reception was one of those black-tie dinners for visiting foreign dignitaries, in this case the president of an incidental but amicable banana republic, the guest lists for which our own chiefs of state like to sweeten by throwing in an intellectual or two. The practice has declined since the Kennedy days, of course. Still, there we were in the fabled East Room, plucking drinks from a passing tray, I in my tuxedo, Amy, dazzled and dazzling, in a gown of pink chiffon, with a square shirred neckline and a bouffant skirt. She had been escorted on the arm of a military aide come to greet us as we sprang out of our taxi. The sound of my name when announced turned heads and created a stir among guests already sipping their cocktails. Two women asked for my autograph, which I scribbled on the envelopes containing the cards specifying their table numbers.

We had time for only one drink. Then we heard, "Ladies and gentlemen, the President of the United States." There was the ruffles-and-flourishes fanfare, instantly followed by "Hail to the Chief." We set our drinks down wherever convenient and stood at attention as the Presidential party and the guests of honor came down a long red-carpeted corridor, accompanied by a color guard. They lined up quickly for the presentations, for which we had been briefed, and as I preceded my Amy down the receiving line I found my heart beating high. I was rather impressed with myself. You spoke your name, clearly, into the ear of another military aide in full uniform, who sent it rolling down the line according to established custom, beginning with the President.

When President Nixon heard mine he wrung my hand and beamed a hearty welcome.

"I'm a great admirer of yours," he exclaimed with obvious sincerity. "I listen to the show every chance I get, and I happened to catch your, what shall I call it, maiden performance. Incredible what you know about the Bible."

"Thank you, Mr. President. I'm honored to be here."

One knew better than to prolong such an exchange beyond limits determined by the President himself. He passed me along to the South American President and his wife with something like, "He's a walking encyclopedia," already then smiling at Amy. He murmured something complimentary about her dress, noting its resemblance to Mrs. Nixon's, adding archly behind his hand, "But don't say I mentioned it."

Mrs. Nixon, indeed comparably gowned in dusty rose, instantly took up what she must have overheard the President say to me. "We *were* impressed. He mentioned something about it at a White House prayer breakfast the next Sunday. Such an example in these irreligious days. We're honored to have you."

"The honor is ours, Mrs. Nixon."

The next face brought me up short. I had not expected to encounter the Vice President, I don't know why. I'd simply never given it any thought. Agnew was then at his peak as the Savonarola ranging the land with his clarion calls to the traditional virtues. Now the gimlet eyes, so familiar an aid to caricature, seemed to drill right into me, divining my guilty secret. Because for the first time I felt a pang of guilt over the corners I had cut, the compromises I had here and there made, the moral wind to which I had perhaps a little too closely sailed, in gaining the kudos that had landed me here. I was unnerved despite the warm handclasp and the friendly smile. "Glad to have you. Hope the kids in the country are inspired by your example. So many dropouts, such lack of discipline . . ." He shook his head as I murmured some now forgotten words of agreement. I had not voted for the administration. All the keener my sense of falling short of its proclaimed standards, its summons to national honor, to patriotic dedication, to law and order. Here I was being complimented by a man preaching moral fibre as it had never been preached. No wonder that I sensed something avuncular in his emanations, there in the reception line. He was an uncle of formidable probity looking straight at an erring nephew. One on the take! I felt skewered on the term for the first time that night. *Did* the end justify the means? This high-minded public servant would not have thought so. It was an unexpectedly jarring, curiously chastening confrontation.

Not that it cast its pall for long. On to the State Dining Room where I found myself at Table Seven, seated across from a nuclear physicist and between the wife of a western Congressman and a Detroit banker who had confessed to me *sotto voce*, as we orbited the table looking for our places, that he "hadn't the slightest notion why he was invited." He laughed and added, "Probably an oversight."

Conversations rose, fell, rose again amid the tinkle of crystal and silver. We had three wines. A California Chablis with the fish mousse, a vintage Margaux with the beef fillet, and for champagne a Dom Perignon. When that was poured with the dessert, the President rose to offer a toast. I froze. I had not prepared a response. But the danger passed. It was to the chap from the banana republic. I drew a sigh of relief. Afterward there was dancing, and as I swept the First Lady across the gleaming ballroom floor she prettily recalled a line I had on the show so easily identified as from Tennyson's "Maude." "And I said to the rose the brief night goes in babble and revel and wine." When a successor claimed her favor, I proffered another line from the same poem as I bowed in withdrawal, "Oh when will the dancers leave her alone!"

When the revels were over, Amy and I flung ourselves in collapsed ecstasy on our beds at the Hay Adams, in a room overlooking the palace from which we had freshly come. She stirred herself, still in her ball gown, to phone home. We had taken a long chance in leaving Chip there alone, not that there was anything else we could have done. Everything seemed all right — I could hear the Veiled Threats belting out something in the background — but God knew what recesses of the house he was prowling in our overnight absence, what private effects he might even now be rummaging among . . .

That other worm again burrowed the apple of the evening. I could sense Agnew's beady eye fixing me in fancy once more. The pang of guilt was now compounded by the chill of fear. Was disclosure possible? The specter had not before raised its head: one's own had too much been swimming in glory. And one justified the corners as having been cut for the sake of a cause far worthier than a personal hour in the sun. But having in triumphal climax rubbed shoulders with a high official seen as voice of the national conscience, I felt my own begin to throb. The peacock perquisites given in return for the risks taken had all along been tinged with misgiving. From now on the pleasures enjoyed were to be increasingly self-cancelling, edged always with anxiety. It was like basking in a sun destined to scorch. It was like drinking vintage Burgundy out of a dribble glass. I had had enough. I would get out. I would take my money, put it into escrow for the settlement, and see what the IRS would let us keep. Maybe a good tax lawyer could help us keep it all.

It was therefore interesting to get back, with the intention of phoning Versprunk immediately to say I wanted out, to find a message saying he had called, and would I call back. I did. "How about lunch Monday?" he said. I agreed.

That was a Friday. Between then and the appointed hour, two incidents occurred in rapid succession that sharpened my sense of uneasiness, and one of which hinted indeed that I was riding a tiger.

Friday evening Amy and I had dinner at her parents', under circumstances roughly constituting a reunion of the old salon crowd, when Mrs. Wintermoots had had her "Sundays." Everyone wanted to hear about the White House. Amy's and my account rambled on through dinner, and we were still at it over brandies and stingers later. Jake was quiet, seemed tired, somewhat morosely so. Whether this was the result of overwork or of having to listen to tales of triumph from a guest freshly back from a place to which he had himself once aspired was hard to say. Possibly a combination of the two. Notwithstanding the cares that infested the day, or maybe owing to the overeating consequent on them, he had gained a lot of weight in a short time, so that his clothes were grievously in need of letting out, the modishly thick pants belt in particular looking like a boa constrictor with a death-grip on him. Political ambitions put by, he had reverted to loud neckwear (prompting a renewal of josh-ing about his underworld ties) and shirts that were statements. He dropped off after a sip or two of his brandy.

Now a man asleep in an armchair is going to dominate a conversation. Any conversation. We chattered nerv-ously, trying not to look in his direction. The queasy spell he had us under could not have been long borne; I thought of nudging my snifter to the parquet floor with my elbow, of asking Miss Canfield to thump us out some Scriabin on the piano. She was the local university musi-cologist whom I had met at my first "Sunday." She was dilating, rather jumpily, on contemporary Russian music, and every time she said, "Khachaturian" I was afraid Jake would come to with a start, kicking his feet out, and say, "Gesundheit." Something did bring him to, the telephone, whose jangle penetrated his slumbers without undue reflex. He just twitched erect. The houseman presently materialized to say it was for him. He excused himself to take it in his study, with sighs of deliverance all around. He reappeared at the end of the room after a few minutes. Having caught my eye, he summoned me over with a jerk of his head. I joined him in his study, the door of which he closed. He was wide awake now, and very sober, the laugh lines etched deeper than ever.

"That was Carter Pippin. He says there's blood on the moon."

"Of course."

He took a step forward, till he stood planted squarely in front of me. He gave me a look as pointed as a cat's ears.

"Is that show fixed?"

"You'll have to ask the producer that," I said, forcing my tongue as though through another clot of peanut butter. "Maybe it is for some, or here and there, or partly. It probably varies. All I know is, I climbed aboard honestly," I went on, honestly enough. "I'll see what I can find out if you'd like. Why? Where did Carter get this?"

"Some kind of rumor going around the studio or something. A contestant they once had named Frumkin threatens to sing. Feels he didn't get enough of the gravy while he was on it. Others, with all your charisma and all, got so much more. Sore because they dumped him after a couple of weeks."

"Well, as you know, I'm not 'getting anything.' It's not for myself that I —"

"Yes, I know all that. But the celebrity, the White House, one thing and another." Jake began to pace, packing a meerschaum slightly less in size than the smallest of the known saxophones. "That property'll be worth a million dollars next season. One of the few decent things coming out of Chicago. We don't want anything to happen to it. Something like this could blow it sky-high. Prick it like a balloon, not worth a nickel."

"I realize that. I'll check into it I tell you. I'm sure there's nothing to it. They can give Frumkin another whirl. Bump me with him any time. Welcome to it. I want out, it's too gruelling. Let them arrange it."

He looked at me hard again, this time through a dense cloud of smoke.

"Bump? Arrange? What the hell do you mean?"

"Arrange to put him on with me, on his own turf if he wants. I think it's sports. I'm game. I'm more than game. Christ I'm tired." I passed a hand across my forehead in what I instantly realized was one of those gestures in which I had been coached to accompany some particularly racking though counterfeit prodigy of memory, there in the sweatbox. "Let's join the others. Isn't it a little warm in here?"

I felt Agnew's beady eyes watching me from behind as Jake and I marched side by side back into the drawing room.

The next day Amy and I had scheduled one of those Saturday afternoon back yard barbecues we periodically threw for the boys in the settlement club. We expected about twenty, some better, some worse, than the redoubtable Chip Griswold. As usual, I shopped for the provisions while Amy made the party preparations. I entered a nearby supermarket clutching a long marketing list.

First to be selected were the weiners, and here I looked as ever for our old Hot Diggety Dogs, climbing steadily among the best sellers in the frozen frankfurter category. Third by now, I believe. I had formed a habit, when shopping, of coming armed with a magnifying glass, then a jeweller's loupe, to research foodstuffs for packaging and other flaws, as well as make out the print with which mfrs. meet Pure Food and Drug requirements without making the rollcall of ingredients discernible to the naked eye. I was squinting through the loupe at stacks of weiners already jumbled by previous shoppers when the manager bustled over in his orange duster.

"Sir, is it necessary to look at every package? You're disorganizing the entire display."

"Yes, quite necessary. For myself and all shoppers, as a matter of fact." The scene he had himself created drew several customers, and I figured I might as well make the most of what had necessarily become a soapbox speech. "How many of us, for example, know how to spot a package of spoiled meat? I mean one bacteriologically on its way to putrefaction."

"I do!" said a woman, raising her hand like a pupil who knows an answer in a schoolroom. "It swells up like a balloon."

"Right," interjected the manager, "and I defy you to find a single bloated package in that freezer."

"I don't expect to," I said, "and if I did I'd be more reassured about your honesty than if I didn't. Because a single pinprick — *poof* — makes the stuff salable again. *To* the naked eye. That's why it behooves us never to go shopping without our trusty magnifier. I have here in my hand a package of frozen Hot Diggety Dogs. Would any of you care to conduct an examination with this loupe?"

"I would."

I felt sorry for the manager. There was nothing he could do to establish his personal integrity but accept the challenge. Screwing the relinquished loupe into his eye, he took the package and ran his gaze minutely across it. Finding nothing suspect on its top surface, he turned it over. My sympathy for him deepened. He would have to spot the telltale perforation I had, and that he knew I had.

"Why, there's one. On the underside." He looked wildly around. "Whoever is responsible for this . . . Heads will roll . . . I hope you don't think the management here would stoop to . . . Things like this could happen at the packing end. They're kept in storage there for a while . . ."

"Of course. No offense."

"Because I don't want any trouble. I have a wife and three . . ."

"We'll say no more." Snatched from his hand by one of

the women, the loupe now made the rounds as one after another they peered at the frankfurters through it. "Ladies, please! Leave eight at least."

"Eight?" the manager said.

"Yes. I'm giving a barbecue this afternoon, and not being one of the Borgias I don't want to poison my guests, however much they may deserve it. Little peculiarity I have. So if you'll all excuse me . . ."

"Aren't you James Tickler?"

"Yes, and I'd like my loupe back. Thank you."

I stowed eight seemingly acceptable packets of wurst into my cart and trundled it off, leaving the gaggle of indoctrinated housewives behind me.

As I was stowing my bags of provisions into the back of my station wagon, I was aware of a woman watching me from beside a car parked in a nearby slot. She was holding a sack of groceries and a six-pack of Würzburger. She smiled tentatively, then, chucking her goods into the front seat, clapped the door shut and came over.

"Mrs. Flamsteed," I said, recognizing her. "My God, it's been ages."

"I was at your wedding."

That was the second time I had seen her, the first having been my baptism at the salon when I seemed to remember we had rather tipsily traded satirical reflections on Judge What's-His-Name's landmark pornography decision. Her famous round heels did not seem to rule out a stern morality on other counts, as she again proved on characteristically short notice.

"We never see you at the Wintermootses' now," I said.

"I don't approve of them. Or of Jake, actually. And by extension you, for that matter. We're on opposite sides of the fence."

"I suppose. We keep aware *of* you though. Stormy petrel of the consumer cause. How's the *Review* doing?"

"We have nearly a million subscribers."

"Of which I'm one. Where I got this little gismo about the pinprick, matter of fact."

"I heard that brouhaha. Surprising. So the prostitute has this crusader trying to get out of him. Or is it just a sop to your conscience, making a public stink. Isn't Hot Diggety Dogs one of your accounts?"

"I thought of the name."

"Good God." She laughed, shaking her head. "Aren't you ashamed?"

"I think it's pretty awful myself. I only suggested it as a gag, but they all went for it. It was my Big Break. That's how it all got started."

Her full red lips still parted over gleaming teeth in the lingering smile, she cocked her head to one side as she appraised me critically. I was aware of the shapely bulk encased in snug mulberry slacks and a white silk blouse, as a breath of wind tousling her short-cropped tawny hair blew the scent of perfume my way.

"Hard to figure types like you out. Whether you're just cynical, or have been corrupted by stages so delicate you don't realize how far you've gone."

I began here to lose the tone of bantering good nature with which I'd tried to hold up at least my end of the chat. Bristling a little, I said, "What do you mean, how far you've gone?"

"I've caught you on the tube. Brilliant. Wonderful. But have you no trouble sleeping? Don't you think at times you'd like to make an honest living?"

Here the sensation of fear again plucked me. Following

so closely on the heels of Carter Pippin's phone call, her words provoked a wild alarm. "What do you mean?"

"All that for such a sponsor. You must realize that all those pots of muck they peddle to unsuspecting wretches of middle-aged women who think they'll have beautiful complexions overnight, and all the rest of it, that it's obscene. It's all such a pigsty. The corruption of this country is appalling, even without the bunch we've got in office now —"

"Look here, I didn't vote for them."

"Then why did you go to the White House?"

"Home-keeping youth have ever homely wits."

"I suppose that's from something."

"*Two Gentlemen of Verona* I think. And I was curious to see what it was like inside. What the hell harm could it do?"

"To you. Our Beamish Boy. You're an expert on the Bible. How about this? Be ye not unequally yoked together with evildoers."

"I think it's unbelievers, not evildoers. And they're all believers there, believe me!" We laughed together, somewhat dissipating the tension. Mrs. Flamsteed's tone became rather more good-humoredly chaffering, as my own mood eased.

"You know, you look like the Nixon type. All those clean-cut young chaps he's got around him — none of whom I'd trust any farther than I could see them, if that far. I think they're all as crooked as ram's horns."

There was no evidence then that her diatribes were all that justified. Mrs. Flamsteed was either raging irresponsibly, or she was clairvoyant. That she considered the latter to be the case was plain in the way she continued her strictures, which rose in a fair crescendo of denunciation. One is used to austerity among certain kinds of liberals, those who over the years scolded you for taking vacations in Spain and Greece, chided you for buying lettuce and grapes when striking labor unions asked you to boycott them, and gave you short shrift indeed for walking through a picket line. At the same time, the emotions clearly boiling within her as she warmed to her subject hinted at something out of kilter, even unstable. She had the hot heart — a term I was later to hear her fling about in praise of a sort of fanaticism not to be considered untoward in one directing it to salubrious ends and humanitarian goals; but she was guilty of the uncharitableness and intolerance that often simultaneously characterize rebels. Those who in my parents' day criticized you for fostering racial caricature by listening to Amos 'n' Andy on the radio. Bigotry is by no means a monopoly of the right-winged and the strait-laced.

"I think we're going to see exposures of corruption and dishonesty the like of which this country has never seen. I mean in high places. And all those prayer breakfast hypocrites. And all those silly little American flags in their lapels, when they go on the air. Surely there ought to be a law against using our country's emblem for a vote-getting trinket. Don't you think? And everybody on the take, and all the poor suckers who vote for them. 'Everybody does it.' That's the really alarming part. What's to become of us? That this glorious land could have become such a terrible country . . ." She laughed again and gave off. "I'm getting carried away. It's just that that evangelical zeal I saw in there doesn't jibe somehow with working for the fat cats and the exploiters."

"Let's say I haven't lost my ideals, just mislaid them."

"Anyway, if you ever want to come over to the side of

the angels, we have openings for bright young men. We're growing by leaps and bounds. You must come see our campus in any event —"

"Oh, I'd love that! I really would. How you test products and all. May I give you a call next week sometime?"

"Here's where I'll be for about two weeks." She jotted an address and phone number on the back of a scrap of paper for which she troubled me. As she bent to her task on the top of my car, I experienced again a definite physical response to the woman who had been thus morally dressing me down — a paradoxical reaction for which psychological explanation is no doubt available. "Here you are. Couple of weeks. Then after that at *Consumer Review*. That's in the book, of course. Nice to see you again. Best to all the Wintermootses."

Versprunk was at least interested in hearing all about the White House. I wasn't long at it over our luncheon cocktail, however, being myself concerned about something else. I broke my account off after a minute or two and asked: "What's all this about Frumkin threatening to talk?"

"Nothing another whirl on the show and a bit more boodle won't fix. I'm not worried about it. Which brings me to something." He grinned across the table in characteristic fashion. "Time to go."

"I've been meaning to talk to you about that, Bob. I think I'd like out. I've come to that decision."

"Good. Then we understand each other. You've had a good run. Roll up more than anybody before you're through."

"It's not for myself that —"

"Yes. Juvenile delinquents, isn't it?"

"Some citizens of tomorrow who have gone astray. It was never the dough I wanted. Omar's 'Take the cash and let the credit go' isn't my line. Other way around with me."

"We'll put that in the swan song. We thought a literary category would be a good way to kiss you goodbye. What else do you know? What was that you said once about some writer saying another wrote fiction as though it were a painful duty?"

"Oscar Wilde said it about Henry James."

"Let me just make a note of these things." I looked away as he scribbled on the back of an envelope. "Let's say we have the one and two ball. We'll see that you roll up six or seven more, then with the eight ball — farewell. You've had it. O.K.?"

"Yes, but wait a minute. Frumkin on literature? I thought you'd have to bring him back in on who knocked, duh, who out in the sixth round in Los Angeles, or what's the runs-batted-in record for a single game in a World Series."

"We'll brush him up. He's a quick study. And that's what he wants. He's not a Neanderthal, he's cultured, like the rest of you. Sticky stuff, but we're stuck with it. We had a woman lined up to bump you, an extremely personable housewife from Roanoke, but we'll use her to bump Frumkin when the wheel's been greased enough to stop it squeaking. But we may have to let him rack up enough to beat your record. He seems capable of being nasty. He's going to amaze his friends all right. Especially resents the play you and Trotter got as the Beautiful People. The in crowd. Well, we seem to understand each other all around. Shall we order now? I'm suddenly famished."

All might have gone according to the scenario had the eight ball not presented such a delicious surprise, and along with it the irresistible temptation to double-cross the mob. Pride is so very much a two-sided coin: on the one hand what goeth before a fall; on the other eliciting the finest within us.

I had pocketed the first seven balls with answers to questions tailored to fit what the producers knew I knew, on the basis of those preparatory conversations. Again, replies were never glib or instantaneous, but made to seem the product of profound self-lacerating concentration as, biting lip and mopping brow, one dredged up the requested fact from the Sargasso Sea of memory while the world watched, on tenterhooks itself. Then I heard Falconer say: "That gives Tickler twenty-eight points and another twenty-eight hundred dollars. Now for the eight ball, traditionally a hazard in any poolroom." I was keyed up now. I hadn't been told what the question would be on which I was expected to take a dive. Suppose I knew the answer? That would presumably be a remote possibility. Adjusting my clammy earphones I heard him go on: "As you know, Tickler came on as an authority on the Bible. This next quotation, which we're going to ask him to place, has a kind of Biblical ring to it. Ready? For eight hundred dollars, in what book are these words found? 'God tempers the wind to the shorn lamb.' "

The bastards, I thought as my heart jumped into my throat. The line wasn't from the Bible at all; they had suggested it might be to throw me off, or, equally likely, to let Frumkin come back with an especially triumphal flourish. A trick question. A curve. But I knew the source. What should I do?

I hesitated, gnawed my lip and ran a finger under my

collar in what was now all too genuine a struggle. At the same time, I relished the suspense in which I held everyone. I swung the studio audience as I would the country like a yoyo on a string for a quarter of a minute. I toyed with it, teased it. I looked over at Falconer, who was himself clearly tense with worry. He frowned, with a barely perceptible nod of his head, an impatient cue. I grinned back in a way meant to convey that I knew damn well they had pitched me a screwball.

"Oh, I'm sorry," I said, "but that's not the Bible, though many people mistakenly think it is, because, as you say, it has a Biblical ring. No, it's from Laurence Sterne, who was, of course, a clergyman as well as a novelist. From . . . let me see . . ." I drummed a tattoo on the old noggin, shutting my eyes in thought, though I knew the answer damn well. "Not *Tristram Shandy* . . . No . . ." I muttered to myself, bleeding it. I raised my bowed head. "*A Sentimental Journey.*"

"Rrright!" cried Falconer, who wished me dead and in hell. I knew he was fit to be tied as he went into a commercial. That completed, he gave me a covert glare and read off the nine ball. I got that one too. What artist said, on failing a test that flunked him out of military school, "If silicone had been a gas, I would have been a general."? Whistler. Falconer was at his wits' end, and I knew Versprunk was having kittens in the control room. Lucky all around I muffed the next one — absurdly enough, a sentence known to every man, woman and child in the English-speaking world. "The female of the species is more deadly than the male." I hadn't known the source — Kipling. Probably Frumkin hadn't either, until briefed. As he had been on all the rest as well. He ran what was left of the table and won the game, 75–45.

So now we had a new winner, who next week would face his own challenger. I staggered out of the sweatbox, glad it was finished. The ride was over, so was the strain. I could go back to private life — I thought. Anger still flashed in Versprunk's eyes when he emerged from the control room, sweatbox enough for him this night.

"That was dirty pool."

"Listen to W. C. Fields."

Thus I ended my run as I had begun it, on the up-and-up. I had restored some honesty to what had become a thoroughly shady enterprise. A blow had been struck for integrity. Decent folk the wide country over had, thanks to me, for a few straightforward and validly dramatic moments been at least that much less the dupes and butts of base and venal men.

14

MEANWHILE, BACK AT THE RANCH things continued
hairy with the Griswold. He proved a harder case even
than originally divined. Resisting all efforts to refine him
by example. Even more proof against tutorial illustration
than poor old Jake Wintermoots (backslidden into "each
and every" and "shape, manner or form"). Fins and sin-
gles continued to be abstracted from one's wallet, causing
one to tote it on one's person at all times, at last to sleep
with it under one's pillow. Or lie wakeful there, as might
betide, the night filled with music from the cluster of
humanoids called the Veiled Threats, sinister representations of whom, fondling their electrical instruments like
Sten guns, decorated the LP albums brought into the
house. Cultural counterattacks, say in the form of
Debussy arabesques and Chopin nocturnes, availed little.
Neither did any of one's more felicitous traits seem to be
rubbing off at table. There, despite all efforts to keep the
conversational ball rolling along lines one had proved

one's ability to prosecute, in drawing rooms reasonably to be regarded as touchstones in this area, a steady descent instead was noted in the stories with which the guest tried to crack us up. Did we know about the couple dancing too close together on the ballroom floor? Big navel engagement, lots of semen lost. Yes, yes, of course. Quite. One tried to take such diversions in stride, never revealing them to be found boring rather than shocking (that would never do), laughing with a conspiratorial wink intended to establish a rapport as between two buddies on a father-and-son basis, together seeing how far we could go with the lady of the house. Such palship remained inefficacious. One's own stories, lacking in filth quotient, were not reciprocally laughed at. Aimed at offering that civilizing influence so abysmally denied the object, they would fall flat. And ever and anon the cuds of bubble gum, enough to vulcanize half the tires in Illinois. Disappearing from the bedposts where one sternly disclosed one's wish never to see them again, they turned up on the undersides of chairs and tables, or along the walls of closets one regularly patrolled for beer bottles, seldom in vain.

"I just don't understand it," Amy said. "We give him a decent home, you the only decent treatment a man ever has, apparently. You stick up for him in public, give him pocket money, even if it's only to buy some more Veiled Threats — and incidentally wait till you get a load of this new bunch, the Viable Alternatives — and he plays hooky to go down to the lake front and smoke cigarettes and eat candy bars he probably shoplifted."

"Well, it's only a few more days," I said. "The Edmondsons *are* coming back this time, aren't they?" We'd had Chip well over a month now, as their return from the

West Coast was postponed. "I shouldn't have given the impression in the cover story that we've more or less adopted a kid. The researcher did read it back to me over the phone." When Amy failed to answer, rather turning away, I said, "Isn't it? Three or four more days?"

She mumbled something all too minimally affirmative, if that at all. Suspicions sprouted deep within me, like mushrooms in a dank cellar. The sister in Seattle was not at all well, beeeetcha, the operation by no means a success, indeed if not downright fictional. Weeks would drag into months, the sister lingering on, the Edmondsons themselves loyally doing so as well, in that faroff port . . .

Amy sighed, then as though girding up our joint loins, said: "Well, what we've got to remember is that his background has been so *aw*fully traumatic —"

"Like our foreground?"

"— so deeply so that miracles simply will not happen overnight. It'll take far, far more good example to offset the bad, and bring him around."

The next day I saw, in a wastebasket in the guest room the nonesuch was using, several newspapers and magazines that had been scissored up in a curious way, together with a lot of snippets of paper. Inspired by the discovery to go through some desk drawers, I found at the back of one of them a jumble of letters and numbers of various sizes and colors, of the kind from which kidnappers and the like paste together anonymous communications. What the hell was this? Was our friend up to some such shenanigans? We had recently together watched an F.B.I. television drama the plot of which had concerned a youth in cahoots with a gang trying to milk his own old man for ransom, hiding out meanwhile in an abandoned warehouse. How high would I go, in payments demanded to get this one back? Interesting question. I could not find it in my heart to say that it would be a very exorbitant figure. Quite the reverse. Nothing in four digits, or even three. Ten, maybe fifteen bucks would be my top figure. Take it or leave it.

Evidently it was my lot perpetually to play the Pygmalion, one destined never, however, to fall in love with any of the end-products. Other mythological parallels might include that of Odysseus united at last with a surrogate Telemachus, were it not that he was in this instance trying to shake free of him.

"*I* didn't have much of a father figure," I said aloud, there in the empty house, standing at the window with my hands in my pockets, watching a gentle rain begin to fall. Modesty forbade my adding, "And look at me," though the implication hung clearly in the air.

My presence there in mid-week was explained by my spending more time at home in order to "be with Chip as much as possible," so that as much might rub off as could be within the time allotted — whatever that might turn out to be. Also to keep an eye on the little bastard — not yet, just then, returned from school, or wherever he was. It was also a fact that I could work as well at home anyway. At the moment, I was trying to concoct a commercial for the makers of a deodorant called Zephyr. The idea that had occurred to me was to have someone spray the preparation on a slab of Swiss cheese, with some such snapper as, "Not even Swiss cheese would sweat with Zephyr on it." Maybe I was tired, beginning to show the strain. Maybe I was burnt out. That tensions were unlikely to abate in the foreseeable future was indicated by a phone call just then from Jake Wintermoots.

"Carter Pippin just told me something very disturbing."

"Blood on the moon?" I said, wearily.

"You damn tootin', if it's true. The rumor he hears is that it isn't Frumkin who's going to sing now at all, it's that young woman who first got the ratings up. What's her name again?"

"Angela Burwash."

"Yes. Apparently going through an emotional crisis, involving a religious conversion. All mixed up with guilt about the show. She's been seeing a psychiatrist, and it seems the only way she can purge herself is to make a clean breast of it."

"Oh, for Christ's sake."

"Those are her exact words! She must do it 'for His sake.' "

"So. The Jesus bag. Sounds a bit cracked."

"So does your voice, buddy boy. And well it might, because do you know what the cream of the jest is? It was your dazzling performance on the Bible category started her thinking along those lines. Both how important it is to know God's word, and also not to put it to such purposes. It's all been a lesson to her, and her newly found faith won't let her rest until she's made a full, public, all-out confession."

"My Bible performance was on the up-and-up. I'll have you know that, Jake, in fact you know it already. Making Jesus freaks out of a lot of my listeners was not my purpose and is not to my taste. And I would like to say that to Angela Burwash's beautiful but bovine face. She probably didn't know who the father of her country was until somebody told her. Just because *she* needed — I mean if it's to be that Jesus freaks will nail me to the cross —"

"All right, all right. It's no use going ape over it with me. It's just a rumor around the studio. Maybe it'll all blow over again. I hope so. But meanwhile, Jim, maybe you'd better . . . I mean it might be wisest in *case* the roof caves in that, particularly with the Jeepers scandal still hanging fire with the FTC, we aren't any more, you know, intimately associated with it than absolutely . . ."

"I understand. I get the message. Not any more intimately linked to me than necessary. Of course, Jake. Consider me resigned. This is my resignation from the firm."

"It'll only be a leave of absence as far as we're concerned, I mean privately. Between you and me and the gatepost. But to all public intents and purposes, *if* there's a blowup, the firm will then be able to say you were let go."

"Sure. Fair enough. Consider yourself deodorized. And Jake? Don't worry about it. Because I've got something else lined up."

15

FOR A LONG TIME, I got through things by refusing to believe the testimony of my senses. This is the protective mechanism familiarly brought into play by muttering to yourself, "I must be dreaming," or, "This is simply happening to somebody else." The period in question spanned roughly some five months beginning with the afternoon of the day following that colloquy with Jake, when I found myself sauntering up a gravel path toward the address given me by Mrs. Flamsteed. I had phoned her and, after being shunted among what I took to be a battery of secretaries and domestics, taking a length of time requiring the deposit of a second dime, I was rewarded with Mrs. Flamsteed herself saying, "Oh, hello. Yes, do come on over."

The place for which I made was an old Victorian manse on the far West Side vaguely reminiscent of those on South Prairie Avenue where Chicago society had flourished at the turn of the century, the original Gold Coast in whose modern North Shore mutation we have seen me the twinkling rage. I now fancied myself a blade of the Dreiser-Wharton era making a sally on what I assumed to be part of the estate left by the late Harvey Flamsteed, legatee in turn of a family fortune he had chosen to sink into consumer advocacy before his untimely demise.

At a bend in the path, past a clump of silver spruce, I encountered a thin boy in a sweater flicking bits of the gravel onto the lawn with a guilty smile. He snicked the pebbles one by one with his thumb, from a supply in his palm. He glanced apologetically at me as I walked on past, before scooping up another handful for similar projection onto the grass. Perhaps he was Mrs. Flamsteed's gardener, caught in a wayward moment? Or the gardener's son, a witless lad who did no one any harm, really.

Waiting to be admitted after pressing the doorbell, I turned around to survey the ample and opulently landscaped grounds. The grass was like that on a putting green. Old lawns, old money . . . Revolving this line of rumination, I glimpsed at a far turn of the serpentine walk an older woman strolling on the arm of a younger, the latter in what seemed a blue cape over a white dress. Possibly a cap on her head. I couldn't be sure. They vanished around a clump of shrubbery the instant they were seen. A guest of Mrs. Flamsteed's, perhaps an infirm aunt humanely seen to, sojourning with a medically trained companion. Closer note now revealed stretches of the gravel walk to be flanked with benches, on one of which two men, one in tattered evening clothes, sat playing checkers, or backgammon.

There was a sound behind the door at my back, urgent yet discreet, a repeated flat, muffled noise as of innumerable flapjacks being rapidly hurled against a wall. As I wheeled about, the door, a heavy portal of glass and grillwork, was swung open by a smiling young man in a dark suit, over whose broad shoulders I caught sight of a wide, elegantly curving stairway up which another man soared in hot pursuit of a woman with thick auburn hair, piled in complicated tiers on top of her head in a ponderous coiffure that even from this distance could be seen to be in acute danger of disintegration. "If you want to go to Paris to freshen up —" the man seemed to be saying as they vanished round a twist in the stairs. The kin toward whom Mrs. Flamsteed was extending such Homeric hospitality would seem as numerous as they were picturesque, arguing a lady of almost preternatural heart and responsibility, if hypothesis survived closer inquiry.

"Yes?"

"I'm here to see Mrs. Flamsteed."

"Oh, yes. I think she's expecting you. Come in."

"Thank you."

I stepped inside, after wiping my feet on a mat the shape and size of North Dakota.

"I'll announce you," said the young man, whom I had at first taken to be a butler, or houseman, a conviction seriously undermined by the sight of a wicket at the far left of the foyer at which a man in a tight green suit who twitched rather a goodish bit seemed to be paying a bill. A calculating machine clattered softly in what must be a small office there. Speculation shifted to the theory that Mrs. Flamsteed spent her widowhood in some well-staffed condominium-like establishment of which the upper quarters would bear out the idea of an old mansion cut up and converted into apartments, with at least its quota of eccentrics considered par for such haunts. Yes, that was it. Henry James's story *The Great Good Place* came to mind, the substance of which was the delineation of just such sumptuous quarters where absolutely every need was fulfilled — by a staff, and for a price.

The young man ran up the stairway two at a time, leaving me a moment to inhale further impressions. Inhale is good, for hanging not heavily but palpably in the air was some dense, no doubt wisely chosen scent, neither exactly cosmetic nor medicinal, reminding me fleetly again of Mom's peaches that appeared to have been poached in cologne. Mom — filial *devoirs* to whom had been neglected and must be again observed — hinted that the reconciliation I had effected was being undone by another of Oompah's peccancies: he had got mixed up with a certain Mrs. I'msmith-Buffington, and she was again saving her blue stamps for a divorce. All that must be looked after, tidied up if at all possible. I sighed heavily at the thought of such a job of work.

These reflections were dispersed when the twitcher shot past me toward the door, having paid his rent for the month, or whatever, and was now no doubt keen for an afternoon movie or a chat on a bench with some of the other tenants. A pretty girl in attendance at the cashier's desk waved and smiled at still another man hurrying along in a checked coat from a pocket of which appeared to protrude a bit of rubber tubing, as of some instrument, by association vaguely clinical, hastily tucked into it.

The butlering young man's handsome head appeared over a turn of the balustrade.

"Mrs. Flamsteed says to come on up. First room to your right on the landing here."

The past few moments had been among the first of

those in which I had begun to doubt the testimony of my senses. By now some credibility began to seep back in as to them, the element of doubt shifting rather over onto the prospect of my getting any gainful employment out of this visit. That didn't make me any less eager to see Mrs. Flamsteed. On the contrary I was never keener to clap an eye on anybody. The door of the room indicated was open, and she was sitting on a handsome flowered settee with her back to the window, drinking a bottle of beer of the brand, Würzburger, I had seen her clutching at the supermarket.

"Hello, hello, nice to see you," she said rising to shake hands. "Will you have a drink? Anything you want."

"I'll have a bottle of that, if they've — if you've got another."

"Plenty." She picked up a phone and pressed a button which evidently got the kitchen, because she asked to have two more bottles sent up "from her supply." "I'm mad about beer," she then told me. "It's my one weakness." She heaved a bright sigh. "Now then! Let's have a good talk. Do sit down."

No warm body of male persuasion in a facing chair could not take acute note of Mrs. Flamsteed's getup. She wore a white flirt shirt with lemon wedges all over. A man can recognize such a body blouse from a certain skintautness especially at the waist, where the tails go down into a skirt or slacks, a tension recognizable to the trained naturalist as exerted from the point of convergence where the two snaps secure such a garment. Her burgundy trousers were nearly as form-fitting, snugly encasing as they did loins as opulent as the breasts bursting from the shirt.

I felt a sudden weariness, or rather a clairvoyance of

weariness to come, something in the cards one wished were not there; not physical so much as emotional; a depressed torpor not unakin to our old friend, post-coital *tristesse*, come calling even earlier this time; as though I had already lain (as mentally indeed I was) with this woman exerting despite her eccentricity a tidal pull not to be denied, under the right conditions not long to be resisted either: so that in fancy one were already abed, "paying," amid the sheets on which one had so lately thrashed, leaden with fatigue, sodden with remorse . . .

Spreadeagled on the coffee table between us was a book entitled *Metempsychosis*. Something about the structure of the word, in this environment, made it seem the name of something you might be in for, rather than believed in. Maybe the unlettered often think that's what it means. The thought flashed over me for what it's worth.

"I see you're interested in my book."

"Do you believe in the transmigration of souls?"

"Oh, yes. Too many things in life that can only be explained by reincarnation."

"Eastern philosophies espousing the doctrine hold that we may come back as animals, or have been here in that guise before."

"Isn't that how most people live, this time around?"

"But what I've always puzzled over is, if we've been here before, why don't we remember it?"

"Oh, we do, we do! I have haunting memories of several identities. Mystical certainties. One in particular —"

A man in a white coat appeared with two bottles of beer and a fresh glass on a tray. As he set them down and began to pour, Mrs. Flamsteed rose and began to pace, chattering volubly in quite another key altogether.

"Yes, it was while working in the CIA that I discovered

the Russians have been spraying American sidewalks with an invisible poison that makes our bodies decay from the feet up. In a few years we shall all begin to rot — *irreversibly*. De ankle-bone connected to de leg-bone, de leg-bone connected to de knee-bone . . . They don't need military conquests. Oh, no, no indeedy! They're going to decompose us. And they're going to do the same thing with Red China. Well, they found out I discovered their secret, and have been after me. That's why I'm here, being given asylum in an American embassy."

"Or embassy in an American asylum," I thought.

By this time the St. Bernard had finished pouring the drinks and trotted off with the tray. Mrs. Flamsteed, breaking off her recitative, strolled to the door and watched him out of sight.

"Imagine an American embassy in its own country," she laughed.

"You mean . . .?"

"Yes. I rattle on like that for their benefit. Because as you've probably guessed, I'm here as a plant." I glanced wildly at the ferns and geraniums decorating the room, any one of which might be the real her, returned from a prior tour of mortal existence when she was something else altogether, while the person who was addressing me was anybody's guess. But she straightened it all out.

"Yes. We're doing a study of nursing homes and sanitariums. Conditions in many of them are scandalous — which was what we'd heard about this one. But so far I've found nothing scandalous, except of course the rates, which is nothing consumerism can do much about. It's not too badly run, the personnel seem decent as well as efficient."

"And they let you out."

"Oh, of course. To shop and so on. I'm voluntarily committed, naturally, and can sign myself out. Which I think I will soon. I sail pretty close to the wind with the stuff I go on about, because it's hard to get the proper fix on them if they're onto you, and suspect you're just giving them the once-over for a newspaper story or consumer review. But I had them going. I had you fooled, too, didn't I?"

"You certainly did! When we first met —" I must be on guard myself here. I was about to blurt out the facts as experienced, that I had long thought she was O.K. but now saw she was nutty as a praline, but I caught myself, realizing she wanted to hear the reverse — about what was happening now on this visit. "You took me in all right. All that stuff about the Russians and rotting from the feet up. To say nothing of the transmigration of souls bit. That psychosis."

"Oh, that's perfectly true."

We were both seated again, and, gulping back a good cold mouthful of the Wurtzburger, I watched her settle back on the sofa. Her manner indicated a revelation of some intimacy was forthcoming.

"I said I know who I was in a previous existence. Long, long ago . . ."

"How long ago, Mrs. Flamsteed?" I asked softly.

"Two thousand years," she answered, ominously enough. She reached to the coffee table and took a swig of her own beer. "People ask for proof. Well, 'poof' goes proof in the barren logical sense within which our paltry minds remain all too sadly imprisoned. What proof is there for anything, even that we exist? There are much more convincing mystical intimations of great truths. The phenomenon of *déjà vu* is one for which there is no explanation except that we are reliving memories of other existences. I once experienced a *déjà vu* that went on so long it took the good part of a minute, not just the usual split-second to which people testify."

"Tell me about it."

"It was on a shopping trip to New York. A woman in a red hat came through a revolving door I absolutely knew she was going to get her umbrella caught in. I absolutely knew she was going to get both it and herself wedged inside as it accidentally opened up on her. Knew that when she got out on the sidewalk and finally yanked her umbrella free it would be ruined, that she would turn to me and smile, shrug, and throw it into a trash can."

"That's interesting." I might have offered in return a similar experience of my own, but all I could think of was having heard a man at a party the week before begin, "You can fool all of the people . . ." *and known exactly what he was going to say.* And I was more interested in something else. "You say you have an inkling of who you once were, in a former karma, as I think you call it."

"I know exactly who I was."

"Anyone I know?"

"If you've read your Bible, and you evidently have!" she went on with a laugh, "judging by the mint you've made on it."

"Mrs. —"

"I'll give you a hint," she said, becoming sober again. "Who I was. I lived," she continued, lowering her eyes modestly, "on locusts and wild honey."

I expressed my amazement in a soft whistle. After a few moments spent in absorbing what I had been vouch-safed, I asked the inevitable question, and not that con-

cerning John the Baptist either. "What was — you know
— He like?"

That line of inquiry proved a dead-end, and was regarded as frivolous. Mrs. Flamsteed was not required, any
more than another claiming trans-millennial pedigree,
to justify private intimations to that effect by producing
thumbnail sketches of personages with whom she might
have had contact in a previous embodiment, or to remember details of that embodiment itself for that matter. That
was reasonable enough. Whoever's shoelaces she might or
might not have been worthy to untie had no bearing on
what she saw herself, and quite validly, as constituting
today: a voice crying in the wilderness of shoddy merchandise and reprehensible practices.

The conversation went forward and the beer flowed.
We had another, then another (what a lot of shopping
she must be let out to do!). I was wondering what previous incarnation might accommodate natally relayed
memories of umbrellas and revolving doors. The latter in
particular did not go very far back in time. Mrs. Flamsteed
herself was regarding me with a kind of musing
speculation.

"I suppose I was having a little fun with you in not
telling you what you'd find here. A little harmless sport,
putting you on like that. It's my one weakness. I was
curious to see how you'd play it. And how a future
employe does when he's discombobulated says a lot about
him. Do you want a job?"

"Have you a place for a marketing counselor? It was
while marketing that we met. It's the other side of the
same coin. I'm interested in merchandise, after all."

"As a drinker in his liver? Forgive an old woman's
curiosity," she said, spreading both arms along the back of

the sofa in a manner that made her breasts resemble the headlamps of a vehicle bearing down on me at high speed, "but why do you suddenly want to give up pimping for the exploiters?"

"Aren't all conversions sudden?"

"We can't pay much, you know. How much have you been making as the fair-haired boy over there?"

"Well, with cost-of-living adjustments, Christmas bonuses—"

"Spare me hearing about salaries of forty and fifty thousand dollars for junior executives. Harvey left me as many millions as you hear, but I pour it all into the firm. You'd have to give up that chic hobo jacket for a hair shirt. Let's discuss it sometime in greater detail, perhaps over lunch. Here's my home address. It's not listed. I'm going to check out of here over the weekend, I've decided that now. This line of research would be much too expensive, though I was glad to have the rest. Massages, whirlpool baths! Have you ever tried one of those? I do have my sybaritic side. That includes good food, it's my one weakness. Do you know Cavendish's steak house on Michigan Boulevard?" It was interesting to watch the crusader in her unbend, if not positively unravel, as she went on, smiling at me with the sense of easily ignited camaraderie, of negligently traded confidences, wildly contradictory as were those she herself dispensed. "You remind me a lot of Harvey. He would probably have worn one of those patchwork jackets too, with the same sense of just-for-the-unadulterated-hell-of-it you do, not as slavishly following a style. The piece about you said you popularized the word 'twang,' or even coined it, for what somebody simply has or hasn't. You've got twang, so did Harvey. We liked living it up, and live it up we did. You know the

217

speech of Cinna the poet's in *Julius Caesar*? How he dreamed he dined with Caesar? We dined with Caesar once."

I kissed the job goodbye again, this time I was sure for good. Metempsychosis *was* what she was in for. She *was* nutty as a praline. In for, among other things, delusions of being a tycoon, a goose with delusions of gander you might say, the rabidest conceivable projection of feminism. There wasn't even a research center, leastways one she had anything to do with. It was all a figment. That reduced to zero the likelihood of finding employment in it. Getting a job with an outfit that doesn't exist can be tough taffy.

"We're all on loan to one another, so let's enjoy each other to the full while we can," the rhapsody went on. "I myself am determined to 'love that well which I must leave ere long,' believe you me. Or as Omar put it, 'Drink, for once dead you never shall return.' "

"But you just said you believed —"

"Oh, for God's sake, Jim Tickler, don't be so dull! You quibble the way people do who point out that Hamlet goes on about the bourne from which no traveller returns no more than he's just seen his father back from it."

The rebuke, unexpectedly sharp in tone, silenced me, generating a somewhat awkward pause. She herself seemed to regret its severity, quickly reaching to pick up her glass again. I drank back a copious mouthful from my own, set it down and, licking the foam from my lips, leant toward her. Gently I said:

"Tell me about the time you dined with Caesar."

"All right I lied, it was just lunch. President Kennedy had us to the White House. Nothing as toney as your dinner with Nixon, but more twang there in those days, wouldn't you agree? Oh, it wasn't I who rated the invitation of course, it was Harvey. He and Jack were friends. Jack admired him. It was a state luncheon for the then President of Ecuador, Arosemena. Later deposed. Drank a bit too much, I gathered. But there were a lot of interesting people there. Lillian Hellman, Edward Murrow, one of the astronauts."

I put a hand to my head, in reflex fear of the scalp blowing off, like the top of a pressure cooker. "When was that?"

"I remember the date as though it were only yesterday. A great golden occasion engraved on a schoolgirl's heart, don't you know. A memory like a rose pressed in a treasured book. I don't think we should ever lose the capacity for enchantment, do you? Sophistication must never dehydrate us, experience dry us up. It was Monday, July 23, 1962."

The wish to remain emotionally arable was no doubt more than half my motivation for calling on Mrs. Flamsteed in the first place, certainly for not letting the matter drop there — Mrs. Flamsteed herself vanishing into oblivion through a gap in her own credibility, like a mountain climber into a crevasse — but rather hotfooting it over to the Chicago *Tribune* to see whether its back issues had anything to say, either as news or in the society columns, about the date she had given as that on which she had at least lunched with Caesar. I had to do my research with a microfilm copy lent me in the newspaper library.

The news pages yielded nothing. Then there it was in a society column, a small item about Mr. and Mrs. Harvey Flamsteed having attended a White House luncheon for President Arosemena of Ecuador, on Monday, July 23.

A few days later I telephoned her at her apartment, to which she had repaired as promised, and made a date to lunch with her at the steak house suggested. We would continue conversations about my possible employment, talks that had clearly reached, as the diplomats say, a sensitive stage.

"What's the matter?" Amy asked.

"Why? What do you mean?"

"You don't act right. Look right. You look . . . guilty."

"What would I be guilty about?"

She set her homework aside under a parlor lamp and straightened in the chair in which she had been curled up reading a folder. Not looking quite at me nor exactly anywhere else, she asked: "Is there anything, you know, fishy about the show? Dad says there are all sorts of rumors about a big stink. That it's fixed. Crooked as a ram's horn. Was it that way with you?"

"If you mean were there duplicates of those famous questions in sealed envelopes kept in a bank vault till the last minute, no. Nobody ever handed me answers just before show time."

"Did they ever, well, like help you over a hump? So the show could go on?"

"I made my debut on the up-and-up and that's how I made my exit. You know that nothing comes at anybody cold, any more than the questions you get at college finals. You cram for them. And the 'briefing' discussions with the producers, on the categories, fishing out of you what you know, and then tailoring the questions to what they've found out you do — I've never kept any of that from you."

She heaved a long sigh, ambiguous as to whether

expressive of relief or anxiety. Perhaps a combination of the two, but more the latter, because she said after a moment: "All the same I'm worried. Christ, I wish . . . I don't know what I wish."

"You don't wish you didn't have a dime in the bank to pay the settlement bills, as of old, and the state forever in coughing up appropriated funds. That you don't wish. I think I'll go up and see what Buddy Boy's doing."

"Oh, he went out. To the corner for an ice cream cone or something."

The sister in Seattle seemed farther than ever from being on the mend. The illness that had laid her low, mysterious enough in the first instance, increasingly baffled the doctors. Nothing terminal. No, rather interminable. That seemed to be the prognosis. The Edmondsons themselves remaining on as might be expected of decent kinfolk, not derelict in familial obligations, an example to all. The fortnight was now in its third month, filled with behavioral goodies on the part of our nonpareil, the dry run providing an experimental crack at parenthood bidding fair to become a long voyage, seas ranging from choppy to turbulent, and no harbor in sight. Love and affection, as from the surrogate father one was supposed to be, were returned only with hostility. That was what I again thought as I strolled into the empty but well-lighted room — to see something on the wall that brought me up short.

There was the cover of the news magazine in which the story had appeared — my picture in full color. This poor misunderstood boy's pinup! How wrong I had been, how inept in reading the signs. Of course! Beneath the antagonism lay a reciprocal affection the hard crust was only meant to conceal. I stood smiling, not at the likeness, but rather at what it now symbolized as evidence of a spirit being redeemed when we suspected it least. After gazing a moment, I turned and started out. I stopped short at the door, arrested by something odd about the picture only now registering on my mind. I walked back and peered at it more closely, bending forward to do so.

The features now seemed that of a subject afflicted with some kind of pox, at least with very large pores in his skin. Tiny holes punctuated them, especially the nose, which was profusely peppered with them, as — what? Perhaps the bull's eye logically to be regarded as such by one pitching darts at it from the middle distance? That seemed the only deduction. A dartboard had been one of the presents we had given the boy on a recent fifteenth birthday. A search of a desk drawer readily uncovered the five darts. A look in the clothes closet turned up the dartboard, itself pristine of any such punctuation as riddled the old physog in the pinup.

"He doesn't like me," I told Amy.

Mrs. Flamsteed was late to lunch. We had agreed to meet at Cavendish's at one. When she hadn't shown up by a quarter to two I went ahead and ordered. I had one of the restaurant's justly celebrated "New York cut" sirloin steaks, with a baked potato and coleslaw. This, sluiced off with two steins of the Würzburger here obtainable on draft (forever securing Mrs. Flamsteed's graces, not to say my own), left me quite replete, to say the least. I could hardly move. That I was to be required to do so, and to look alive at it, within a very few breaths, I did not, at twenty-five minutes after two, expect. I had of course given Mrs. Flamsteed up. One would have had to be nutty as a praline oneself not to, what?

Imagine my horror therefore when, just as I was lifting the last of my beer, the check paid, I saw her profile swim rapidly across the front window of which my table commanded a view, a crimson scarf streaming in her wake.

"Oh, you've begun."

"No, I've finished."

Such, or something hideously like it, would have to be our obligatory exchange were something not done. It would have been insufferable. What to do? The wheels of my brain spun like tires in the mud.

There stood nearly at my elbow a folding service table of the kind on which waiters set down used dishes for busboys to cart off. There was a tray on it heavily loaded with such rubble now. Acting on blind instinct, I sprang to my feet and began to tumble everything from my own table onto the mound of crockery, cutlery and assorted debris. The plate with the sirloin, another containing a scrap of foil in which the baked potato had come swaddled, the coleslaw ramekin, the beer stein, sloshing the dregs of which I had not been able to avail myself — almost in my haste and confusion the dollar bill and change left on a salver as a tip.

That done, I threw a queasy glance over my shoulder, to find Mrs. Flamsteed just inside the door, looking breathlessly about for me. To turn around and expose myself to identification under these precise circumstances — that is, playing busboy to myself — would have been more embarrassing than the scene I had tried to avert. "I thought, you see, I'd get rid of some of this . . ." No. Flight alone remained. Hoisting the tray onto my shoulder, I trotted off toward the kitchen, trusting that I would not be recognized from the rear. I plowed through the swinging door, stiff-arming it like a football player, and moving with such rapidity that the entire scene had something of the fluid delirium of the old silent two-reelers, the kind that in turn possess something of the fluid delirium of dreams. I imagined myself caught up in one such, and began to pick my feet up and set them down with the exaggerated speed of the old flicks. This led force to the experience as pure illusion, something happening to somebody else altogether, if at all, no need to believe the testimony of your senses, etc. Setting the enormously heavy tray down on the nearest table, to the astonishment of ectoplasmically white gaping cooks and other such functionaries, perhaps a cup or two clattering to the floor, I shot on through the long kitchen and out another door.

I found myself in an alleyway. To the right was a dead-end brick wall. The left led, over a short paved stretch strewn with incidental abominations, into a street. I stood in that a moment to catch my breath and straighten my clothing. That done, I rounded a corner and returned to the restaurant. I looked around semi-wildly as Mrs. Flamsteed had for me, spotting her installed in a booth on the side opposite that in which I had so copiously fed, waved, and strolled over.

"Well. I figured you gave me up for Lent."

"Actually I gave you up for lost. I left, despairing of your arrival, then saw you come up when I was out on the street, up the block a way. So I hightailed it back here. Whuh hop?"

"Would you believe two flat tires?"

Mrs. Flamsteed, whose antic gifts were never more in evidence than when she was unaware of their being opera-tive, would have me believe that, driving down in the "landau" of otherwise unspecified construction, first one blowout had befallen her, blessedly contracted smack *but smack* in front of a filling station, where an attendant grievously wanting in wits but mechanically apt had, with the speed of a functionary working for a racer making a pit stop at the Indianapolis 500, plucked off the flat tire and thrown on the spare, which then, several blocks later, and that many from a garage mechanic, had in turn given out.

"We shall be very acid about Goodyears in future. But here I am. So sorry. Nice of you to wait. God, you must be starved. What'll you have? I could eat a horse myself. Probably what I should be riding."

"I'm not very hungry, for some reason. But have a good steak for yourself. I think I'll just toy with the tidbit plate."

"I always have the T-bone. Never liked fillet mignon. But first we'll want some of the Würzburger. It's on draft here, you know. Rarest of miracles! Waiter, bring us two steins?"

Sodden with satiety, and waterlogged by lager into near immobility, I did my best to hold up my end of the conversation. Midway which, having furtively eased my belt a notch or two, and keeping my face ever averted to avoid recognition by the waiter on the other side of the room who had already seen me scarfing it up within the hour, gripping the handle of my stein for support, I asked a question about a matter that had not in my stupefaction escaped my curiosity. "How, by the way, did you get here? After the second blowout. If as you say you had to leave the car there so they could fix the tires."

"Hitchhiked. That is to say, a passing motorist was kind enough to pick me up."

"Kind! And aspired to lunch with you himself, no doubt," I prettily put in. Women like that sort of thing — and one's bladder was about to net us blowout number three. "Excuse me a minute, I —"

"That's right. A smarmy sort — wait, let me tell you about it. Thick black hair greased to a fare-thee-well, and reeking of cologne that must have cost at least fifty cents an ounce. I was glad to get out with my virtue."

"If you'll —"

"Goodness." She stayed me with a hand on my wrist. "I hope we can find the the car."

"With a little bit o' luck . . . I'll be right back."

The hydraulic exigencies attended to, and having leant a moment against a wall to clear my head with a few lungfuls of violently deodorized fetid air, I was able to settle back in the booth and talk at least without emitting audible groans. Mrs. Flamsteed again had her stein pleasurably aloft. "Malt does more than Milton can to justify God's ways to man."

The archly appraising glance was one I had in the past weeks become quite accustomed to, from people putting me on. Yes, I could place this one.

"I agree with Housman there. Never better put."

"Well so. We can have a brandy up at my place if you want."

The question now was merely one as to when Mrs. Flamsteed would throw the definitive pass. We located her car — a Lincoln brougham, not a landau model at all — in a remote corner of London and drove to her apartment. She had paid the garage in advance. Behind the wheel, she struck out on a long monologue on the subject of open marriage, to which she had apparently given a great deal of thought, every bit of it enlightened.

"Promiscuity no. Absolutely not. But any legitimate pleasure not destructive to another. Once, I was that third party. I learned Harvey had a bit of fluff in Oak Park. This was after several years of marriage, and I accepted it. And it wasn't long afterward that I had a little side order to the main course myself." Waiting for a light, she turned to me. "You know how I'd put the whole thing in a nutshell? The way Bertrand Russell did. That marriage should be permanent if at all possible, but that it should not exclude other relationships. What do you think?"

"I never argue with intellectual giants."

"So at last we see that we can make a distinction between loving someone and being in love. With someone else — however briefly. Because the bubbles go out of any champagne. Everything becomes routine, even humdrum. Profane love as well as sacred, affairs as well as marriage."

"That's what's wrong with Paradise. Not the snake in the tree, but the worm in the apple."

"Well, here we are."

It was an apartment of probably no great size, but the living room was enormous, a long assemblage of large, low-lying couches, deep chairs, broadly spreading plants, and a grand piano at one end. Mrs. Flamsteed promptly sat down and began to ripple off some Chopin. I leaned over the edge of the instrument holding a brandy and watching as much as listening to her.

"My tastes run strictly to the romantic, I'm afraid. Not for me the cool symmetries of classical music. Even Bach . . . I agree with what Colette said about him."

I "gave up," the expert stumped. "What did she say?"

I said, swirling my brandy about with a knowledgeable air.

"She called him a golden sewing machine."

The nocturne came to an end. She sat for a moment with her hands on the keys, then withdrew them into her lap. A hush closed in on us. She raised her head and smiled faintly at me across the waste of gleaming walnut.

"I've noticed something about you. One eye is higher than the other. It's what gives you that look at once astonished and informed. What have you noticed about me?"

"Right now! That way you have of cocking your head to one side, like . . ."

"Like what?"

"Like a robin listening for a worm."

She rose and stood beside the bench, as though revolving the pros and cons of such a parallel. Then she came toward me, a hand outstretched to my cheek. "You're a handsome gargoyle."

I laughed nervously, eluding the projected blandishment by sidling, in a kind of slithering motion, along the curved inlet of the piano toward the keyboard edge.

"What's the matter?"

"Nothing. It's just that, when it comes to left-handed compliments, you're a real southpaw, Mrs. Flamsteed."

"Call me Rosé."

This was a bridge anticipated as difficult to cross. The guess was that, finding herself, as a romantically overheated adolescent, to have been saddled with the name Rose, she had snatched it from banality by the introduction of the accent. I answered nothing for the moment, promised nothing. That would have to be played by ear, muddled through . . . She was coming closer.

"Your rise in the firm could be meteoric."

Again the discomfited laugh as I slid back again to the narrow end of the piano. From there I drifted toward a window hung with heavy draperies decorated with loose, Matisse-type flowers. "I've often wondered, why do we say meteoric rise? Don't meteors usually fall?"

"Well, we'll see." She came toward the couch on which I had subsided, installing herself with some perceptible sharpening of her features as she leaned an elbow on its back, the fingers of a hand buried in the dense whorls of tawny hair. "Why don't you report for work Monday morning then, and, as I say, we'll see."

That was the day I should of stood in bed. Having welcomed me in her office at the "campus," as they called the *Consumer Review* plant sprawling over several acres on the far south side of the city, she marched me outside to my first assignment. We traversed a wide expanse of lawn on which some men were pushing hand mowers, figures in a de Chirico landscape, toward a long wooden fence.

"We keep painting this in several of the outdoor white lead paints, to check on comparative brightness, durability, resistance to cold and heat, and so on. Each section is marked according to the brand used there. We can't test all products that thoroughly on the lot, but we do in every case where they can be used as part of our own maintenance. I'll have Bascomb give you a bucket and brush, and of course fit you out with a pair of overalls, and then you can hop to it."

"But I thought my duties were to be administrative."

She smiled into the bright sunlight. "We all start at the bottom here. I mean you wouldn't want to sit down at a desk without your basic training, would you? Would you?"

"Well . . ."

So that was how the cookie crumbled. I was to be punished for my virtue. By a woman scorned. Was that it? Or was it merely a bit of cat-and-mouse before installation in the proper executive post to which some prior thought should, in any case, be reasonably given?

I worked all morning, slapping away at one end of the fence. Toward noon, the boss appeared again. Since the fence now blocked my view of the main building, I didn't see her till her head appeared around the end post.

"Well, Tom Sawyer, how's it coming? Do you have to do this whole thing yourself, or will your friends come along and offer to help?"

I slapped silently away, refusing to dignify her taunts with a reply. I had my pride. I had committed my share of misdemeanors slaking the thirsts of the flesh, but the role of gigolo I did not fancy. One could not live in an atmosphere of moral squalor, the era was much too permissive, as Spiro T. Agnew had been preaching anew to properly responsive audiences. I went along with him there. Standards must be upheld, a line drawn. Let Mrs. Flamsteed do her worst in retaliation for my having resisted her advances. I would not prostitute myself, as she had accused me of doing — I was not blind to that little irony!

"I suppose you think I'm doing this to you because you wouldn't go to bed with me. Hell hath no fury like a woman scorned and all that."

"You said it, I didn't." Slap, slap.

"You're a fast worker. And you're doing, shall we say, a slap-up job?"

"I like painting. I've always wanted to be a painter, but the combined examples of Picasso, Braque and Kandinski broke my spirit."

"How would you like to go to Florida with me?"

"Isn't that a little banal? Wouldn't the Virgin Islands or Martinique be a trifle tonier? Have more twang?"

"We have a branch there you should see. Part of the orientation course we give all those who are being groomed for executive posts. We could fly to New York to clear up a little business there, then I like to take the overnight train to Fort Lauderdale. Think it over. Meanwhile your wearing that Schicklgruber outfit like a suit of armor you're protecting your virtue in is not to be missed. Come, it's time for lunch. We've just opened a cafeteria, but we'll have a bite in my office."

As we sat in her rather sizeable quarters munching chicken sandwiches brought in from the cafeteria, it began to cloud up outside, and what we first thought a brief shower settled down to a steady rain threatening to become a feature of the afternoon.

"That does it for outside work. Or do I wander around the campus testing a line of water-repellent trenchcoats? Or maybe crash-drive an automobile at high speed into a locomotive or two to evaluate it for safety?"

Mrs. Flamsteed replied quite seriously. "Cars are something we haven't taken on yet. *Consumer Reports* does that so well, and so thoroughly. They use the race track in Old Lyme, Connecticut. I suppose we could use the Indianapolis Speedway, but it's too expensive a category for us to take on at this time. We're expanding though. You noticed the cafeteria is in a new wing we're just finishing off. There are floors to be mopped and waxed."

"I get the message."

I remembered Potiphar's wife saying to Joseph, "Lie with me," and Joseph's refusal, and how it came to pass in her fury she did then accuse Joseph of seeking to lie with her, and of then fleeing when she cried aloud in resistance, leaving his garment in her hand as evidence, and how the master Potiphar then cast Joseph into prison. Well, we would see.

She did then take me unto a man named Lumpka, who was in overall charge of maintenance, saying unto me as we went thither that, though they ran formal tests on most products, here again was an area where appraisals could be made in the normal line of duty. "For instance, this carpeting we're walking on, we keep a strict record of how long we've had it and what kind of wear and tear it gets. Ah, there's Lumpka."

Lumpka was a hulking Balkan closer to seven feet tall than six, with, if memory serves, eight to ten fingers on each hand, judging by the force with which he wrung mine on presentation. Me and Lumpka together began mopping a long corridor running at right angles along the new wing, using buckets with pedal wringers into which we introduced a brand-name detergent.

"You the new janitor?"

"I guess." There seemed little point in explaining that I was in fact a minor deity driven from Olympus for a season to do penance in disguise as a lowly mortal, by gods of higher rank jealous of my probity which was tantamount to a moral hubris — a merry mythological mixup that would soon be straightened out.

The corridor mopped, me and Lumpka waxed it, using a rotary bristle power waxer that made the asphalt tile floor gleam like a skating pond. The wax was a new preparation "low in slippage risk." All this would prove temporary. I envisioned the day when hordes of us menials would simply chew slippery elm and spit on the floor at intervals guaranteeing uniform sheen.

When I had mastered the use of the waxer, Lumpka went off to see to some other aspect of his domain. I swung the machine back and forth across the hallway in great arcs, like a reaper his scythe. After a time, Potiphar's wife again appeared. She stood watching a moment, her face illegible as to what precisely she might be thinking. I made no secret of what I was.

"This is a day that will live in infamy."

She paced back and forth in my path — that is, at my rear, as my progress down the hallway was backwards. I could sense her milling about with great emotion there. If one person can mill.

"Would you like to enter a sanatarium?"

"Why not? You seem to want your help fully committed."

"I believe in the recoverable ecstasy. I believe in the ever-renewable dream. That we are all involved in something dark and conspiratorial when we mate. 'Much madness makes divinest sense,' said the New England poetess, who, however, never availed herself of what she celebrated, preferring to flit about in that Amherst house in a white dress. Well, I do not intend to flit about in a white dress — or black. It's not idly that I talk about loving well what we must leave 'ere long. I won't tell you what it is, or how long I've got. It's borrowed time, is all."

"The worst betrayal of an innocent man since the days of Judas Iscariot."

"I believe in living to the hilt, I believe in gathering

rosebuds while we may, I believe in not standing there wasting gas when the green light has been flashed —"

"I believe this should be rated Acceptable. And the detergent too. It says goodbye to old-fashioned methods, and it gets out stubborn stains."

"*You're* a stubborn stain." She came around in front of me, with such stern deliberation that I switched the machine off. "It apparently has not penetrated that thick pate of yours that I really do not have much time, and that I want this outfit — a multi-million dollar investment sunk in a desperately important cause — left in the hands of competent young people who must be *trained in the field*. I'm only having a little innocent fun with you. I suppose I like to put people on. It's my one weakness. But that's all it is. Do you think I'd attach any strings to hiring a Boy Scout just because I find him palatable?" She rolled her eyes to the ceiling. "Right there is your office. If you want it. We're bursting at the seams and really do need more room for more comers. But there's your office — where you'll work as — oh, I'm not sure what. Maybe in charge of all outside laboratories we engage for special tests of a kind we can't conduct here. Chemical analyses for example of — well, the hot dogs you've dedicated your talents to. Christ, don't you feel relieved, purged, with a chance to be honest for the first time in your life? Hoh! You are something. Come on, I'll show you the new offices here. You want to be an executive, this is where you will execute."

"We're Puritans. That's what we are," Mrs. Flamsteed was saying. "Puritans."

I nodded dully from the great round bed in which I sat propped on a mound of striped pillows against a white buttoned-leather headboard, a sheet gathered tight about my chest and secured under my arms, sipping hot bouillon she had herself prepared in the maid's absence. No stranger to post-congressional blahs, I was now sunk in funk to a degree that can be imagined. Guilt being a cardinal ingredient in the sodden torpor in which I stared at the window embrasure in the opposite wall, I was more than a little interested in how she came by that designation for us. I was all ears for the reasoning behind it.

"Puritans," I said, half in query, half in dazed echo of herself, by way of prompting her back to the discourse she seemed in danger of abandoning for some other conversational tack as she plowed the carpeted floor in ruffed mules and a belted aquamarine wrapper of watered silk, sipping her own beef tea. I mean this I had to hear, this promise of fresh perspective, nay justification, to one very much on the hunt for that.

"Puritans of the market place are we, that's us. Intolerant of sham, unresting in our censorship of those who would perpetrate it upon us. The professional scourge of commercial sinners. Yes, I see it as a Puritanism transferred from the sexual sphere — where of course we've all been quite liberated —"

"Oh, quite."

"— totally freed for lovemaking, the supreme cure for all the ills of men."

"All," I said, with a tongue tasting as though it had been marinated, like a thick slice of sauerbraten, for the five or six days recommended by epicures.

"Transferred from that sphere to one where it's sorely needed, the economic and political. Holding merchants to as rigid standards as possible in the sale of goods and the promulgation of services. Sinners! That's what they are and how we must view them. That's our profession. To keep a hawk's eye on them at every turn. Oh, it's not only liberty of which the price is eternal vigilance!"

"Far from it!"

"Puritanism," she dilated, warming to her subject, "has always been a deep-seated strain in the American conscience —"

"Up to now a strain *on* it?" I proposed tentatively, wishing to be epigrammatically helpful, however necessarily the straight man.

"Yes. And though it no longer operates as personal self-denial, the prohibition of healing pleasures to me and my neighbor, it surfaces publicly, in crusaders like us, for what I call this morality of the mart. We must be as rigid as our Colonial forebears as to that, giving no quarter to corporate devils, polluters of earth, sea and sky while bilking and short-changing their fellowmen."

So that was what we were. This was an apocalypse indeed, one arriving just in the nick of time! This was an intellectually cogent as well as emotionally bracing exegesis of her point, in the first instance cryptically enough stated, now to be clapped with all due haste and fervor to one's breast. This made sense. This was a thoroughgoing credo one must only find admirable, especially as expounded by one of God's creatures so toothsome when already so relatively long in the tooth. It bespoke a clear mind as well as an austere morality. Mrs. Flamsteed had every virtue but virtue.

As I set aside the cup of restorative broth and helped myself to a cigar from a bedside humidor, one of a store of Jamaican panatellas to which Mrs. Flamsteed herself was partial, she gave off elucidation and launched one of those brief resumés of what had just happened: the pleasures collaborated on. The joys of epilogue dear to all lovers of lovemaking. The act of love was not at all a hard act for her to follow.

"You were great," she said with a smile, fishing out a cigar for herself, "after you got over the hump."

"Allow me." I snapped on the lighter with which I had set fire to my own cigar, and extended it to hers, the end of which she had trimmed with a gold cutter also a nightstand accessory. She puffed the cigar to a fine coal, then resumed her articulate pacing.

"You're as involved with giving pleasure as with taking it. That's by no means to be taken for granted in a man. Huh!" She rolled her eyes in a manner bespeaking ample private backlog for this generalization. "Murmured inquiries, whispered solicitudes, these are so important. I mean a woman doesn't want just to be *plowed*." She strode a bit more, in clouds of smoke from the cigar on which she puffed. She removed it from between her teeth and smiled over again. "I liked your tongue in my ear."

My foot in my mouth had been a matter of greater early concern, that having been my specialty on openers. I had made the booboo of telling her she looked like a certain cinema star. The actress's having been a great beauty was beside the point, in the *gaffe*. It's the kind of thing a boy tells a girl, not a man a woman; notably one of strong ego who is going to bristle with more than normal resentment at the implication that she is not unique. Then of course I was bogged in this confounded post-coital *tristesse* setting in far, far more in advance than ever, as might be divined for such circumstances.

237

The pall had descended before we had our clothes off, indeed as we sprang out of the cab and entered the foyer of her apartment building, under the eye of a doorman in full mulberry livery (the color of my spirits). Nerves made me blurt out such inept flatteries. This adventure would never get airborne. *I was prophylactically sorry for what I wasn't going to do as a result.* I had watched in mesmerized stupor Mrs. Flamsteed dig a passkey out of her bag and fit it into the lock. I followed her into the apartment, the remorseful freebooter given a shortcut to the sort of crystalline fatigue that is the goal of all priapic struggle.

Tearing off my clothes and wildly flinging them every which way as we made for the bedroom was a ritual courtesy owing to Mrs. Flamsteed and an aid in momentarily camouflaging my inoperability under a guise of Not Being Able to Wait, a courtly response to her own stocking-peeling, slipper-shucking, cotton-picking goddamn lather of preparation for what she could not dream would be a fiasco, my violence at least half-valid as a rage that all this must be so as I dove into a bed from which I had ripped back the covers in an earnest of bacchanalian revels the like of which had not been seen. I mean, languidly unknotting a cravat as one casually commented on propped photographs and inquired as to the source of etchings on the wall, carefully draping trousers over a chair-back as one nudged off an Oxford with only moderate haste, that would have been a less than knightly thing to do. I ripped off the tie and nearly kicked a shoe into a Venetian pier glass in my Need to Have Her. She joined me in the scented sheets, ones of peppermint stripe, into which I then plunged face-down, burying it in a blessedly cool pillow of matching design.

"Well?"

"Well what?"

"Are we playing hide-and-seek?"

I rolled over to rights, and, lying on my back with outflung arms, I gazed at the ceiling with glutted eyes.

"You satisfy me more than any woman I've ever known."

Propped on an elbow, she peered at me under a tendril of hair, in lieu of oral inquiry.

"I mean . . . I feel so contentedly weary with you. I mean in your mere presence."

I looked around with the leisure of the practised technician who does not rush things, who is mindful of the value of foreplay. "This room. This hour. Together trampling the blue grape of dusk . . ." Here an image of bloodstained tootsies slogging in tandem a large vat of empurpling pulp-mash imperilled the fragile spell I was attempting to weave, indeed provoked a nervous laugh out of me, removing any remaining confidence that we would be hearing from Johnny Jump Up in the very near future.

Yet Mrs. Flamsteed set everything to rights. By the most delicate caresses, bestowed with the most exquisitely shaded sense of understanding, itself in its way aphrodisiac, she roused responses themselves immediately electric with the urge to return them, so that, whispering and fondling, trailing with our fingers delicate flowers of sensation across each other's limbs, we were soon enough swept toward Mrs. Flamsteed's objective. The results were everything she celebrated in the afterwords to which she proved so partial, and which she prized as part and parcel of the pleasure itself. These epilogues in turn acquired an earmark: "our" bit in the errant hours together. I would fish two cigars out of the humidor, light them both, and hand one over to our moment-seizing friend.

16 ━━━━━━━━━━━━━━━━━━━━

OF COURSE MOMENT-SEIZING TAKES TIME. It is one of
the most time-consuming of all human activities. Hours
of careful planning and execution are required in the
administrative exactions necessary to any rendezvous, a
far cry from the reckless abandon in which they culmi-
nate. They are like the minute and painstaking attention
to detail a pastry chef pours into the concoction of a tart
gobbled in three minutes, whether by himself or another.
The hammock one must oneself weave, stitch and assem-
ble before, with a moan of joy, briefly flinging oneself
into it. To many this is all the candle making the game not
worth it. That everyone must decide for himself. Naturally the botheration is halved in a case in which one of
the parties is independent, leaving the strains of conspiracy to be borne only by the other. Insofar as these
might consist in domestic testimony to the effect that
one will be working late at the office, the problem is further reduced in a marriage in which the other is frequently doing just that.

My own office was modest but comfortable, when at last finished and furnished. I was, as originally suggested, put in charge of all testing farmed out to commercial laboratories outside the campus. I negotiated with these laboratories, arranged for the samples to be supplied them, studied and coordinated the reports for final inclusion in the *Review* sent out, by now, to a million subscribers. We were growing by leaps and bounds. This was in part due to a dedication on the part of our personnel to the cause of consumerism bordering on moral fanaticism. Mrs. Flamsteed had so rightly gauged and pegged us! We *were* Puritans of the market place. Nor did we forget our work when we left the office either. We took it home with us, took it everywhere, ceaselessly subjecting everything eaten, drunk, ridden, worn, played and plied to unresting scrutiny. We were the foe of the shoddy, scourge of the second-rate. For example, I myself test-rode a neighbor's bike before dictating the following report to my secretary, Miss Tumulty, to be shot to the proper department. It was typical of this kind of extra-curricular effort brought by total commitment.

"Hamilton bicycle: Sturdy construction on the whole, but on braking must be considered dangerously over-responsive, an evil little better than sluggish response. On hard- and sudden-braking test, pitches rider over handlebars" — here I felt a goose egg on my head — "when front brakes over-respond, reverse when rear brakes do, causing front wheels to rear up, leaving rider like a general on a horse in a public statue. Tipping completely over backwards off mount not inconceivable. Must be rated unsafe."

"Unsafe, you damn near fractured your skull," Miss Tumulty said. "Mr. Tickler, now that you're an executive and all, I don't think you should do so much actual, um, stunt testing any more."

"Nonsense, Miss Tumulty. Whoso having put his hand to the plow looks back is not fit for the kingdom of God."

"What?"

"Anybody who won't put in his time on the barricades is no soldier."

"That Band-Aid has got unstuck. Here, let me just . . ." She rose and came over, pressing one end of it back onto my brow. In doing so, she bent provocatively over me a frame I had myself in fancy test-driven over the old Mattress Mile. Oh, well, I thought, in the attempt to quell myself, take away the miniskirt and what have you got.

"There, that's a little better."

"Thank you. You have the touch of a Florence Nightingale, besides being a damn good secretary. Shoot that as a freebee to — I guess Murton, to file under bicycles. Then let's get that batch of reports from the Wilmot Laboratories on frozen frankfurters. We're trying to get that all lined up for a feature in the April issue."

It was with more than normal interest that I digested these. My curiosity about Hot Diggety Dogs can be well imagined. Regrettably, my child was wayward, must be chastised.

"Subject: vacuum-packed frozen frankfurters," I dictated. "Brand: Hot Diggety Dogs. Since last reviewed found to have introduced perceptible portions of pork under an all-beef label, besides exceeding permissible limits of fat content. Recommendation: to be stricken from Acceptable rating."

"You do come down hard on wrongdoers, Mr. Tickler, if I may say so," Miss Tumulty remarked. "Like a crusader for moral, um, righteousness."

"Can't relax standards. The minute we compromise, we're worthless. It's almost lunchtime I see. But before you go out, would you get Mrs. Tickler on the phone? I think she's at the settlement now."

She disappeared into her outer cubicle, disrobed, flung to the floor, plucked and eaten before she had reached her desk. She got Amy on the phone, buzzing my own.

"Top of the day. How are you?"

"Up to my ears in case histories. You?"

"Up to mine. Say not the struggle nought availeth. How's the devil incarnate?"

"Complained of being sick this morning, so I let him stay home from school."

"Nothing trivial I hope."

"Jim, we've heard from the Edmondsons. Long letter describing the situation there. It's not good, but they're coming back anyway, though not for a couple of weeks. The real trouble is with Chip. I've had a long talk with him, and, well, I'm not sure he wants to go back to the Edmondsons. He prefers us, which makes it so much more baffling why he wants to give us such a hard time. Especially you. I don't get it. I think he hocked that pocket transistor radio that's missing. It beats me. The more you do for him the harder time he gives you."

"He threatened to run away at one time. Whatever happened to that plan? And what about dinner tonight?"

"There's that pork roast in the refrigerator. You might pop it in the oven when you get home. I'll be a little late."

"And I like a nice Pommard with roast pork. Cuts the grease, you know. Much better than applesauce."

"You are a brick."

"Rumor has it that marriage is a give-and-take. Or is that too arcane for you this early in the day?"

Cynics who believe that no good deed in this world goes unpunished will be gratified by the fruits of all my charities toward Twinkletoes. The more I gave the more he took, the better I was the worse he got. He snitched my old prep school jacket from a storage closet with which he made free, one afternoon in the absence of both foster parents pro tem, and wore it, rather derisively it could be sensed, to the public school he favored with intermittent appearances. But seeing him sporting it, I was at first struck by something other than the theft. Beneath the gold insignia over the breast pocket was stitched my old private school motto: *Laboribus Iudicamur*. What did it mean, again? I couldn't for the life of me remember. True, I'd never taken Latin — but not knowing what your old school motto meant! By your labors you are judged. Was that it? It seemed to ring a bell.

One was doing one's best to live up to that slogan in real life, and all the good it did. I had to judge myself a flop as a surrogate father figure, despite all efforts to fulfill that complex and delicate office. I gave up. I quit. I threw in the sponge — or was about to. Then all of a sudden it all changed. Overnight something happened that gained for me the end I had for weeks and even months striven in vain.

The blow finally fell. The preliminary tremors we had uneasily been feeling became at last the earthquake we feared. Angela Burwash spilled her guts and in so doing strewing ours collectively across the United States, Great Britain, and parts of Europe.

I was watching the seven o'clock news with a TV dinner in my lap. Amy was on a house call of the kind social workers can sometimes only make in the evening, when the father, or working mother, of a delinquent can be caught at home, or for some such reason. Chip had eaten and was in his room, probably getting in a little dartboard practice or pasting up another anonymous letter. I wondered to what use, if any, he put those scissored-out letters and numbers I had discovered. Maybe they were just part of a harmless fantasy. Maybe he did glue up ransom notes that were never sent, just to amuse himself. Maybe he actually sent out poison-pen letters. Who knew what went on in the mind of a boy like that? At any rate, I was watching the news alone when Angela Burwash's name galvanized me. She was shown in a clip of a press conference held that day. There she was, before a battery of mikes and cameras, seated in a silver gown on a dais such as she had never occupied when enthroned in her brief hour of glory as quiz queen, in a recovery of the limelight for which she must have fretted in the interval, fatally hooked on fame, "purging" herself of the burden this recent religious conversion made it impossible for her to bear.

"I can't go on with it any longer," she said, her face like tinted Dresden, every platinum hair in place, the most frightening piece of narcissistic wallowing I have ever seen. "My Maker tells me to make a clean breast of it. The show was rigged. My time on it was a lie, a fraud. It was just a show. They gave me answers to the questions I would be asked."

"How about the other contestants, Miss Burwash?"

"I cannot answer for them. It is between them and their own consciences."

"Miss Burwash, a Special House Subcommittee on Legislative Oversight, to give it its full name, is convening in

Washington for hearings on broadcast deceptions such as this. Will you appear before that panel?"

"If subpoenaed, yes. Or even if they just ask me in a nice way. [Laughter] At the moment, I understand they are questioning only volunteer witnesses. So far I've just appeared before a special grand jury investigation. That was yesterday. I've told them all I've said here. I shall withhold absolutely nothing . . ."

I shut the set off and stood a moment in the middle of the room. My guts were a bag of garbage. The house was absolutely still. I set down the plate of food, now turned to mold, walked to the cellarette and poured myself half a tumbler of bourbon. As I raised the glass to my lips the telephone rang. I stood in an agony of indecision. Would it be the first of the reporters, now certainly to be viewed as a gathering wolfpack, slavering for "statements"? I would have to face them, or in some way take them on, eventually. I might as well begin now parrying them with whatever evasions might be necessary to buy a little time. "Miss Burwash will have to speak for herself. She has ample means for breasting the tide of her own publicity." No. "I wish they'd handed me all the answers. I'd still be on . . ." Yes, something in that vein would be better. Keep my twang, hold my cool . . .

Between rings I heard the creak of footsteps overhead. If I didn't answer, Chip would, with his sardonic butler's "Tickler residence." I snatched up the extension nearest me.

"Yes?"

"What on earth is this all about?"

"For God's sake, Rosé, I've told you never to call me here at home. It's just fool's luck I happen to be —"

"I'm only calling as an employer, wondering whether you're in any hot water."

"I'll be in hot water if you ever do this again."

"Naturally anything that reflects on you. I would follow the old Christian principle. Hating the sin but loving the sinner."

"Just a minute."

Something about the acoustics on the line hinted another extension had been picked up. I set the phone down and shot on tiptoe toward the bottom of the stairs, in time to hear, rather than see, other footsteps racing into the spare bedroom. I stood a moment listening, trying to evaluate what sounds came from overhead. There was the faintest last rustle, then complete silence, to me taut with eavesdropping. I went back to the phone, wound the conversation up as quickly as possible, and headed back to my drink, cursing through gritted teeth.

I was pretty well smashed by the time Amy showed up, looking quite pale herself as she came in the front door. She shot me a look when she set her briefcase down in the hall, and as she hung her coat up in the closet I knew she had heard, possibly on the car radio. My head was light as a Christmas tree ornament, and I returned her gaze with rather a foolish grin.

"The whole show is rigged," she said.

"How about that."

Discussion went forward as best it could, after she had mixed herself a drink, a device rarely resorted to, therefore a spectacle now sobering in itself. I related everything that had happened from beginning to end, omitting nothing either to my credit or the reverse, splitting hairs, be it granted, in a piece of casuistry that would have done credit to a Jesuit disputant. Everything was relative, and to expect an answer or dispense a judgment in black and white was to ignore the intermediate shades of gray applying rather to the delicate moral transaction on which I had embarked and which I had over the weeks sustained, with a soul-searching of which I would now like to be quit, but with which in the hideous forthcoming sequel I was apparently to be revisited in triplicate. "It was a tricky piece of bookkeeping, but I think my ledger balances," I finished.

Amy sighed, rubbing her hands together as she rose from the sofa on which she had heard me out, and began to pace the television-room-library-den to which we had repaired.

"Well, I believe you. I mean I've got to. You couldn't be married to somebody this long and know them that little as to think the explanation must leave them very far apart. Has anybody phoned?"

"Only Rosé Flamsteed. To ask what gave, and offer me moral support. Didn't sound as though she was going to fire me because of what might reflect on the firm. Your father's probably glad now I quit his."

Continuing to walk the floor, Amy seemed to be revolving other aspects of the crisis.

"What will this do to Chip? I mean if in the end you are, well, tarred with that brush. Everything you've been trying to give him in the way of a good example down the drain, just when he needs it most. A scandal would undo everything, it would . . ." She flung her hands upward in a pantomime of demolition.

The doorbell rang. She shot me a look of alarm, one quite certifying us as In This Together.

"I'll get it. You keep out of sight. If it's a reporter I'll tell him you're not in."

It was, as a brief exchange overheard from behind the draperies indicated. He was told Mr. Tickler was out, that she herself had no statement to make, and gently shoved out onto the porch from which he had been trying to ease his way in. The door closed and she returned.

"You'd better make yourself scarce."

"You mean *run away*?"

"Till you can think things through, sort them out, figure out what to say. Time for homework in earnest now. What with grand juries, Congressional investigating committees and what not."

"Perhaps you're right. I'll pack a few things and head for the tall timber."

"May I be of any help?"

I wheeled around. Chip stood in the doorway, grinning like Beelzebub.

"See here," Amy scolded, "it's not nice to sneak around listening to other people's conversations."

He ignored her.

"You taking it on the lam, Jim?"

At last he called me what I had been trying to get him to all along: the first sign of the palship striven for.

"I'm going away for a bit, for reasons I suppose you've been eavesdropping on. You mustn't believe everything . . . A man is innocent until —"

"Don't worry about anything here. Mrs. Tickler and I will hold the fort while you're gone. Batten down the hatches and stuff. Will the heat be after you? Will they accuse you of fraud I mean, or anything like that?" he asked hopefully. "Could you go to prison?"

"Goddamn you!" I raised a hand in a threat to give him the back of it, a gesture wilting in midair as he smiled in return. He wasn't being ironic, his manner was sincere, as Amy and I realized in a moment when the scales suddenly fell from our eyes. Chip sent about his business, Amy dropped once more onto the sofa, her legs out, a hand clapped to her brow.

"My God, and I call myself a psychologist. The whole explanation was under my nose all the time. This is what he's wanted from you all along, what he's been needling you to give him. Some evidence, any evidence that you're not all that much the prince of a good guy as to make his own old man look like a bum. Which is what you did with every kind word you uttered, every good deed you did him. Jesus Christ! the last thing he needed was a hero to worship. That only made him hate you all the more, the world all the more."

"I get it now too. His home life was so traumatic that he seethed with rage at the sight of any house with the composure and integrity of this one, couldn't rest till he had reduced it to the same shambles as his own, or something did it for him. So the ill wind blows some good."

"I can see now what it is for a boy to endure humiliation from his father. Absolutely festering in his case. You've made yourself a little easier for him to take. All you'd have to do to close the gap is beat him up some, the way his own old man did. That's the surrogate who would really restore his ego."

"I still may."

Amy dropped her voice to an even lower whisper than that in which we had been conducting the discussion.

"One thing we must be careful of. We mustn't let him think you 'did it for him,' for the cause. That would spoil it for him. Let him believe the worst. You've been on the take and now you're on the lam. Might even make it a little dramatic. It's as a hunted criminal that you must continue to gain his confidence and win his respect."

"Well, all right."

We next discussed whether I should, and how I might, disguise myself for a bit. My face being known to millions, it seemed impractical to take a powder without some sort of self-editing. Measures short of plastic surgery were calmly evaluated and objectively agreed on. My hair I had let grow moderately long in the espousal of twang (despite Mrs. Flamsteed's slurs at the supermarket about my clean-cut Nixon-regime look). I now had my head strip-mined by a barber into whose chair I slipped unrecognized the next morning, after being spirited out of the garage by Amy under the noses of a couple of newsmen lurking about the house, after a long night with the phone off the hook and the bottle uncorked. I lay down on the floor in the back of the car, huddled under a blanket as well, with a hangover on spin-dry, as she wheeled down the alley, leaving the now most genuinely cooperative Chip to pull the garage door down after us.

I was now made to look like a wholesome administration chap indeed by a barber working in a silence atypical of his profession. He only asked once as he clipped away, in fact all but shaving my head, "You going into a convent?" I took it he meant monastery, but said nothing. The convent might be a good idea at that, were one prepared to go into ecclesiastical drag. A refuge from the folly and perfidy of this world. A false mustache and Vandyke left over from some bygone party revels completed the transformation. We being a two-car family, Amy left me the one in which I had made my escape, walking the few blocks home. We bade goodbye in the street, with the agreement that I would keep in touch.

Then, in dark glasses and a soft hat pulled over one eye, the collar of my topcoat turned up, I got behind the wheel and set out, somehow braced, rather than the reverse, by the melodramatic sense of myself as a hunted animal.

I drove southward from town to town, aimlessly, with no real sense of itinerary or destination. I put up in a motel in Crawford, a town near the Indiana border below Terre Haute. I sat propped in bed with a fresh bottle, keeping up with myself on television, as I had throughout the day with snatches of news reports on the car radio.

After breakfast I got behind the wheel again and resumed my ramble, only this time more or less doubling back on myself in a vaguely northeasterly direction that had me crossing and recrossing the Wabash River several times. At dusk I fetched up in an all but nonexistent town on its western bank, where I had a sandwich in a bar and grill. I took a stroll through its two-block Main Street, and then, acknowledging to myself what had been at the back of my mind all along, climbed back into the car, and, rattling eastward over a bridge one last time, headed for the old home town.

17 ━━━━━━━━━━━━━━━━

I SAT IN FRONT OF THE HOUSE on Jefferson Street with the car lights and engine switched off. The lamps weren't on in the front parlor either, but through the white lace curtains, illuminated by a nearby streetlight, I could dimly see on to the dining room where a faint glow made visible a ghostly figure moving about against walls remembered as brightly papered in a "Birds of Middle America" motif, from whose family selection, long years ago, one had flinched, and chosen to disassociate himself. Once or twice I thought I recognized Mother's equally familiar blue and white checked flannel bathrobe. Had she been catching her wandering boy on the evening news? Was Oompah home? Unlikely, this being the middle of the week which customarily found him plying his trade among the numberless Indiana apothecaries whose wholesale custom had for so many years fed, clothed and sheltered so many of us. Was he still seeing this Mrs. I'msmith-Buffington?

People hurried past along the sidewalk, bent on concerns equally important though hardly as checkered as my own. How many of my townsmen now gave me disenchanted thought? Would Tickler Avenue (past which on the outskirts of Wabash I had shot with head averted) be dismantled as such, and rechristened? Probably — and the assurance of the honorary degree revoked. One hustling passerby, wrapped in a voluminous overcoat, struck a chord. Picked out by a streetlight he revealed himself as Mr. Drummond, husband of Mother's crony Lolly, who had deplored (among other of his culinary perversions) a habit of seasoning his breakfast eggs with snuff.

I climbed out of the car and rang the bell.

"We don't need anything today, and why at this hour —? Oh, it's you, behind all that spinach. I've been praying a blue streak for you. Come in."

"Hello, Mom. It's good to be home. Is Oompah around?"

"He's on the road. And for all I care he can stay there. I don't know where I went wrong," she said, as though he was someone she had somehow unsuccessfully raised along with a few of the rest of us. Mrs. I'msmith-Buffington, later inquiry revealed, was a widow who owned one of the motels where he regularly put up when travelling. The trading stamps once more being amassed with a will were now within fifteen books of the divorce she had, this time, firmly promised herself.

"What's the latest?" I asked. "I didn't catch the news."

"The committee in Washington have decided to go full-speed ahead with the investigation, not leave it to grand juries, and have a subpoena out for you. But first let me fix you some supper."

"I've had dinner, but I could use some coffee. That will do fine. I'll just put my bag in my old room."

Mom had already dined in her customary solitude, on a joint of cold lamb and a glass or two of Gallo wine. She seemed to tipple just enough to get herself through these evenings in an otherwise empty house. There were not even any pets on the scene just then. Conversation at the kitchen table was spasmodic, constrained. In one especially prolonged silence Mother pondered me over her own coffee cup, her elbows cocked on the table-top. At last she set the cup down in its saucer.

"Wherewith shall a young man cleanse his ways?"

"By taking heed unto thy word, O Lord, Mom."

"Rrright! One of the Psalms. And for twelve points, what is it the Lord will not despise?"

"A broken and a contrite heart."

"Rrright! Ab-solutely correct!"

"Don't, Mom."

"We both know what's to be done. Nothing will ruin your character faster than a life of dishonesty."

With every turn in the discussion I died a little. When she bewailed my folly as having been committed just when I was "at the pinochle of success," I wanted to pitch over onto the floor and never get up again. Old Hobbes was right. Hell is truth seen too late. I had identified the quotation on the show. Now I knew what it meant. I had lost a lot of weight. I looked pale and drawn by Aubrey Beardsley. Mom gave the wringer through which my entrails were being sent another quarter-turn.

"To think a son of mine would run into a corner and hide."

"Instead of having the guts to kill himself. Yes, suicide. What about that?"

"It's not a viable alternative."

That did it. I must be worthy of this heritage. My

course was clear. All that remained was the question of how to play it. That was what my soul-searching had really been all about, on this brief, time-buying flight. Two scenarios must be chosen between.

The first was to carry off my appearance on the Big Quiz, as journalistic wags were already calling what would certainly be picked up by newsreel cameramen, with the same twang that had marked my hours in the public eye before. What was twang? In essence, a vibrant cool; a quick yet easygoing resonance of mind; a bow-string-taut sensibility assuring that one would always, again in the words of the beloved Eliot, find:

> *Some way incomparably light and deft,*
> *Some way we both should understand.*

Waving offhandedly to the ranks of reporters and cameramen among whom I squeezed my way, disdaining counsel, I would embark on what would be in effect an exchange between myself and the chairman of the committee, a homespun country-lawyer type from a border state given to moralistic drolleries and complicated oratorical cadences liberally studded with Biblical and Shakespearean allusions of his own. We would be a match. Such a skirmish was daydreamed on my old bed in great and extended detail.

"You seem to regard the end as justifying the means," he would say, raking his iron-gray hair and speaking in the mellifluous gravel-growl that was another trademark. "How, suh, do you justify that postulate?"

"In the same way, Mr. Chairman, I suppose, the same way that you would justify voting against a civil rights bill you knew in your otherwise famously humanitarian heart was to be favored. In order that, rather than be liquidated by your constituency at the next election, you would return to these hallowed halls for the contemplation of other, equally worthy, legislation. I accept your reasoning. Why cannot you accept mine?"

"You are, young man, I see, wise as a serpent. Whether you are blameless as a dove remains a matter of doubt. That is what we are gathered here to determine."

"Other injunctions of our Lord I have tried to heed to the letter."

"Such as?"

"Such as making friends of the Mammon of unrighteousness. Which I might add, my lord, I should have had equally to do were my career that of politics with its eternally recurring need of campaign funds, shortcuts, compromises."

"I congratulate you on your casuistry. You regard yourself, then, I gatheh, as a sort of modern day Robin Hood."

"In a sense, yes. I take from the corrupt and give to the maladjusted."

"In addition to the Scriptures, you evince a wide knowledge of the Bard. You are familiar with the line, 'How my achievements mock me now.' Do you not feel in the least mocked by this . . . how shall I put it . . . deflating turn of events?"

"I do not feel in the least deflated, my lord. To face you as adversary is an honor better than which one could not hope to climax his career with."

And so on. I would come out of it all with my poise intact — the Quiz Champ retaining his crown. Slippery, evasive, his footwork unfailing. But it would have been the choice of scenario egotistically blind to a certain cardinal consequence. My moral dilemma was one having nothing to do with the question of honesty or dishonesty. The histrionics in the isolation booth might have been seen now in amused public retrospect as the struggle of a man wrestling with his conscience — in final cynical determination a match also fixed. The problem here was one requiring no dramatization since it cut quite simply to the bone. There had been enough of personality, it was time for character, as I told myself in one permissible soliloquy. The crisis was summed up in what was preying on my mind when, lying in the dark with my hands under my head, I thought, nearly aloud: "Cagney."

There is an old movie in which he is ready to go to the chair with all the swagger and bravado that have made him a hero to a bunch of street toughs. But he is persuaded at the last moment that it is for their own good he is undone as such in their eyes. He must walk the last mile cringing and snivelling in a way that will make his name forever anathema to the delinquents. My problem was not too dissimilar. If I came out of this smelling like a rose, it would set me back with Chip Griswold into whose affections I had just begun to worm my way as a sinner, having failed to do so as a saint. As, finally, the unflappable hot shot, he could never after abide me. It would be the end as far as cultivating any burgeoning companionship was concerned. He would hate my guts forever, unless I spilled them. That was how I knew I must play it when, the next day, I finally sent a telegram to the committee offering to turn up.

"You've been courting disaster. This is your wedding day."

So it had happened. I was talking to myself.

Mother having somewhere along the line learned of

Oompah's monkeyshines at the Colony, she could hardly be expected to forego tracking my own character back through the genes responsible. "Let's say you came by it honestly," she said, and gave her Edna May Oliver sniff.

Yet the lash of Mom's wit was as nothing compared with a development springing from maternal loyalty. As this one was packing to leave, after one more night under the parental roof, there came the thud of luggage being hauled out of a back storeroom closet. It turned out to be the matched set for which I had got her to redeem the bulk of her trading stamps, dissuading her, at least temporarily, from the divorce for which she had been amassing them. The suitcases had not been used since the "second honeymoon" to which this one had then played Cupid. I stepped out of my bedroom to find her lugging them into her own.

"What are you doing?"

"Doing, I'm going with you."

"Where?"

"Where, to Washington of course. Where else. I'll be right there at your side."

"No." The protest came out in a strangled bleat rather than an intelligibly articulated word. This one sagged against the corridor wall, cackling again, "no."

"Yes. What kind of a mother would it be who didn't stand by her son in his hour of shame. Of disgrace. Of degradation as he returns to that city he so recently visited in triumph —"

Here I felt that I must at last disintegrate, go crazy like the priest in my cherished "Absolution," sliding to the floor babbling incoherently, found there, when they finally came for me, flipping my lower lip with my fingertips in lieu of the speech of which I was no longer capable. However, I got a grip on myself.

"If you go, then I won't. Whither I go, thou shalt not, and that's that. Put those bags away or I go out that door and get in that car and drive off, never to return, never to be seen again, by anybody, a wanderer on the face of the earth, vanished without a trace, like Judge Crater, Ambrose Bierce . . ."

She sighed, shrugging. "Oh, all right. But it seems unfair of you not to let me share this hour."

Her loyalty seemed not altogether untainted by a taste for the limelight, acquired during the days of the cover story when she had cooperated with the researchers with rather more zest than they had bargained for. But the realization of what I was doing her out of by no means made me relent in my determination that nobody was going to Stand By me in any damned Hour of Need.

"Call it the human element," I said, in one of her own serviceable clichés.

She sighed again. "Ah, yes. If it wasn't for that what a good life people would have."

I don't know whether you've ever appeared before a Congressional investigating committee, or whether, if so, it was in the caucus room of the Old House Office Building, scene of so many tumultuous hearings. It's a high-ceilinged chamber with Corinthian columns, beneath which a seated witness faces a long curving dais accommodating a tribunal of whatever number may be conducting the inquisition — in my case five representatives in addition to the chairman. As a lens louse in his own right, he filled the spotlight with a great deal of ham power, a certain pawky, deliberately projected cracker-barrel zest in which his own Bible and Bard were rolled into action like heavy artillery with visible pride and relish. It was an avuncular wisdom and erudition. Not much twang but plenty of bang. Yet without malice. The place was packed with spectators, the largest crowd any witness in this hearing drew, the star of the show. Every seat was taken, and they were standing two and three deep at the back.

The chairman beamed at me.

"Well, you're a drawing card," he said.

"Well, Mr. Chairman," I answered, "you know what Voltaire said when someone remarked on the mobs who watched for his carriage in the streets of Paris."

"Yes, I do, suh," the chairman said, obviously pleased with the opening I had given him. " 'Alas, there would be just as many if I were going to the guillotine.' "

There was a long period of general cross examination during which I testified as thoroughly as I could to the history and motivation of my own participation in the show. It was when I defended myself with the reference to cultivating the Mammon of unrighteousness that the exchange took a definitely combative turn. The chairman objected smartly to my construction of that charge.

"I believe, suh, you rather strain if not distort the moral of that parable about the unjust steward," he said, and you could feel him happily revving up his motors for battle. "It is admittedly subject to more than one interpretation, and the Biblical scholars have scratched their heads over it for centuries. But I think the accepted one, and my own, is that Christ meant that we should use money to give alms to the poor —"

"*Well?*"

"— who will then intercede for us in heaven." He cleared his throat archly. "I trust the recipients of your largesse will be in a position to intercede for you there? [Laughter] Perhaps for the moment you might more relevantly quote Goethe, that 'This is hell, nor am I out of it.' [Laughter]"

"You flatter me by equating me with Faust, my lord. [Laughter]" I felt it would have been churlish to note that he had quoted Marlowe, not Goethe.

All that was fine. Couldn't have been better. It broke the ice. Letting him pick up the marbles had been wise. Now the atmosphere was warm as I read a prepared statement saying that after a lot of soul-searching I had decided to do away with all the rationalizations and self-justifications in which I had in the past few minutes been briefly tempted once more to indulge, and come right out and tell the truth and admit my guilt — and express my regret.

There was a hush when I finished and pocketed the handwritten note. The chairman thanked me for my honesty, as did the other Congressmen in turn, each commending me for my cooperation in arriving at a decision which cleared the air. All but one, a Congressman Pettigrew from Kentucky, who said that he did not think a man of my intelligence and endowments should be complimented for telling the truth, only to be rebuked for having hitherto betrayed it for so long, in a manner deceiving millions of men, women and children gulled into making a hero, and very nearly a folk hero, out of a miscreant who had lent his skills and learning to a piece of national deception. As a figure revered in the councils of a moralizing administration, he cut to the quick. After a pause, he fixed me with a beady eye and said:

"Don't you feel remorse for what you've done? Not just regret, as you say. Remorse. Deep, scalding remorse."

The "scalding" probably did it, as revelatory of no mean knack for dramatization on his own part. There seemed more than a touch of ham here as well. You knew how many of his constituents would be watching this on the evening news. One would be on the tube oneself, the star for one last time. Competitive histrionics made the urge to lay it on thick overpowering. I felt myself being swept along as the principal in a great Self-immolation scene, yet not without a certain gleeful sense of secret parody. I sank to depths of which I would not have thought myself capable. "I've been living a lie," I said, and hung my head in shame at that moment genuine enough.

Thus the image of the princeling was struck down, and that of the penitent stood before them, brought low, in sackcloth and ashes, as the hearing was declared adjourned by a chairman now once again shoved into a bit part and the spectators, in greater numbers than I had ever known, rose from their seats and surged forward to wring my hand and clamor, as people never had before, for my autograph.

18

SO THAT'S THE MORAL. There's nothing like a fall from grace to land you in people's graces. Because Chip was not the exception by any means. Everyone liked me better, especially holdouts during my hour in the sun, such as Carter Pippin, whose resentment throughout my term of celebrity I could sense seething within him every time we met, which hadn't been often in recent days. Now all that was changed. He shook my hand warmly when next we did. People were wonderful, nice as pie, glad to see me fallen. I made them feel so much better. I could see them positively shimmering when they approached. Oh, that I would have known the answers to three fourths of the questions on the show in any case, that they could forgive. I had relieved them of the grudge that is itself three quarters of the burden of admiration.

Not even the sterling Mrs. Flamsteed was sensed to be altogether free of this taint to be expected of lesser mortals, relishing, as she visibly did, the fact of one's having oneself cancelled all remaining doubt or possible refutation of her principle that the country is a cesspool. Or in more ornate invective, an "electroplated society" existing on surface impressions rather than human realities, a packaging and packaged hoax of a nation, its statesmen no less than its commodities the product of the image makers (to say nothing of their being the hirelings of business). I had myself been such a concocted image, in a piece of entertainment selling pots of useless muck in a multi-million-dollar swindle of simulation. "Like the administration itself."

"What do you mean?"

"Wait and see. It will reap the whirlwind, mark my words."

Life is a paradoxical and bewildering amalgam indeed. Now it showers diamonds upon us unasked, now exacts our blood for paste. Mrs. Flamsteed's jeremiads might have been better reserved for the home scene, which proceeded to come apart next.

I had only been back from the wars a day when Amy, silent throughout a dinner during which it remained for Chip and me to keep the conversational ball rolling, beckoned me shortly afterward into the den off the living room.

"Have you been sleeping with Rosé Flamsteed?"

"Not a wink."

"I'd like the truth, not brittle dialogue."

"What brings this up?"

She showed me a letter come to her in the mail in my absence. Inside the envelope, which was addressed in ink in printed figures, was a sheet of paper on which were glued letters of various sizes and colors cut from newspapers and magazines, spelling out in rather uneven lines: "Your husband is having an affair with another woman. Ask him about a certain Rosay."

"Do you have any idea what this is all about?" Amy asked.

Swann (halfway down a left-hand page in my twelve-volume Chatto and Windus set of Proust) receives an anonymous letter telling of Odette's sexual profligacies. That was what shot into my mind, no doubt as a psychic stratagem for appropriating this outrage to myself — for, momentarily at least, acquiring the grievance. I identified myself with poor Swann in a manner making me the recipient rather than the subject of this scurrility, as in fact just for that instant I was. And with some justice, not merely as a cunning rationalization engineered by the ego with its twenty-four-hour switchboard service. For in all conscience I was as much a victim of the letter as its addressee was of the infidelity it retailed.

"I said can you shed some light on this."

"Yes. Our mutual friend. Remember I told you I saw this scrabble stuff lying around in a drawer in his room, back when he first began to enliven our hearth. God knows what he's been using it for up to now, or who's been getting what in the mail."

I stepped to the foot of the stairs and with a very sharply barked summons fetched the culprit down. I marched him into the den by the ear and thrust the paper at him. "You're hurting me," he said, with visible gratification.

"Will you explain this please?"

"I don't know what you're talking about."

"The hell you don't! You sent it, you —. Listening in on extensions to private conversations that are none of your damned business, sending people who take you in and befriend you — Have you no — Is this how you show your gratitude? Is this how you repay kindness, you god-damned little sonofabitch!"

It was here that, my patience exhausted, charity run out, I belted him one across the chops — completing the swing that I had checked in midair the last time. He staggered back against a chair and then down to the floor with an exaggeration that was something to behold. He touched a hand to his lip and examined his fingers as though he were bleeding where struck, which wasn't in the least the case. Determined to make even more of it, he gingerly felt a few front teeth, to see how many might have been loosened. It was quite a performance, which I was for some reason glad to see Amy watch silently with folded arms. The interesting, and significant, part of it was the way he lay there on the floor for a moment, as though felled by a proper brute, yet grinning up at me.

So he'd got what he wanted. I was no better than his father, who was now that much less the Huck Finn's-old-man the very thought of whom he had been unable to bear. This was proof positive. There was nothing left of my self-righteousness to rub in, as salt into his wounds. And all the while, in training for parenthood, I had wanted him to think me the greatest thing since sliced bread!

"Amscray."

His exit was equally something not to be missed, glancing over his shoulder as he made away, as though at a monster for whom hanging was too good, and at the same time continuing to grin a bit in the slightly lupine way he had, assured that this was the case, had at last been so established.

I turned back to Amy.

"Well, you were right. It's what he's wanted. To reduce this household to the same shambles as his own. It's what he's been egging me on to do all along. Your analysis was right on target. He can live with it all now. Shrewd piece of sociology. Your case history parses out beautifully. I congratulate you."

"Let's not get off the subject."

"What do you mean?"

"How does a thing like that get started? I mean apart from her being in the public domain."

"Well, there was a certain community of interest. A sense of shared values and ideals. A kind of Puritanism, even, in the work into which she drew me, a rigid morality of the market place she always calls it. Even a bit of a bluenose if you will, which sometimes goes hand-in-hand with being left of center sexually."

"You will forgive me if I find this reasoning a trifle baroque."

"With all my heart."

Amy paced the room with folded arms, her lips compressed. "Saint Jezebel."

"Wonderful. Love it. Did you think of that just now? It says so much about her . . . this paradox. You're really hitting the bull'seye these days, ducks!"

"I should have known. Your meteoric rise in the firm, an executive overnight, those pay raises. What a fool I've been!"

"Oh, come now, it had nothing at all to do with you."

"Just a harmless little obligato to the main melody."

"That's well put too. You're being ironic, but you do put the case. For — extra-marital affairs, to use a rather degrading mouthful. Why do you think they're the rule rather than the exception? Among people we know, our friends, everywhere. Why? You answer me."

The argument was like a boiling cataract in which I could only keep afloat by paddling faster than the current that swept us on to God knew where. Calm waters, a demolishing rock. So that when Amy retorted, "No, you go on. I'm all ears. Take up the cudgels. You don't believe in sexual monopolies, is that the leitmotif?" I continued rapidly:

"That's probably a fair statement, too. That man isn't naturally monogamous, and too short a tether is often bad for the nerves. I don't see what harm there is in a bit of quiet womanizing. I don't think a change of erotic scenery necessarily hurts the other party, except in the discovery. No one person fulfills every need of the other. We all have unplucked strings to our harp, unused portions of ourselves that another may bring out. I don't flatter myself that I've tapped all your potential, and we'll both go to our graves the poorer for beautiful music — I shrink not from the cliché — we might have made with others. On this brief day of sun and frost, as Pater put it. A man, or woman, may be legitimately refreshed by the kind of experience we call affairs. Yes, maybe even a better companion on the home front, if it comes to that. I'd go so far as to say *our* life together, with all the hazard brought into it lately, has been as good as it's ever been. To sum up, I have a sneaking suspicion that adultery has kept more marriages afloat than it has sunk."

"Well, don't think bandying paradoxes is the way to salvage this one. God, what a riddle you are, Jim. A saint as a foster father to a homeless waif, while as a husband you're carrying on —"

"I'm not carrying on, my dear," I answered quietly, "you are."

"Not for long. Only long enough to say I wasn't born yesterday, and in view of that am leaving today."

"But don't you see. We've won. We've won through with him. It'll be smooth sailing now that he knows I've got feet of clay."

"It's not what my head is made of. Let me by, please."

She seemed to mean it, to my horror. "For God's sake, Amy," I said, blocking her passage through the door, "you can't do that. Don't think of me — think of the kid. Just when we're over the hump with him. Not that he deserves it. We've taken a viper to our bosom. But we can't throw him back into what we just fished him out of — the victim of another broken home!"

She pushed me aside, though turning in the doorway to which this gave her access. "Maybe this time it'll be good for him. Maybe the best thing is to let him face the facts. That this one didn't deserve to last any more than that first awful one did. Why wean him back to this — hothouse ideal? Christ, it's the same mare's-nest as the Little Red Poolroom. Besides," she flung at me with a toss of her head, "he won't miss me. It's not a woman's companionship he needs. It's a wholesome adult male example — remember?"

With that she marched out of the room and upstairs, where presently could be heard the thump of suitcases being pulled out of remote closets.

Chip and I remained on in the house together. Amy moved into a nearby motel, checking out of that after a few days and moving back in with her parents. She saw no objection to doing so once they realized there had been a separation. I wrote her daily, sometimes just general communications, a few conveying matters of greater pith and moment, such as that I had broken off with Mrs. Flamsteed (still love that "Saint Jezebel") whose employ I had then also necessarily left, the situation at the office being far too sticky in consequence. Without a job, I couldn't keep up payments on the house. We must get together, at least long enough to see about putting it on the market. Meanwhile I did what I could to befriend or, as sometimes was the case, rub along with my young charge.

"Can't you keep your room picked up, damn it?"

"Did you always want to have youngsters of your own, Jim?"

"I wouldn't mind children, if they would just mind me."

Parenthood by aphorism? We would have to see. This one seemed to appreciate a sharply turned phrase no less than a well-placed cuff. "Living with an adolescent, you see, my dear chap, is like spelling pfeffernüse. No one really knows how to do it." Ah, echoes of the old salon days . . .

I fixed breakfast every morning in the now fair expectation that when he set off for school he would go there and stay there through the day. Breakfast is a pleasant meal for a man to cook. The smell of brewing coffee and of discreetly sizzling bacon. And there are few sights on earth more satisfying than a frying egg.

"Not a fried egg," I elucidated to our young friend one morning as I presided over the skillet. "A frying one. A perfect piece of pop art."

He preferred to dwell on other subjects just then.

"You're a stinker, aren't you, Jim?"

"I guess."

"A real bastard."

"You're no bargain yourself. I wouldn't trust you any farther than I could see you. If that."

"Me too. We're a pair."

So that was how I plucked one brand from the burning. That was how I saved one boy for life in modern society. But there was a fly in the ointment here, a complication that might have been foreseen. The Edmondsons in the end frankly conked out on the role of foster parents. New "residential custody" must be found for Chip who was still on probation for that spot of shoplifting. I could not fill the bill alone. There must ideally be two parents on the scene. Thus the problem was thrown directly back onto Amy. It was a cruel choice, to which she proved equal. She came back.

She stayed on. We marked time, saw what we saw. We signed papers, tread water, played it by ear (while well knowing the score). Meanwhile, life was rich enough in other complications to offer intermittent respite from our own. I gathered that my parents were a rough echo of us, continuing to live more or less estranged under the same roof also. I phoned from time to time to ask about life on old Jefferson Street. Evidently Oompah remained serious about the woman he had taken up with. I remembered then his long-ago, oft-muttered assurances that "the geezers aren't going to get me." Meaning that "that thief and donor, Time," as one of the better lines in his plagiarisms put it, would never find him among the ranks of those old men who sit in the park playing checkers or in the library reading newspapers on a stick, if an at least autumnal affair might help you hold out against winter.

Mother had the reverse opinion about sex at his stage of the game. "Doesn't he realize these are his *golden* years?" She claimed in this regard that more than passing interest had been shown in herself by a man identified only as a noted glazier, which strongly suggested the widowed owner of a certainly profitable local window-glass business. She continued to amass her trading stamps against that day when she would redeem them on a divorce. It was when, having got wind of the plan, Oompah expressed approval of it for his part since he wanted to marry the other woman as soon as he was free, that Mother promptly changed her tune. That put another light on matters altogether. "I wouldn't divorce him if he was the last man on earth," seems to be her final word on the subject. What use will eventually be made of the stamps is anyone's guess.

All that hangs fire, as does the Federal Trade Commission's case against the Jeepers people over the contest. The quarrel will probably go on and on, never to be resolved. Either the FTC or some consumer group is egging a number of disgruntled losers on to bring a so-called class action suit against the Jeepers Corporation, who probably couldn't in any case turn around and sue us after all, as originally feared that black day when Jake cried out that I had made an apple vendor out of him, since we really didn't run the contest, only dreamed it up. The Poolroom scandal, with the show off the air forever of course, drowned deeper than did ever plummet sound, will likely fade from the national consciousness, lingering on at last only as an entertaining memory, nudged into the background by no doubt more important scandals. The dust showing signs of settling on both those fronts, Jake Wintermoots offered me a job with the firm again,

which there was nothing for me to do but take and probably nothing for Jake to do but offer, Carter Pippin
having gone over to another agency, "hopefully," as Jake
continues to say to my utter despair, "where there is not
so much blood on the moon all the time."

"While I've got you on the phone, Columbia Foods
want to test-market a new frozen ready-made pancake
mix. They haven't got a name for it yet. You might put
your thinking cap on about that."

"Batter Up."

"What?"

"Batter Up. It hits the spot."

Seeing a strong man cry, or even just hearing him,
can be an unsettling experience. Jake could hardly speak,
and when he did his words came out in a kind of Stan
Laurel squeal. "I'm sorry. It's just that . . . just that, after
everything's said and done, you're the greatest."

"I know. It's hard. See you Monday morning then,
Jake."

Amy and I didn't resume our relationship as husband
and wife until we suddenly found ourselves alone in the
house once more. That was when, our personal finances
again stabilized, as well as augmented by the stipend
provided by the state to foster parents, we were able to get
the Griswold into a decent private school, one specializing
in troubled boys — at heinous rates of course. A place in
Ohio. We drove him out for his first semester on a Friday,
returning homeward the next day in an unexpectedly,
yet understandably, pensive mood. We came along sweet,
still green rolling countryside, on a day balmy with white
clouds and bright sunshine and a steady gentle wind

under whose ruffling touch the hills lay like fondled breasts.

We wrote Chip every few days, taking turns on the chore. It wasn't until over a month later that we got any reply. The place was lousy, the food stank, the teachers nowhere. All par for the course, standard in our boarding-school years. There was one ray of light. He had made friends with a marvelous cat named Mike Frawley, both an amiable companion to drink beer with and an intellectually stimulating friend. He opened vistas. He considered the bourgeoisie the bane of society, source of all human ills. He espoused a brand of anarchy suited to today's problems. He didn't believe in money. Chip hoped to bring him home for Thanksgiving.

"He sounds O.K.," I said. "Especially the part about not believing in currency as a medium of exchange. Maybe now I can leave my wallet lying around again."

Amy smiled at me across the dinner table at which we had read and digested the letter. One of her first really genuine smiles since the rupture, though even that slightly edged with irony. For a long time, she eyed me with a hint of inner qualification, the perhaps familiar gaze of a wife making do with the materials at hand. Yet there was something more. One caught in her expression a note of resentment; as at something, so to speak, for which she could not quite forgive me. The words with which she at last broke the silence conveyed something of this mixed feeling.

"You're the salt of the earth, you louse," she quietly observed.